GRAVE ON GRAND AVENUE

NAOMI HIRAHARA

BERKLEY PRIME CRIME, NEW YORK

THE BERKLEY PUBLISHING GROUP
Published by the Penguin Group
Penguin Group (USA) LLC
375 Hudson Street, New York, New York 10014

USA • Canada • UK • Ireland • Australia • New Zealand • India • South Africa • China

penguin.com

A Penguin Random House Company

GRAVE ON GRAND AVENUE

A Berkley Prime Crime Book / published by arrangement with the author

Berkley Prime Crime Books are published by The Berkley Publishing Group.
BERKLEY® PRIME CRIME and the PRIME CRIME logo are trademarks of
Penguin Group (USA) LLC.

For information, address: The Berkley Publishing Group,
an imprint of Penguin Random House,
375 Hudson Street, New York, New York 10014.

ISBN: 978-0-425-26496-6

PUBLISHING HISTORY
Berkley Prime Crime mass-market edition / April 2015

PRINTED IN THE UNITED STATES OF AMERICA

10 9 8 7 6 5 4 3 2 1

Cover illustration by Dominick Finelle (The July Group).
Cover design by Jason Gill.
Interior text design by Kelly Lipovich.

To Denise Blanco,
who always was at least a chair ahead

ACKNOWLEDGMENTS

This book is completely fictional, but research led me to fall in love with the Walt Disney Concert Hall and the Los Angeles Philharmonic. I feel so lucky to be so close to this Los Angeles treasure. Thanks to the usual suspects, including Wes, but mostly to my agent, Allison Cohen, and my editor, Shannon Jamieson Vazquez, whose blue and green editing bubbles showed me where Ellie was going astray. And also to Chiwan Choi, the great conspirator of Writ Large Press and all things literary in downtown Los Angeles.

*I know who I am and who I may
be if I choose.*
—Miguel de Cervantes, *Don Quixote*

*grave (It.) (grä-vĕ.) . . . a deep low pitch in
the scale of sounds . . .*
—Elson's Music Dictionary (1905)

ONE

The Green Mile is gone. Not everyone will be bummed about it. After all, it's a green boat-sized 1969 Buick Skylark, no air bags and only twelve miles to a gallon. My best friend, Nay Pram, calls it sick, but not the good kind of sick. She means puke, or at least its color. But I'm devastated. There is something about that car I love. The Green Mile makes a statement. A statement that I'm not your average LA girl. Or your average cop.

I don't know how I'll break it to my grandmother Lita (short for *abuelita*; even though she's not Latina by blood, Lita taught Spanish to high school students for forty years and inspired me to pursue my BA in Spanish). She's the one who gave me the car in the first place. It used to belong to my grandfather, my father's father. Mr. Anonymous. When I had to do a family-tree project in elementary school, I had branches going from Los Angeles to Okinawa, Japan, on my mother's side. On my father's side, I had Lita's Scottish ancestors, but one tree branch abruptly ended with my grandfather John Doe, the name my father told me. I was so naïve back then that I thought that was his actual name.

But Lita, thankfully, is out of town, on one of her exotic getaways. This time she's in Puerto Rico. I don't know how she's going to react. I feel like I've let her down. And I'm not too proud of myself, either. I mean, to have your car stolen out of your own driveway while you're home is pretty embarrassing. Doubly so when you consider that I'm supposedly one of LAPD's finest. I'm a P2, Police Officer II, no longer on probation after a year of patrol. My goal is to make detective by thirty, though right now my friends joke that as a bicycle cop assigned to downtown LA, I'm barely a glorified security guard. I don't need to give anyone more fodder. In other words, I won't be Tweeting my car theft anytime soon, even if I was on Twitter.

Detective Cortez Williams of the Robbery-Homicide Division can't believe it when I call him to file a report. Again, embarrassing, as I relate how I'd last seen it parked in my driveway just a couple of hours earlier. "You didn't hear the engine? And your dog didn't bark?" Cortez asked.

Shippo, the fattest Chihuahua mix in the world, bark at a car thief? I forgot that Cortez never met my dog. Shippo may play watchdog when I'm not around, but once I'm home and he's snoozing on my stomach while I'm lying on my couch, surfing the web? Not even sirens responding to a five-alarm fire would cause Shippo to bend an ear.

"Well, I'll tell the Robbery section to keep tabs on it. But I wouldn't—"

"I know, I know." *Don't expect it to ever be found.* "So,

you've been busy," I say. It's a loaded statement. More like, *Why haven't you called*? Although I'm pretty sure I know the reason. Cortez and I got close a few months ago, back in February, but professional issues overshadowed our personal attraction. It's complicated. He's seven years older than me, and has a kid. And, most important, we both have the same boss—the LAPD—and having a relationship wouldn't be good for either of our careers.

"Yeah, well, the Old Lady Bandit," Cortez says.

How clueless could I be? The Old Lady Bandit has been the talk of the station for a week. A woman who looked to be at least seventy years old on security camera footage had hit ten banks around downtown LA, the latest one in Lincoln Heights last Wednesday. Only this time, the robbery left a security guard dead. It was strange to hear of bank robberies these days, especially in Los Angeles. Totally old-school. We used to be the bank robbery capital of the world, but a recent *Los Angeles Times* article said we are getting beat out by San Francisco and even places like Atlanta.

"No leads?" I ask.

"No, not a one," Cortez says, but I know he's lying. Why would he tell me, a lowly P2, anything? He knows better from previous experience.

"Well, thanks," I finally say. "I'll, uh, see you around."

"Take care of yourself, Ellie."

The end of the conversation—*très* awkward. It's not like I'm begging for a sympathy date, or even to go out again at all. But maybe calling him wasn't the best idea. We both know that I could have handled this on my own. But didn't the Green Mile deserve the best? And everyone in the department knows that Cortez is the best at what he does.

When I call my folks with the news, my parents, of course, go ballistic.

"I'm sorry, Dad," I say. "I know it was your father's car and everything—"

Dad doesn't seem to care at all about the car, or about his bio-dad. "You okay? Maybe you need to move back home." A bicycle cop who lives at her parents' house with her teenage brother and eighty-eight-year-old grandmother? No, thank you. That's all I need to lower even the small amount of cred I've got now.

My folks want me to move to Pasadena, South Pasadena, somewhere outside of the city of LA, even though my parents' own house in Eagle Rock is still technically within the city limits. My dad may work for the city and constantly sing Randy Newman's "I Love L.A.," but when it comes to his daughter, he'd like me to get out of town. Even my fellow police officers tell me it's not a good idea to live where you work—we know too much about local gangs, drug trafficking, prostitution. And I have firsthand experience to show they're right; I recently had to move (just a few blocks from my old place) because there were unfortunately too many bad guys who knew where I used to live. That's something my parents don't need to know about. The thing is, even though I'm making pretty good money for a twenty-three-year-old, I have Shippo. And having a dog means needing at least a little yard. Highland Park is the best I can do, and that's fine with me.

Mom sighs. "I guess it's just as well. That car was going to kill you one of these days."

My brother, Noah, is just concerned about what I might get to replace the Green Mile. He immediately texts me—*no hybrids.* He can't wait to get away from the hybrids in his life (Dad's Honda and Mom's Toyota). One reason that he still doesn't have his license is his refusal to be seen driving anything remotely environmentally friendly. He's counting on me to come through for him with something cooler.

After I break the news to my family, I wander aimlessly around my small rental house. The TV is on, but I'm barely watching. I can't relax. What a waste of a day off. Today is officially Cinco de Mayo, but most of the festivities were this weekend when I was working—my legs are stiff from all that pedaling and standing these past few days in Olvera Street. I look out my kitchen window. It's May, so there's still some light even though it's after six. My driveway is empty, only a sad oil spot left by the Green Mile remaining as proof that it once lived here. I start to feel jittery, violated, angry. What did I learn in psych class? Anger is part of the five stages of grief and I don't want to be in it alone.

But I know where I can go.

I toss Shippo a chewy treat, replenish his water bowl and grab my jacket. I get on the Gold Line light rail—I may be missing my car but unlike some Angelenos, I know how to use public transportation; my dad is an engineer with the Metro—and get off at Little Tokyo.

Two blocks east from the station is Osaka's, the best ramen in the neighborhood. Inside, I find my friends—Nay, my ex-boyfriend Benjamin, and the fourth member of our little posse, Rickie, the ultimate Mohawked diva—right were I knew they'd be.

"You won't believe this," I announce. "Someone stole the Green Mile!"

The whole table begins to clap. I hate them all.

"Wow, I had no idea you all thought so highly of my car," I say bitterly, sinking down in an empty chair. How many times had I given them all rides? How often had the Green Mile come to their rescue (especially Nay's) in the middle of the night?

Nay is sensitive enough to backpedal. "Girl, don't get us wrong. We're not dissin' the GM."

"I am," Rickie spouts out, his mouth full of noodles.

Benjamin lowers his eyes. He doesn't dare say anything negative about me or my beloved car. Things between us have still been pretty awkward since last year, but, well, as good as they can be. We're polite to each other. But we don't go out of our way to make one-on-one conversation. I've told myself that I have to forgive him. I mean, really forgive. Our breakup was both of our faults (well, maybe his a little more than mine, but who's keeping score, right?). We've been the Fearsome Foursome since freshmen year at PPW, Pan Pacific West, and even though I've gone in a different direction (I graduated in three years, while the rest of them are working on their fifth), we still hang out together all the time. I'm not going to let a little thing like a breakup get in the way of that, right?

"Shut up, Rickie," Nay says, then turns back to me. "Look, Ellie, you have a real job. You're not a professional Dumpster diver like *some people*." She gestures toward the Mohawk.

Rickie swallows. "Ah-ah, I prefer *upcyler.* You should have seen what I did to an old lampshade frame. Covered it with my *lola*'s old nightgown. Sold it for twenty bucks on craigslist."

The rest of us cringe in unison at the image of Rickie's

grandmother sans nightie. I shake my head free of that picture, as Nay directs her attention back to her food, generously sprinkling Japanese chili powder on top of her ramen. "Look, what I mean is that you can afford a new car. Like, actually new. "

"Yeah, get some decent wheels." Rickie devours a plate of *gyoza*, which had probably been Benjamin's order. Rickie describes himself as a free spirit. Unfortunately, we're the ones who usually end up paying for his freedom. "Last time we all went to that fund-raiser for the Legal Center, everyone was giving the Green Mile dirty looks. I even had to apologize to the valet."

But you didn't feel bad enough to give him a tip, I think.

The four of us continue chatting about nothing of consequence—our specialty—as we finish our meal. Even though I don't get much love for the Green Mile, I do feel better. But then, I always feel better after hanging out with my friends, especially Nay.

As I lay ten dollars on the plastic bill tray to pay for my meal, Benjamin unexpectedly grabs my wrist and holds it tight while Nay and Rickie continue to jabber away on the other side of the table.

"We need to talk sometime. Just you and me," he says softly, so the other two can't hear.

"Okay," I say, trying to sound as casual as possible. He's wearing his faded red plaid shirt, my favorite. And he's close enough that I can smell the soap on him. "How about right now?"

"Hey, guys," he then announces loudly, getting Nay's attention. "I have to take off. See you around."

And like that, his backpack on his shoulder, he's gone.

What just happened? I'm not sure what I'm supposed to do. Follow him? He didn't give me a chance; he disappeared too quickly.

In any case, we've paid the bill and are all about to leave, so soon I'm also saying my good-byes to Nay and Rickie, who are off to the PPW library to do some studying. The streets of Little Tokyo are relatively empty for a Sunday night. There are a few groups of people our age mixed in with single Japanese men in T-shirts and flip-flops. Before I walk to the Little Tokyo station, I text Benjamin:

When do you want to talk?

But he doesn't call or text back, and I start wondering whether I, again, am reading too much into nothing.

The next day at work, Johnny Mayhew and I are assigned to patrol Grand Avenue, just past the courthouse around Walt Disney Concert Hall. Apparently, a bunch of jurors have been jaywalking across First Street from jury parking to the courthouses, and yesterday a DASH bus sideswiped one of them. Luckily, the bus was pulling into one of its stops, so it wasn't traveling too fast. The pedestrian got away with her life intact but her leg broken. And now we're here to try to keep the other pedestrians in line.

I remember a teaser I saw for the six o'clock news last night—something about a bus running over a pedestrian, as if the woman had been innocently strolling on the sidewalk or within the crosswalk lines when the bus mowed her down. No mention that she'd actually been running through a red light and across four lanes of traffic during rush hour.

Plus, we found out this morning that she was actually high on painkillers at the time. That juicy detail is not going to make it on tonight's news.

Because of all the hype, Johnny and I are essentially crossing guards on bikes today. Even Grandma Toma could do what I'm doing today, and she's eighty-eight with hammer toes on both feet.

"This is so lame," says Johnny. He has a slight stammering problem, but it doesn't seem to come out around me. Which I can either take as a compliment: he's comfortable around me; or as an insult: he doesn't view me as intimidating. I choose to take it as a compliment, because why not? It's going to be a mighty long morning regardless.

We're on the side of the concert hall. Thanks to my father, Mr. "Rah-Rah" Los Angeles, my brother, mother and I were all in the building the day it opened. There was a free concert to show off the hall's acoustics, which are definitely state of the art. The stage is made of cedar from Alaska, and the whole thing is built so that it sounds awesome from every seat in the house.

Johnny, who's more into extreme sports than the arts, has never stepped inside the concert hall. "Looks like a crushed beer can," he says about Frank Gehry's masterpiece.

I don't bother to tell him that the "beer can" cost close to one hundred fifty million dollars.

Both of us need to use the restroom, so after the jurors are all safely inside the courthouse, we ride down Grand Avenue toward the artists' entrance. There's a fancy restaurant connected to the hall, and we've used its bathroom in the past. Johnny goes first while I watch his bike on the corner.

Businessmen and -women go in and out of the restaurant, their eyes fixated on their smartphones. People of my parents' generation complain about millennials being addicted to social media and high tech, but I'm not the one posting food porn on Facebook after every three-figure meal. In fact, the academy advised us not to have much of a presence on the Internet. Not only could it affect our professional career advancement, but it could be plain dangerous, especially if a pissed-off perp started following our activities.

That's not to say that law enforcement isn't all over social media. LAPD has an official Facebook and Twitter account, and we have investigators checking social media all the time. While community relations people are sending out Tweets and photos of smiling police officers volunteering at toy drives, detectives are combing through public Facebook photos and posts from criminal suspects and persons of interest, monitoring who's hanging out with whom and where. It amazes me how stupid people can be—flipping gang signs with known underworld figures on Instagram while claiming to be as innocent as newborn babies. Those images aren't going away, not even when the subjects attempt to delete them.

Unlike a lot of my peers, not having a presence on social media isn't that big a deal to me. I was never much into Facebook, anyway. The PPW Athletic Department used to post photos from our volleyball games on its page; then a bunch of pervs—old ones, too, who hadn't been in college for at least twenty years—would try to friend me. It made me kind of paranoid, knowing I was being watched by strangers. I didn't like that feeling.

So once I got into the Police Academy, I got rid of my

existing social media accounts. I did open a new Twitter account, for Shippo Wan Wan, which literally means, "Tail Bow Wow" in Japanese. I only follow a few people, namely Nay, because sometimes she'll read a Tweet before a text message.

Being friends with Nay, the Queen of Social Media, also means I'm hardly missing out—she keeps me filled in on anything juicy. Rickie's totally not into social media, either—he says he's not going to let the government or Big Business spy on where's he's shopping or eating—even though his main activity usually involves a Dumpster, not an exchange of currency. Benjamin does have a Facebook page. He uses a night scene from São Paulo (he's ethnically Korean, but his family's originally from Brazil) as his avatar, but he only has posts from other people wishing him a happy birthday. Instagram is more his thing. He's into taking photographs—never selfies, unless he's there with other people. Instead, there's shots of stuff like a cactus in the Mojave desert, the stairs in Silverlake, a man selling paletas from his cart near MacArthur Park, where Rickie lives. Benjamin even has photos of us still in his account. I don't know why, but recently I've started to look up those old Instagram photos. It makes me remember when life seemed way less complicated, maybe even more peaceful. It's become a bad habit, though, and I have to remember to turn my phone off before I get sucked in too deep.

My phone's not on right now as I stand on the sidewalk on Grand Avenue. Above me on the wall of the artists' entrance at the concert hall is a huge banner advertising their current performance, Eastern Overtures, and an over-sized image of the star cellist, Xu.

I have no idea whether "Xu" is the guy's first or last name, but it really doesn't matter. You know that when a musician is known only by a single name, he or she is bigger than life. Aside from being really bad at both the piano and the guitar, I know hardly anything about classical music. I do know that Beethoven had killer hair, while Bach had either really bad hair or a really bad wig.

But even I have heard of Xu. I may not actually be sure how he sounds, but I know exactly what he looks like.

Even if I didn't, it would be hard to miss the seven-foot-tall image of his face on the banner right above me.

Nay would call him hot. Heck, *I* would call him hot, although he's not exactly my type. He's got one of those anime character faces, a little emo or femme, some would say. A definite pretty boy. Nice big, sloped brown eyes and a refined chin. A nose that any surgically altered actress would die for.

Johnny comes out and catches me staring at the banner a few moments too long. I quickly avert my eyes and put on my sunglasses. The last thing I need is the squad room hearing that I was ogling a photo of a male cellist. I'm already considered the biggest nerd in the LAPD Bicycle Coordination Unit. Not only am I a college graduate, which not all my fellow officers are (many just went straight into the Police Academy from high school); I actually got my degree in three years. Add to that my connection to the assistant police chief (aka my aunt Cheryl), and I'm definitely prima donna material.

Johnny, thankfully, doesn't seem to have a problem with me, but Mac Lambert, a slightly more senior officer in our unit, has already pegged me as a police princess. We've had words and most of them haven't been good. Like with Benjamin, I'm currently in truce status with Mac, but relations can break down at any minute.

Mac's on the radio now, asking us where we are and telling us to get back to post.

"We better go," Johnny says.

"I will," I say. "Eventually. It's my turn to pee." Mac's not my commanding officer; Tim Cherniss is. I'll get back to the intersection when I'm good and ready.

Johnny's face colors slightly, and before he can stammer out anything else, I hand off my bike to him and walk past a series of concrete stairs in between a building for the artists' entrance and the concert hall.

The stairs lead to a small garden that's wrapped around the oddly shaped building. The gardeners must be adding more plants because I see flats of seedlings and pots of flowers on the stairs. One gardener in maybe his thirties is using a gas-powered blower to brush away dead twigs and dirt from the walkway, and an older guy has his hand around a potted bush with pretty lavender flowers.

My dad is always on some kind of environmental kick. His latest campaign is drought-resistant plants. He vows that he's going to transform the front lawn into Joshua Tree. Noah, of course, is hoping to move out before that happens.

"What do you call that?" I ask the older man about the lavender blooms, wondering whether it's something Dad might be interested in. The blower that the other gardener is using a few feet away is pretty loud, so the man holding the plant doesn't immediately respond.

I repeat the question louder, and switch to Spanish.

"What you say?" the man asks me—in English—when the younger one gives all of us a break from the blower.

"The lavender plant. What is it?"

The gardener smiles widely. I can tell that he's really into plants. "Gracias."

Uh, what? Why is he thanking me? Maybe his English isn't that great.

The gardener must have read the puzzled look on my face. "That is the name. Gracias. Gracias sage. Don't need much water. Grows real strong."

Oh. "I like that," I say. "Well, *gracias* for Gracias." I smile back at him, then continue to the restaurant. The maître d' and I are acquainted with each other, and he knows why I'm there. I take off my helmet and head for the ladies' room. Inside, it's cool, the perfect temperature. I wonder for a moment what it would be like to have a regular day job. To wear cute outfits and carry a purse or leather bag to work. To be in an air-conditioned room twenty-four/seven. I consider it for a few seconds and then think, *Naaah.* I'd go stir-crazy. As I wash my hands, I look at myself in the mirror. My face is a little flushed from being outside all morning. Hair back in a messy French braid. Yup, I'm not meant for the corporate world, and it's not losing anything by not having me in it.

When I go through the restaurant, the maître d' is no longer at the door.

I soon find out why.

It's mass chaos outside.

A crowd has gathered near where I left Johnny, who is now off of his bike and kneeling next to something on the ground.

But that something is actually someone: the same

gardener who told me about the bush with the lavender flowers. Though he's not talking now. In fact, he's not moving. His body is lying at the foot of the stairs, near the Gracias sage, now uprooted from its broken planter, brown soil spilled down the flight of stairs.

Leaping over our sprawled bicycles, I get close to Johnny, who's kneeling down beside the gardener. "What the hell happened?"

"I'm not exactly sure. Called it in already. The ambulance is on its way." Johnny puts an ear to the man's face. "He's still breathing."

"Barely." I take his pulse. Weak. "Mister—" I'm at a loss for what to call the gardener. "Sir, sir, can you hear me?"

"Maybe you should try Spanish."

"No, he can speak English. We were talking just a few minutes ago."

The gardener's eyes flutter open for a second. He mouths something, though I can't quite make it out.

"Ba-ra-baaaa," he says.

I hold his hand. It's rough and callused. Working man's hands.

Some loud talking in another language breaks through the din of the crowd, mainly from a middle-aged Asian man in a white button-down shirt and blue sports jacket. I can recognize enough to know that it's probably Mandarin Chinese. The man is clearly upset; sweat drips from his eyebrows even though it's only about seventy degrees, cool for LA. I notice that he's clutching a huge, shiny purple instrument case, most likely for a cello, from the shape of it. There's some sort of silver design on one side of the case, but I can't make out what it is.

Directly behind and above the man, I spot a familiar pretty face. Specifically, Pretty Face with the aquiline nose and soft brown eyes. Xu. He's much taller in person than I expected, closer to six feet than my five foot six.

"Is Eduardo going to be okay?" A thin, middle-aged woman with a spray of freckles on her face approaches us and I get up, knowing that Johnny is keeping an eye on the injured gardener's vitals. "I'm part of the crew. I was up in the garden when it happened."

I could probably take notes faster on my phone, but I opt for the old-school method, pen and paper. I remove my notebook from my pocket and ask for her full name. Wendy Tomlinson. "Tell me what you saw."

"That man." Wendy gestures toward the older Asian man holding the cello. "He pushed Eduardo down the stairs."

Before I can even write her accusation in my notebook, another Asian man, this one in a bright neon polo shirt, breaks into our conversation. "I'm the translator for Mr. Xu," the neon man says. "He would like to make a statement." He pronounces the name something like "Chew." I mentally file that away. This whole time I'd thought it was pronounced "Zu."

I first think he's talking about Pretty Face Xu. But based on his body language, I quickly adjust and realize he's talking about the middle-aged man. A relative?

"This is Xu's father," the translator confirms.

Father? I look back at the older man. He bears no resemblance to the star cellist, who must have been blessed with his mother's looks.

"I can take your statement in a few minutes. Let me just finish up—"

"How *could* you?" It's the younger gardener, the one with the blower. He has large dark eyes, the whites now rimmed in pink. He points a finger toward Mr. Xu. "Why did you try to kill my uncle?"

At the word *kill*, Mr. Xu's face visibly darkens. I suspect he actually knows more English than he lets on. He nudges the translator, who communicates: "That man was trying to steal this cello. Xu's cello." The father is still clutching at the purple case. I can see now that the silver spot I'd noticed earlier is a creepy image of a multiheaded bird.

This is not a good situation. I'm starting to feel that Johnny and I could be in a little over our heads. This isn't just a routine accident situation, an older gentleman taking a tumble down the stairs. We are suddenly talking about an alleged robbery attempt on one side, and an alleged intent to cause harm on the other. I don't know how much that cello is worth, but it's probably a small fortune. Johnny and I need reinforcements. After getting Wendy Tomlinson's contact information, I call Jay Steinlight, the watch commander on duty, and let him know what's going on. "We may need a Chinese-speaking officer, too," I add. "Mandarin, not Cantonese."

As soon as I end my conversation with Steinlight, I see that Johnny has his hands full. The younger gardener and Mr. Xu are starting to circle each other like angry cats. "Get 'em outta here, Ellie," mutters Johnny, who hasn't left the injured gardener's side.

I quickly separate the men, instructing Mr. Xu and the translator to stand on the south side of the stairs with the cello, and the younger gardener to stand on the north side. Xu seems to have left, but then I notice him standing in the concert hall's side building entryway with a leggy redhead, her hair swept back in a ponytail. Someone in a higher pay grade will have to deal with him.

I address the translator. "Sir, you and Mr. Xu will have to wait here until our detectives arrive. And we'll have to hang on to the cello."

Again, Mr. Xu's comprehension of English seems fine as he explodes in a fireball of Chinese. The translator attempts to calm him down.

The tall redhead with the ponytail that I saw earlier with Xu has now come out of the side elevator. At least she had the sense not to take the stairs and disturb a crime scene.

"I'm Kendra Prescott. I represent all of the hall's visiting guest artists." She grips her cell phone as she introduces herself. "Is there a problem here?"

Uh, yeah. A man is semiconscious after being allegedly pushed down the stairs by the father of your guest artist. "I was just informing Mr. Xu that he needs to speak to detectives," I explain to the PR rep. "Also, the cello needs to be turned in as evidence."

"Ah—that's not going to happen. Xu has his concert tonight. Do you know how much this instrument is worth? Five million dollars," Kendra reports, causing Mr. Xu to shake his head as if that information should not have been revealed.

I try to prevent my mouth from falling open upon hearing the value of the instrument. Johnny is obviously listening, too, and he doesn't do as well hiding his shock. His eyes bug out and he starts to cough.

"Well, the investigators will be telling you what to do," I manage to say. "Just don't go anywhere."

I then go across to the younger gardener. Up close, I reassess him as probably in his late twenties. The guy doesn't seem more than five years or so older than me.

"What's your name and phone number?"

"Raul. Raul Jesus Santiago. Most people call me RJ." He then gives me two phone numbers—cell and landline, the latter also serving as his primary work number.

I ask for his uncle's name. Eduardo Fuentes. His mother's older brother. They're obviously close, because RJ is really agitated. Even though he has a tough exterior, I sense that he could start crying at any minute.

"Why did he do that? Why?" RJ keeps repeating.

Sirens announce the arrival of the ambulance. I turn and see that Cortez has also arrived on the scene, along with another guy I assume is probably his partner. I've never met the partner before. He's pretty short with some ugly-ass growth on his face that's neither a goatee nor a beard. He has some gray hair mixed in with some black, and I have no idea what ethnicity he could possibly be.

Cortez is looking good, wearing a crisp white shirt with a yellow tie that only a man like him can pull off. "Best dressed in the LAPD" definitely goes to him. "Garibaldi, Rush. Rush, Garibaldi," is the extent of his introductions.

"Ellie Rush." Garibaldi takes his time looking me over, multiple times. Somehow I feel like I have to take a shower now. "Oh, so you're the one."

What the hell is that supposed to mean?

"You called this in, Mayhew?" Cortez says to Johnny, who nods.

"Xu's in that building." I gesture toward the artists' entrance. "And the cello case, that should be dusted for fingerprints."

"We got this, Ellie," Cortez says. In other words, *Shut up*.

Paramedics have strapped Eduardo onto a gurney and begin carrying him to the back of the open ambulance.

RJ tries to accompany his uncle, but I have to stop him.

"I want to go with him," he says. "Where you taking him?"

"Mr. Santiago, we can't let you do that." Even though RJ says he's a relative, I have no real proof of that. Plus, this is turning into a possible crime scene and we can't have the two men having a private conversation before we question them individually.

"We'll handle this," Cortez Williams tells me. "Maybe you can help us with crowd control."

In other words, *Get lost, little bicycle cop*.

"I did speak to the vic," I add, but by then, no one's really listening to me. Cortez is now getting a full report from Johnny. I notice that he isn't telling *him* to do crowd control.

I spend the rest of the afternoon on the corner of Grand and First. I sneak some glances at my personal phone, searching for any mention about Xu or the incident that just happened at Disney Hall. Besides information about the concert that's scheduled for tomorrow, there's nothing. Either people are too busy to post anything or aren't sure what they witnessed. Johnny eventually joins me on the corner and I can sense that he's feeling pretty good about himself. He assisted an injured man and got to interact with detectives. I'm happy for him, but I have to admit that I'm a bit envious, too. I don't want to stay a bike cop forever. Benjamin used to tell me that I need to slow down, not always obsess about my next step. But a part of me feels like I'm on one of those moving airport walkways, only it's traveling in the opposite direction. I need to be always moving forward just to stay in the same place.

Both Johnny and I have had enough excitement for the day, so we don our sunglasses and station ourselves on different corners on First Street. Nobody even attempts to jaywalk. The only nasty thing that happens is a Jack Russell taking a wiz on my back tire.

It's dark by the time I get home, via the Gold Line. My Glock is safely zipped up in my very unfashionable fanny pack and soon will be resting in the bottom drawer of my bedroom dresser, next to my laptop. As I approach my house, the motion detector activates the light above my porch. I see the lonely puddle of oil from the Green Mile glistening in the light, still mocking me.

I notice then that it's a full moon. Weird stuff happens when it's a full moon, especially in the Central Division. Homeless people come to the station, claiming that they've been pursued by either zombies or alligators from the sewer. Sad thing is that bargain shoppers from Beverly Hills in the Garment District would claim that the homeless men and women *are* the zombies.

Shippo greets me by jumping up and licking my bare knees.

"So, what kind of a watchdog are you, anyway?" I say to him, cupping his face in my hands. It's no use. He knows that I can't really be mad at him.

That night in bed I keep my Glock next to me underneath my extra pillow instead of in the dresser drawer. There's just way too much weird stuff going on right now. Grandma Toma always talks about bad things happening in threes. The stolen Green Mile, and now this incident on Grand Avenue, were one and two—and I'm in no hurry to find out what the third bad thing will be.

TWO

When I get to work the next day, my commanding officer, Sergeant Tim Cherniss, stops me before I head into roll call. "Captain wants us to go to County General," he says.

My heart immediately begins to pound. Don't get me wrong—I love Captain Randle, but I'm also totally scared of him. He's the boss man. My future is entirely in his hands. Second of all, Cherniss says *us*. Which means I'll be sitting in the same vehicle as my CO.

Again, it's not that I don't like Cherniss. It's more that we don't have much in common. He's in his late thirties, a family man, a guy who doesn't swear much, and who goes to church regularly. I know this because he's told me about how he goes over to Tijuana with his church to visit an orphanage in Mexico on his days off. You'd think, considering all we deal with here in the Central Division, that he's already received his gold star in heaven right now and could just be kickin' back with some cold ones in his favorite sports bar during his days off. But that's not my CO.

Cherniss is definitely on the straight and narrow. Nay may claim that I'm Ms. Goodie Goodie, but he makes me look like Lindsay Lohan. He knows that I'm the niece of the LAPD assistant chief, and based on things that I've already managed to do during my first year as a P2, I can tell that he doesn't completely trust me. Heck, I don't entirely trust myself sometimes.

I'm not quite sure what to say to him as we walk over to a patrol car parked in the back parking lot. "What's going on at County?" I finally ask, trying to make my voice sound light and unconcerned.

He checks his phone and says, "Eduardo Fuentes, the vic from yesterday at the concert hall? His family's requested to talk to you."

"To me? Why? I didn't even see what happened. They should be talking to Johnny."

"They already have."

Latino gardeners aren't usually high on anyone's priority response list, so it's a little weird that Eduardo's family can pull the captain's strings. But I'm pretty sure I know what Cherniss and I are doing with this visit at County General: containing a possible explosion. The LAPD Bomb Squad has this thing that explosives are placed in—a containment vessel. That's us. We can't let Eduardo Fuentes's family feel disrespected enough to kick up a fuss that ends up on the six o'clock news. Especially a fuss involving Chinese musical superstar Xu. The mayor wouldn't like that.

Cherniss doesn't need to tell me any of this. I've been

around my aunt Cheryl often enough to absorb the kind of politics she's had to survive over the years. It's not like she talked about it, but whenever she was on edge during family get-togethers—and we have them all the time—I'd check the Internet for clues and always found some kind of dustup within the force. Aunt Cheryl says you have to like living in a pressure cooker to be in the LAPD. Fortunately, I do; I'll take stressful over boring any day.

And today is going to be one of those days. As we walk inside and bypass the metal detector in the front of the hospital, I feel the palpable distrust from everyone in line. I hear someone murmur, "I smell bacon." Whatever. I keep my eyes straight ahead of me. I've been called worse. As soon as we enter the hospital's conference room, a heavyset woman rises from a chair. "We want that *Chinito* to be charged with attempted murder," she declares.

I try not to cringe. Most strangers have no idea that I'm half-Asian, which sometimes places me in uncomfortable situations. Like hearing the Spanish slang word for *Chinese* used as a slur.

Cherniss has his game face on, but then, he almost always does. "I'm Sergeant Tim Cherniss and this is Officer Ellie Rush," he says, extending his hand to the woman, who introduces herself as Eduardo's daughter, Marta Delgado. Also seated at the table is Eduardo's nephew, RJ.

"Is she the one?" Marta asks RJ, glancing at me.

He nods, but I get the distinct impression that summoning me was his cousin's idea, not RJ's.

"I heard that you spoke to my father. What did he say to you?" Marta demands.

I look at Cherniss and he nods.

"Well, he did say something," I tell her. "But I couldn't quite make it out."

"What was it? Maybe it will mean something to us."

"It sounded like 'ba-ra-baaa.'" I suddenly have a flash of an idea. "Is there someone named Barbara in his life?"

"My mother's name was Cristina and she just died last year. Are you trying to say that he was having an affair?"

Cherniss's jaw tightens. I should have kept my ideas to myself.

"No, no. I just heard 'ba-ra-baaa.'"

"Is that all?"

"Well, I did talk to him earlier. When he was working in the garden. But we just talked about plants," I say. It sounds so lame. Lamer than lame.

Marta's eyes mist over. "He loves plants. And he loves his job, especially this one at the concert hall. He was a day laborer for years before RJ got him in his crew." She blows her nose in a well-used tissue. "Why in heaven's name would he want to jeopardize all that to steal an instrument in broad daylight?"

She has a point.

"That's why we would like to talk to your father," Cherniss tells her. "Eventually, when he's able."

"Those detectives were here at the hospital. Like vultures, they are. Waiting to pick Papá's bones before he's dead."

From what I've seen of the guy, that might be true of Garibaldi, but I'm surprised to hear Marta characterize Cortez in this way. Besides being hot, Cortez is smooth. His voice is like dripping honey. During his interviews, people often start to like their medicine enough that they practically beg for more.

"They were ready to accuse him, not defend him." Marta points her finger our way.

Cherniss shifts in his seat, making his leather holster crackle. I know what he's thinking. *I've got nothing to do with the Robbery-Homicide Division. I'm just in charge of Ellie Rush, this P2 here.*

Marta keeps going. "We were in the waiting room, flipping the channels, and on some Chinese news program, they're showing Papá's face. It's from twenty years ago. I don't even know where they got it. I couldn't understand a word of it, but I could figure it out. They were saying he's a criminal. But Xu's father is the one who hurt *him*!"

Marta blows her nose again, even more furiously. I notice a box of Kleenex on a table against the wall. I get up and leave it on the table beside her. She whispers, "Thank you."

RJ finally starts to talk. "You saw him right before," he says to me. "Working hard, not bothering nobody. Did he look like he going to steal something?"

No, in fact, no, he didn't, I think. But I can't say that for fear of being called in as a witness in a possible civil lawsuit.

Cherniss can tell that I'm wavering and he swoops in. "We will be conducting a full investigation in this matter. You can depend on that."

Before Marta can respond, there's a knock on the conference room door.

A young man who looks barely twenty enters. "Mom," he calls out to Marta. "You better come."

Marta is immediately on her feet. She follows her son without saying good-bye.

RJ remains for a moment. "My uncle didn't do what that Chinese man say. He wouldn't do nothing wrong. He a good man." And with that, he, too, is out the door.

Cherniss and I get up, too, and my CO thanks a woman in one of the private offices for the use of the conference room. "Let's get back to the station," he tells me. Thank God. I can tell that the family of Eduardo Fuentes is in crisis. No sense in having "bacon" stink up his hospital room.

Back in the black-and-white, we both strap on our seat belts. "Well, that was fun," Cherniss says. He doesn't mention whether I messed up or not. I guess I didn't, because he doesn't say anything more during our drive back to Sixth Street.

I spend the rest of the day catching up on paperwork, specifically writing up what happened on Grand Avenue. Although report writing is my forte, I'm starting to hate not being out in the field. At first I was resistant to join the bicycle unit, and it was my aunt who encouraged me to do so after my first probationary year. "It's the trend now. Community policing. Being on a bike is one of the best ways to do it. And you get to follow up on cases that you wouldn't be able to if you were in a police car. You'll have more latitude than those patrol officers," she had told me. And while I resent being dissed by people like Rickie, I have to admit that being with the Bicycle Coordination Unit has been kind of growing on me.

Later, as I'm proofreading my report, I see that my personal phone is vibrating on my desk. I quickly take a look, see "Text received from Nay Pram—*CALL ME.*" Well, that's not going to happen right now. I have to be careful with Nay. After hanging out with me on a previous homicide case, Nay changed her major from sociology to communications. She thinks she has a knack for investigative reporting, which maybe she does, but she's taking it way too seriously. Now she's a reporter for the *Citrus Squeeze*, Pan Pacific West's student paper, with access to wire services. She's been keeping tabs on any crime within a five-mile vicinity of PPW, which unfortunately for me includes the same area that the Central Division covers.

"Hey, Rush, who is this Nay Pram? She says that she knows you," Jay Steinlight says to me right now in the squad room. He's always fielding questions from the press, and apparently Nay has made an impression. *Oh great.* Nay must have called him directly.

"Uh, yeah, she's a friend." *Like my BFF, practically the sister that I never had.* But Steinlight doesn't need to know how close we really are.

"She's persistent," says Steinlight. I can read between the lines. She's a crazy nightmare, and I should use my influence—discreetly, of course—to get her to lay off. But Nay's a challenge. Push too softly and she won't feel a thing. Push too hard and it will make her even more curious.

During my break I go outside and stand beside some dying palm trees next to our building. It's times like these I kind of wish I smoked. To hold something in between my fingers, some excuse to let my mind wander miles away from here.

Instead, I hold my phone to my ear and keep my back toward the door. "Hey, Nay, what's up?"

"What's with that guy Steinlight? Wouldn't give me a thing."

"What do you mean?" I am an awful liar, because Nay quickly says, "You know exactly what I mean. Xu. The fight that his father had with that gardener. It was right at Walt Disney Hall. Weren't you saying that you had patrol duty there?"

"Nay, I can't talk about it."

"So you were there! Did you see what happened?"

"I didn't see what happened," I say definitively. That isn't a lie. "And all of this is off the record."

"Of course, of course." I want to believe Nay, but I can't. Even her writing that "some unnamed cop said that she didn't see anything" could possibly get me in trouble.

"But you know what happened," Nay continued. "Did Xu push that gardener down the stairs? I heard that he's not doing well."

"Where did you hear that?"

"I have my sources."

"Nay, this is not a joke. You can't be writing any of this right now."

"Did you meet him, by the way?"

"Who?"

"Xu. Oh my God, he is so damn cute. I could eat him up."

"I did see him." Shoot, did I say that? *Shut up, Ellie,* I tell myself. "Oh, Nay, ah, I got to go, okay?"

I end the call and take a deep breath. Crisis averted, right?

Before I go back in, I set a Google Alert on Eduardo Fuentes, although I know it's probably a pretty common name in both North and South America, not to mention Spain. I add Los Angeles and Disney Hall to limit the category.

I turn around to see a tall redhead walk into the station, and get a closer look as I enter our lobby. The PR lady, Kendra Prescott, obviously here on some kind of mission.

I try to keep my eyes down, like when you're in class and don't want to be called on. I'm almost safely out of the lobby when I hear Captain Randle call out from his office, "Officer Rush, could you join us, please?"

Johnny's already seated in the office. Captain Randle, his graying hair close-cropped, looks as intimidating and as dashing as ever, like that classic actor my father loves, Sidney Poitier. He's dark-skinned like Poitier, and commands the same level of respect. In other words, we P2s are scared as hell of him. Johnny seems about as happy to be there as a dental patient waiting for his root canal.

"I understand from Officer Mayhew that you are acquainted with Ms. Kendra Prescott from the concert hall," Captain Randle says.

"We've met," I say.

Kendra frowns slightly as if she can't remember our previous encounter. *What can I say? I must be pretty forgettable.*

"All I'm saying, Captain," she continues where she apparently just left off, "is that it's absolutely essential that we get that cello back. Today."

"As soon we get an expert to take a look at the cello to confirm its value as well as conduct a thorough examination, we'll be returning it. It's in a very secure place, believe you me."

"Xu's already had to rehearse with another cello. But he says that he needs the Stradivarius. In addition to being an extraordinary instrument, it's very special to him. An anonymous donor from China gave it to him while he was a conservancy student in Philadelphia. It's always represented that his country believed in him. It's really responsible for getting Xu through hard times."

Well, whoop-de-do, I think.

"It seems as if you are very familiar with the cello's history," says Randle.

Do I detect a touch of snark in Captain Randle's tone?

"I interviewed Xu about it for our program," Kendra says, straightening her back in her chair. "He and his cello, in fact, are going to be the centerpiece of a special concert in China this week. So, you see, this is not only a matter of national significance, but also of international importance. I'm sure you don't want the president involved in this."

I exchange glances with Johnny. *Did she just say what I think she said? Did she just threaten to get the president, as in the president of the United States, involved?*

"Ms. Prescott, we are dealing with two serious issues here. One is possible attempted grand theft. The other, attempted murder. No politician can circumvent our legal system, especially during my watch."

"Attempted murder? That's utterly ridiculous. Mr. Xu was just defending himself and a five-million-dollar cello from a thief."

"Do you think Mr. Fuentes, one of your employees, would be capable of such a thing?"

"Well, he's not officially an employee, more like an

employee of a vendor. And you never know, right?" She turns to Johnny. "You were there; what do you think?"

Johnny starts to stammer and I feel so bad for him.

Kendra begins to frown and even Captain Randle seems a bit distressed. A police officer with a speech impediment? I know that Johnny's been working on his issues with a speech therapist (she called the station once), though I haven't mentioned anything to Johnny; hey, I'm part Japanese and know all about saving face.

"Neither one of us saw clearly what was going on," I break in. Both the captain and Johnny seemed relieved that I've interrupted. "Officer Mayhew was at the bottom of the stairs and I was in the restaurant at the time of Mr. Fuentes's fall."

"Why else would Mr. Xu have a conflict with this man? It's not like he knew him," she says.

"We do have a witness."

"The other gardener? She works with Eduardo. She's probably just protecting him." Still holding on to her phone, Kendra crosses her arms tightly around her chest. This meeting is obviously not going the way the she wants. She glances at her screen, and then reports to Captain Randle that she can give him the name of an appraiser for the cello. "He's available right now."

Captain Randle seems skeptical.

"Or do you have another string instrument expert that the LAPD uses on a regular basis?" Kendra has a point. She shares the screen with Captain Randle, who writes down the name of the expert and his phone number. "It's Phoenix Instruments. In Arcadia." Arcadia, home to not only the Santa Anita Racetrack and one of the biggest malls in San Gabriel Valley, but also the best Taiwanese dumplings in perhaps all of Southern California.

"Okay, I'll get on this, Ms. Prescott." The captain then gives her one of his blinding smiles. "See what happens when you actually cooperate with police?"

As soon as my shift is over, I take off for a small rental car company that operates out of a hotel in Little Tokyo. Even though I can manage LA via bike and public transportation, my friends are right—I do need some new wheels. But I've never bought a car before. I'll need some time to research, compare, test-drive. Since my insurance doesn't cover a temporary replacement for a stolen car, I go for the cheapest option. Economy. And yeah, you get what you pay for, because I get a Hyundai Accent. And get this—it's Kermit the Frog green. My friends will not be happy.

Since it's dinnertime, I park Kermit a couple of blocks away in the lot across from Osaka's. My phone begins to vibrate in my pocket, and I pull it out and see that Google Alerts is telling me that something has been posted about Eduardo Fuentes/Los Angeles/Disney Hall.

It's an article by Nay in the *Citrus Squeeze* digital edition. I feel sick to my stomach. Surprisingly, the article is fair and factual, or as factual as Nay can be given the lack of information that's been provided to her. But one quote attributed to an anonymous police source will undoubtedly be linked back to me. She's included a statement from Fuentes's daughter, which is pretty damning. The nephew, although he was on the scene, is not mentioned.

As I enter Osaka's, I'm relieved that Nay's not here yet.

It's only Rickie sitting there at our table. He's stuffing his face with boiled edamame, a bowl overflowing with empty pods in front of him. The edamame are free at Osaka's, and when money is tight, Rickie takes full advantage.

I sink in a nearby chair and sigh, my helmet in my lap.

"Bad day?" he asks, sucking on the end of a soybean pod.

"Don't tell Nay, okay?"

Rickie raises his eyebrows and leans forward. He's always ready for some juicy gossip. "My lips are sealed." Yeah, right. I should know better, but I'm desperate to talk to someone.

"You heard about the thing with that Chinese cellist?"

"Oh, Xu?"

Of course, Rickie would keep tabs on beautiful Asian men. And he knows how to pronounce it right.

"Well, it's becoming a bit of an international incident."

"You mean his dad did kill that Latino gardener?"

"He's still alive," I murmur, feeling so bad for the Fuentes family. I get a familiar pang, the memory of feeling helpless while waiting in that hospital room during Mom's breast cancer surgery. "Anyway, the PR person came by the police station today."

"What for?"

"She wants Xu's cello back for tonight's performance. She says it's worth five million dollars."

A soybean falls from Rickie's mouth. "Does that come with the cellist?"

"No, without Xu."

"Well, that's a bloody shame."

I do a double take at Rickie's use of *bloody*. Is he going *Downton Abbey* on me?

"Hey—" Nay walks into the restaurant toward our table.

Rickie gives Nay the once-over. She's wearing a silver knit dress and ankle boots with killer heels. (They would definitely kill me.) "Who's the new guy?" he asks.

"What?" Nay hangs her purse over one of the empty chairs at our table.

"Mascara, eyeliner—and are those falsies?"

"Dude, this girl don't need no boob enhancements." Nay sashays her ample cleavage. Yeah, I admit it. I'm a bit jealous.

"I'm talking about the eyes. False eyelashes. You have a date."

"Oh." Nay blinks three times fast, and I finally notice the black wedges glued to her eyelids. "Well, kind of. It's with someone who can do it for twenty minutes straight."

"Nay!" I exclaim.

"Girl, can't you take a joke? I'm talking about that cellist Xu and his playing. I'm going to his concert tonight."

"Really?" That thing must have been sold out for months. Plus a ticket would probably set someone back at least a hundred dollars.

Nay immediately reads my expression. (Yeah, I'm pretty much an open book. I have to work on that if I really want to make homicide detective and interview suspects.) She flashes her press pass, her LAPD one. "The power of the press."

Pulling the laminated pass toward him, Rickie studies her photo and her physical description. "You haven't weighed a hundred and forty since middle school."

"Get out of here." Nay gnashes her teeth at Rickie. She then smiles sweetly at me. "You wanna be my plus-one?"

THREE

I agree to go to the concert. It's not that I'm eager to hear classical music after a long day, but I need to keep tabs on Nay. Now that the station knows she's connected to me, I have to make sure that she doesn't do anything to impede the investigation. I'm also super-curious about the cello—is it back in Xu's hands? And if not, will it affect his performance in any way?

The only problem is what I'm wearing, since I came from work. There's no time for me to go home and change, though, so my uniform, shorts and all, will have to do.

Since I have my rental car, I agree to drop Rickie off at PPW before Nay and I head out. As I suspected, the reaction to my wheels is not good.

Rickie and Nay stare in shock at the Hyundai for a moment. "What's with you and the color green? Did some leprechaun mess around with your mom?" Rickie folds his long legs as he gets into the backseat. It's so cramped, his Mohawk brushes against the roof of the car.

"I can't believe I'm saying this, but I think it's worse than the Green Mile," Nay says.

"I'm not buying it, okay? I'm just renting it until I get something."

"You're doing it to torture us," Rickie adds.

"Listen, Rickie, you don't have to ride in it. The Metro bus is a very nice shade of red."

"Well, let's not go there."

I start up the engine and pull out of my spot in the parking lot. Once I've merged onto First Street, I finally ask, "Where's Benjamin, anyway?"

"Not sure." Rickie tries to hide his concern. I have a theory that he's crushing on Benjamin; I mean, my ex's whole scruffy look—his longish hair and plaid shirts—has broken many a heart, including mine.

"He's been MIA a lot. I mean a lot." Nay flips down the flimsy car visor and applies a fresh coat of gloss on her already painted lips. She then attempts to pretty me up, but I wave her off. First of all, I'm driving, and besides, I'm in my uniform and bicycle shorts—some lipstick isn't going to make a whole lot of difference.

"You'd think that he's hiding a new girl, but I don't get that vibe," says Rickie.

"What kind of 'vibe' are you getting, then?" I say with a sprinkle of snark.

"He's been kinda emo lately. I mean, not suicidal, but a little dark."

I start to feel worried. What was it that Benjamin had

wanted to tell me about yesterday? I remind myself to text him tonight after the concert.

Abruptly, Rickie blurts, "You can drop me off here." I'm stopped at a red light in front of a mini-mall with a photocopy place. "Sorry, I just can't be seen in this thing. I have a reputation to uphold." He pops out with his backpack, barely even waving good-bye.

I feel like an unappreciated soccer mom and promptly give him the finger.

"I don't think he saw that," Nay says.

"Sometimes . . ." I say to Nay in a threatening voice, leaving the rest of the sentence unfinished. *"Sometimes."*

"Yeah, but if we don't love him, who will?"

Once I circle around the hall for the garage, I find a spot on the bottom floor of the parking lot, thankful for the truly compact size of the Hyundai. We then enter the building, riding at least three sets of escalators before reaching the expansive lobby. I see plenty of concertgoers here in jeans and T-shirts, which makes me feel a little less self-conscious. This is LA, after all, where you'll find someone in an evening gown in the same room as someone in yoga pants. In the lobby, I spy a guy my dad's age who's trying to look like Bono in blue wraparound sunglasses; I'd say that's a worse fashion crime than what I'm wearing.

Nay checks in at a media table, while I pick up a free program.

"It was cool to meet the flaks in person," Nay says when she rejoins me, studying her press package as if she knows what she's doing.

Back at the media table, I spy a couple of women, including one with a familiar red ponytail. "What's a flak?"

"You know, a public relations person. That's what the media call them."

So that would be Kendra Prescott. A flak. "Sounds nasty."

Nay shrugs her shoulders, like she's completely transformed into some hard-core journalist. She's wearing her press pass around her neck. I fight the urge to mention that we're at a classical music concert, hardly Pulitzer Prize–winning material.

"Too bad we missed the preconcert lecture," Nay says.

"Oh, it's *Don Quixote*," I say, glancing at the cover of the program for the first time. I majored in Spanish at Pan Pacific College and we tackled excerpts from Cervantes's novel in one of my classes. I'm immediately more interested in the concert now. "I actually know this story."

"It's some Dutch thing, right? Has something to do with windmills."

"Not Dutch, Nay. Spanish. It's, like, *the* most important piece of Spanish literature. Don Quixote, the hero, is this guy who's really into being chivalrous, like a knight or something from the old days. But then he slowly starts to lose his mind, thinking that windmills are giants he has to fight."

"Wow, he was really tripping out," Nay comments.

"Oh, you'd like his trusty sidekick, Sancho Panza. He's a simple farmer, really . . . earthy."

"Hey, what are you trying to say? That I'm Panza? I'm your wacky but slow wingman?"

"I didn't say that! Besides, Quixote's the one who goes crazy at the end."

"Hello, spoiler alert." Nay seems genuinely ticked that I've given away the ending.

"It's not like it's a big secret, Nay. This is a classic, like *Romeo and Juliet*, not some TV show, like who got the rose on *The Bachelor*."

"So are you going to ruin that one for me, too?"

Is she kidding? I sigh. "Where are we sitting anyway?"

Nay glances at the tickets the PR person gave her. "Balcony. Row C."

Nay seems to realize that our seats are less than premium as we climb one staircase after another. I bet the *LA Times* music critic isn't sitting way up in the clouds like we will be. But as Grandma Toma likes to say, beggars can't be choosers. *In other words, Ellie,* I tell myself, *give your girl Nay a break.*

The carpet and the seats are dark red with patterns of orange and green. They are abstract flowers, designed in honor of Walt Disney's wife, Lillian, a horticultural lover who pretty much championed the whole concert hall, though she didn't live to see it completed. I can still remember some of the details from the tour my family took back when this place opened.

And since the hall isn't shaped like a cube, oval, or any typical shape you learn about in grade school, the hallways are mazelike. I usually pride myself on my good sense of direction, but I'm certain that I could lose my way in here.

We finally reach the top and discover our seats are about three rows from the back.

"I guess I should have RSVP'd earlier," mutters Nay, fingering her laminated press pass.

There are already some people sitting in our row, so we try to squeeze past their knees to our seats. Nay's ample behind presses against the laps of the seated senior citizens.

A woman wearing a heavy turquoise necklace frowns, but her male companion doesn't seem to mind.

"Man, it's tight in here," Nay comments.

"You think?"

Once we are planted in our nosebleed seats, we take in the scene in front of us. The orchestra is already onstage, looking like toy dolls from up here. All wearing black, they casually chat with their neighbors while tuning their instruments.

"Is that their organ?" Nay gestures toward a giant wooden hearth. It looks like a piece of modern art with shards of polished beams—I've heard it jokingly called gigantic French fries. That nickname fits it for sure.

"Ummm," I say, but nod.

Nay leafs through the press packet again. "That Strauss guy was young when he composed this. Thirty-three."

Wow. He *was* young. I guess Nay had the same impression I did—that only old European men wrote classical music. It's hard to picture someone just ten years older able to create music for a whole orchestra. And not just any kind of music, music good enough to have lasted more than a century.

Nay keeps peppering me with more details and fun facts.

"So Xu's playing the music for this Don Quixote guy?" she asks.

"Yes. The man of La Mancha. It's a place in Spain. I've never heard *Don Quixote* in concert before, but I bet it's like a dialogue between instruments."

"And the viola player is supposed to be the best friend?"

Nay's distracted from her program when a musician carrying a violin enters the stage and the crowd begins to applaud.

"What's that all about?"

I'm actually not quite sure, but I tell her, "It's starting, it's starting."

The tuxedoed man strokes his violin strings with a bow, and soon all the members of the orchestra start to tweet, saw, and blow on their instruments. It's obviously some kind of tuning exercise. Next comes the conductor, a thin man in a tuxedo with crazy wavy hair down to his shoulders. More clapping for him. And then Xu appears, also in a black-and-white tuxedo, carrying a cello by its neck. Is it his multimillion-dollar cello? Outside of that distinctive purple case, I can't tell. It's honey colored. Shiny. Kind of looks like a pear-shaped woman with two curlicue holes in the middle. Basically it looks like any other cello I've seen, but then, I've never really paid attention before. Either way, he's owning it. Thunderous applause for him.

Xu sits in a chair directly facing the audience. As soon as he starts playing, I am mesmerized. When he's not play-ing, he seems otherworldly, like he's a fantasy character, maybe an elf, in an animated movie. But when he lifts his bow and plays, he transforms into a warrior. His head rocks to the music, his hair tossed from one side to another.

"Can I borrow your binoculars?" Nay asks an older woman next to us. The woman seems amused by Nay. Judg-ing from the age of the crowd, the season ticket holders seem only too happy to see young people appreciating classical music. "You can hang on to them," the woman generously offers. "I have another."

As she watches Xu, Nay begins to practically groan, and I don't mean in pain. How totally embarrassing. I take the binoculars to stop her audible aching for Xu. But magnified, I see that the star cellist is even more intriguing. He keeps his eyes closed during some of his performance, showcasing his unusually long eyelashes for an Asian male. Dust explodes as his bow moves through the cello strings. Like a pro athlete, Xu occasionally presses a rolled-up towel against his sweaty forehead during breaks. I notice that some long hairs from his bow have come loose from his passionate playing. I bite down on my lip; I understand why Nay was making such a spectacle of herself.

The viola soloist then comes in. She has a head of platinum blond hair with a streak of pink—more appropriate for a concert on the Sunset Strip than on Grand Avenue, but as far as I can tell, her playing is superb. Her body is at one with the viola; her elbow extended, she moves her arm as vigorously as Xu does. It's almost like they're dancing together.

"Hot, huh?" Nay says, fanning herself with the program.

My body is pulsing. I have to nod in agreement.

I look more closely at Xu's musical partner through the binoculars and gasp in surprise. "The blonde is Asian!"

Nay opens up the program and uses her cell phone for illumination. "Yeah, she's from Taiwan."

"Psst," someone hisses from behind. "Turn off your phone."

I give Nay a look. My "I can't take you anywhere" look, even though technically she's the one who's taken me here to Walt Disney Concert Hall.

"Hey, I'm not the one who's wearing shorts," Nay snaps at me.

"Shh!" the same person scolds us from behind.

I lower my body into my chair. I don't need anyone to see that my back is branded LAPD.

The performance continues with a re-creation of the bleating sheep that Don Quixote and Sancho Panza encounter, the snorts and wailing coming from the tuba and other instruments.

"I can hear the sheep!" Nay says to me, smiling.

I smile back. I can, too.

When the performance ends, the crowd erupts in applause. Some rise to their feet and yell out, "Bravo, bravo." Before I know it, Nay is standing, shouting, "Encore, encore!"

I sock her in the thigh.

"What?"

"You don't say *encore* at a classical concert. It's not like they are going to follow up with Beethoven's Fifth or something."

The lights come up during intermission. The session with Xu and Don Quixote is over. The second half of the concert is dedicated to Brahms and just the orchestra. I wouldn't mind leaving, but there's a meet-and-greet with the musicians that Nay insists we stay for.

"There's somethin'-somethin' going on with those two," Nay declares, looking through her program.

"What are you talking about?"

"The way Xu and that platinum blonde were going at it with their instruments? They are definitely getting it on."

"Nay, these are professionals. Just like actors. They express their passions in their art. It's not necessarily personal."

"No way. You can't fake that kind of stuff. Listen, I know."

I take the press packet from Nay's hands and look at the artists' bios. "Cece Lin. She's been with the Philharmonic for a year. She's based here in LA."

"Un-huh, and that proves what?"

"Well, that she's a professional."

"Duh, you heard her play. Just because she may be

hooking up with a megastar doesn't mean she's shallow or anything. She is a pro." She flips through the program, then stops again at a photo of the platinum-haired violist. "I wonder how I'd look as a blonde?"

I study Nay's dark, uniform skin. She'd look like a Muppet with hair that blond, but I don't dare say that out loud. "I think you're better as a brunette," I say instead. Then I notice that one of her false eyelashes has sprung loose, making it look like a black caterpillar has descended from her eyebrow. "Uh." I mime that something has gone wrong around her eyelid.

"You got a mirror?" she asks.

"Do I look like I'd have a mirror?"

Nay plucks my sunglasses from atop my head and tries to see if she can make out her reflection in the lens, but it doesn't work. "I'm going to head out for the bathroom."

We go out the side doors together—Nay covering one side of her face with her purse. Yeah, super discreet. That's really not going to attract attention.

Once we are on the terrace level, Nay heads for the restroom and I tell her I'll meet her in the downstairs eating area. I'm starving, but everything here is so dang expensive. I can only afford a small bag of potato chips, for almost three bucks. Oh well, the ticket was free and I can't have my stomach growling in the middle of Brahms.

As I'm nibbling on my chips, trying to make them last as long as I can, Nay comes back and practically plows me over. "Guess who I just saw?"

I shrug my shoulders and lick salt from my lips.

"Bono! You know, that guy who's always trying to dig wells in Africa and stuff."

"You know that he's also a singer, right?" My dad is a U2 superfan and, embarrassingly, sings "I Still Haven't Found What I'm Looking For" in the shower. (What he's looking for, especially in the shower, I really don't want to ask.) "Anyway, that isn't Bono. He's just a guy who's trying to look like Bono."

"No, Ellie, he *is* Bono. Really."

"If you say so." I toss the empty potato chip bag in a garbage can and we make our way upstairs.

"Wait, wait, there he is." Nay elbows me and points to the guy I'd been mentally making fun of earlier. He's being tailed by a huge black man with an earpiece dangling down to a radio. It certainly gives credence to Nay's theory that this is Bono and a bodyguard.

"Wow," I say. Who knew that Xu could command the presence of a celebrity that big? Both Nay and I have no shame, and continue staring. Nay takes out her cell phone and starts taking pictures. I worry that might be against the rules, and look around to see whether anyone notices—and jump when I hear a voice behind me say, "Ellie? I thought that it was you."

Oh great. It's the assistant chief of police—aka my aunt Cheryl. I didn't know she was a classical music fan, but here she is, in front of me. As usual, she looks like she's dressed straight out of a Saks Fifth Avenue catalogue. She's wearing a black tuxedo jacket over a shimmering shell the color of blue pearls. She even smells like she has money. Which she does.

I cross my arms and cover my thighs, as if that will make my bicycle shorts disappear.

"You're not working here, are you?" Aunt Cheryl takes a quick assessment of what I'm wearing.

"Last-minute. Nay had tickets. You remember Nay, right?" I push Nay forward.

She's been to a couple of our family parties.

"Love your lipstick color," Nay says.

Aunt Cheryl frowns slightly. "Uh, thank you." She's not a warm fuzzy type; more like an ice cube. Even Nay, who could melt an Antarctic glacier, doesn't try to endear herself, and instead excuses herself to get a drink of water.

"Actually, Ellie, I've been wanting to talk to you," Aunt Cheryl says when Nay leaves.

My palms start to sweat. Even though she's my aunt, she's also the highest-ranking Asian American in the LAPD, and she has that effect on me.

I immediately flip through the possibilities in my mind. For the past couple of months, I've been low-profile. A good girl. Done whatever my supervisors have told me to do. I've even made time to floss my teeth. Maybe this has to do with Eduardo Fuentes?

"I heard that your car was stolen."

"Oh," I say, although I'm thinking, loudly, *Who told you?* My aunt can read my mind.

"Grandma let me know. She wants to buy you a new car."

"I have the money to do it on my own," I say. *But so sweet that Grandma Toma wants to help me.*

"That's what I told her. I don't know why you were driving that old beater, anyway. It's not safe, you know."

"We need to get back to our seats." A figure, at least six feet tall, looms over me. The voice, deep and raspy, sounds familiar. It can't be. But it is. Councilman Wade Beachum is addressing my aunt. He holds an almost empty glass of booze, only a thin line remaining. *You have got to be kidding me. No. This cannot be happening. That nasty old man known for his philandering ways* cannot *be with my aunt.*

The uniformed ushers now move through the lingering crowd, hitting their mini-xylophones with thin mallets. We get it, we get it. The next performance is starting.

Aunt Cheryl and I say our good-byes and I watch to see whether there's any sign that those two are on an official date. Beachum has a hand on Aunt Cheryl's back, but it's a light touch—not necessarily a romantic one. The very thought sends a chill through me. I've dealt with the married councilman before, and I don't like the thought of him anywhere near my aunt.

"Hey, I think we need to get going." Nay's beside me. "What's wrong?"

"Nothing." I know better than to mention my suspicions to Nay. She'll start constantly obsessing about whether the two of them are really having an affair. Rather than allaying my fears, she'll put more wood on the fire.

We settle in for a completely different performance, unfortunately one without either Xu or Cece. I'm not quite sure what a contrabassoon looks like, but the program says this symphony features a famous movement for that neglected instrument. I do a process of elimination and figure out that the musician in the back I see holding a large black instrument must be the contrabassoonist. He's about midthirties, thinning blond hair, a nose shaped like a ball. Not hot at first glance, that's for sure. But, of course, you'd have to talk face-to-face with a guy to see if he's really hot or not. I bend my head toward Nay to share this musical nugget with her but she's dozed off. Thankfully, the bassoons and contrabassoon are making enough noise to disguise her light snoring.

I try to concentrate on the music, but my mind can't help but wander to my encounter in the lobby. Aunt Cheryl has only ever had one serious relationship that I know of. The guy—his name was Steve something—even came to our Japanese New Year's party back when it was at my grandmother's house. (We've been holding them at my parents' house ever since Grandma Toma moved in two years ago, so it was well before that.) He also was with law enforcement, with the ATF—Alcohol, Tobacco, Firearms and Explosives. I think that they met on the job, working together on a gang gunrunning sting investigation. No one in the family ever said it out loud, but I think most of us except for Grandma Toma wondered whether maybe Aunt Cheryl was a lesbian. Which isn't really fair; it's a stereotype that men on the force like to banter about the female officers, especially the ones in leadership. I know that Aunt Cheryl had to sacrifice a lot, especially for a woman of her generation. How could she be a wife and mother, raising babies while helping to oversee one of the largest police departments in the country? Things are a little bit better these days, but not by a lot. And I know I want all those things for myself, but way, way down the line. I don't want to think about any of that right now.

The Brahms piece has ended and someone in the front row begins to clap first, setting off a rainstorm of applause throughout the hall. The noise rouses Nay, who immediately sits up and starts yelling, "Bravo, bravo."

After the concert, there's the Q & A with the artists that Nay insists on attending. "There'll be food, too," she says, and then adds, "Free."

Free food is definitely an added bonus to make an appearance at the reception, which is held in the lobby. In a matter of minutes, I'm loading my napkin with some kind of gooey cheese appetizer and then a shrimp one. I don't care who sees me pigging out. I'm hungry.

Most of the attendees, including Nay, have congregated toward the front of the reception hall to hear a USC professor interview Xu and the conductor. I opt to stay behind, close to the food and drink. Their topic will be on Strauss and *Don Quixote*, whereas I'm more interested in filling my stomach.

I am dying for some wine, but even though I'm off duty, I can't drink while wearing my uniform. Instead I pick up the last glass of mint lemonade and, making myself at home against the wall, I take a sip. This definitely is not my crowd, but then, what is?

I feel that as the months pass, I share less and less in common with the Fearsome Foursome. My coworkers are mostly guys who are married or have girlfriends. Johnny has his biking friends. The one other woman in our unit, Armine, has two kids. I don't fit in anywhere anymore, at least not as easily as I used to when I was at PPW. There, I was just another college student. I could wear my PPW sweatshirt and feel like I belonged to a club (so what if it was a club with a grapefruit mascot; at least it was something).

While the interviewer is talking to Xu at the front of the reception hall, I notice Xu's father taking a phone call in the back. *Rude,* I think. *Isn't this your son's shining-star moment?* But Mr. Xu seems upset. I mean really upset. He raises his voice and then realizes that he's attracting unwanted attention. People don't realize that he's Xu's father and give him some stink-eye. I can't find Nay in the crowd; she's probably positioned herself in the front row.

I'm wondering whether something has happened to Mr. Fuentes. Nobody would think of informing me of his medical status. If he dies, then Mr. Xu could really be in some hot water. He'll have to extend his stay in the U.S.; that's for sure.

After about half an hour, there's clapping in the main hall, and the crowd disperses. Some choose to get more appetizers, but quite a few, their jackets and purses in hand, choose to leave. I search for Nay. Don't see her. Mr. Xu is gone, too.

As I eat more cheese, Nay finally reappears. "Listen, I'm going to stick around. I met someone."

"Who?"

She gestures toward an Asian guy and I catch a flash of orange neon, the same neon as at the crime scene.

"You have got to be kidding me," I say, disgusted.

"You know him?"

"I never got his name."

"Washington Jeung."

I arch my eyebrows.

"Now, now, no need to be so rude," she scolds me, even though I haven't actually said anything. "You know the whole Chinese immigrant thing for presidential names. He can't help what his parents named him."

"Still . . ."

"He's not bad-looking."

"He's not good-looking, either. Or bad enough." I know Nay's type—or should I say *types*—and this guy doesn't fit any of them.

"Anyway, he's a freelance translator. He's even translated for Xu's father in Europe in the past."

"Yep, I know."

"So how do you know him?"

I catch myself before I reveal too much about the case. It has enough complications as it is.

"I heard him introduce himself to some people here," I lie. Weak, but Nay uncharacteristically buys it. Perhaps she's too smitten to think straight?

"Are you sure about this?" I ask. Nay hasn't had the best taste in men. But, as Rickie says, it's Nay's 31 Flavors. If she doesn't like one on Monday, it really doesn't matter because there will be a new one the next day. "How are you going to get home?"

"Well, maybe I won't go home."

"Nay!"

"Look at him. I have a good twenty pounds on him. I'll be all right."

I'm not so sure. I'm worried about Nay. I know she has pepper spray in a sparkly Hello Kitty case, but despite these precautions, Nay could get hurt. Badly. Now that I work in Central, which covers PPW, I hear about many more incidents of assault and date rape than I ever realized were going on while I was attending college. I can't tell her the private details, but I realize more than ever that PPW isn't the protective enclave that we all thought it to be. And beyond its walls, in the outside world, literally anything can happen.

"Listen, you call me if you need a ride," I tell her. "Anytime, okay?"

Nay's already heading back to Washington's side. I try to mad-dog him, give him a fierce look and puff out my chest in my uniform. *You hurt my BFF and you'll answer to me.* Benjamin used to tell me whenever I tried to look menacing, I just managed to look cross-eyed. Either way, Washington doesn't even seem to notice me.

The crowd has thinned considerably and I look for a place to leave my empty glass when I notice someone next to me. Someone at least six feet tall, with a beautiful head of black hair, smooth skin and sparkly eyes. It's Xu, being a wallflower like me.

Shouldn't you be out there, in the center of things, signing autographs or something? I think. Instead, I say, "Oh, hello."

"Hello," he says back. I've never heard him speak before, and wasn't sure how well he spoke English.

"Nice concert," I say. Lamest thing ever.

"You were at the accident site."

He has a slight British accent, which throws me off a little. I know Hong Kong was a British colony, but wasn't Xu from mainland China? Isn't that more New World than Old?

"Yes. And you were, too." *And it would have been nice if you'd stayed around to see if the man your father injured was okay.*

Xu's cheeks are pink and I wonder whether it's from the wine he's holding or from what I'm insinuating. "How is he?" he asks, meaning Mr. Fuentes. He takes a sip of wine as I just shake my head. It's not my place to divulge any medical details, especially ones I'm completely unsure about. "My father was just protecting me. Protecting my cello," Xu says.

"So you're saying that the gardener was a thief?" I can't help myself.

Xu's whole face is flushed now. I wonder if he's missing the enzyme to properly process alcohol, a condition that a lot of us Asians have. "I don't know why he did what he did. Truly I don't," Xu says. *Which he?* I wonder. Fuentes or his father?

"Well, at least you got your cello back." I figure that by making the assumption, it will generate an answer to what I've been wondering about all night.

"I did," Xu says; then his eyes widen. "Did you have anything—"

A woman in high heels and a low-gelled ponytail comes our away. It's Kendra Prescott. "There you are," she says to the cellist. "I was looking all over for you. Bono wants to take a private meeting with you." She notices me beside Xu and frowns, just in the corners of her mouth, before quickly turning up her lips. "Ah, hello. I didn't know the police were here." She still doesn't seem to recognize me from the day before.

"Just here as a private citizen," I tell her.

Before Xu can say another word, Kendra's ushering him away. PR flak—was that what Nay called her? All I can say is that she's very good at her job. I toss my empty plastic cup into the trash can and walk across the expansive lobby to the escalators leading to the parking structure. Most everyone has left, so there are only a few couples—all older ones with stylishly groomed gray hair—on the escalator with me.

I'm parked on the lowest floor, and by now most of the parking spots are empty. Sound carries through the empty parking garage, and I hear angry voices as I make my way to Kermit. I look around warily, and in a section marked

ARTISTS' PARKING, I see a flash of platinum hair. Standing next to a dark BMW convertible, Cece is speaking loudly in what sounds like Chinese to someone obscured by a parking column. I must have been spotted, because she immediately lowers her voice.

I get into Kermit and check my rearview mirror as I back out. The BMW's rear lights are now on, but I don't see Cece or the person she was talking to. As I drive up the next level of the parking lot, all I can hear is the squeak of my tires against concrete, a familiar sound at the end of a strange day.

FOUR

The next morning I check my phone. No calls, texts or e-mails from Nay. Since I'm on a four-day schedule, I'm off today, even though it's the middle of the week. Nay is my usual go-to person to goof off with. Now, thanks to the translator, that option is not available.

I text Nay: *What are you doing?*

About five minutes later, I get a phone call. It's her. I don't bother with hello or any of that stuff. I get right to the point. "Where are you?"

"At Washington's apartment."

"Nay, already?"

"No, it's not what you're thinking. We did some barhopping in K-town and he lives right here. We just came to crash."

She can apparently feel the disapproval in my silence. "This is all for the paper. Really."

"Where is he now?"

"Taking a shower. He lives in a two-story multiunit thing. The outside is nothing special, but the inside is so, so cool. Wait a minute. I'll send you a video clip."

On my phone is a link to a short movie that Nay's made on her phone. The footage is bumpy, like Nay's been in a 7.0 earthquake or something. But I still can make out the room and furnishings. I immediately recognize the spare Scandinavian furniture and colorful throw rugs and pillows from catalogues I get in the mail.

"Nice," I tell Nay.

"He actually has a sense of style."

She thinks he's stylin' just because he knows how to order from IKEA? I'm not going to say anything, however. The video clip includes the view out a large window. I can see a parking lot, palm trees and a weirdly shaped concrete building in the distance. I squint at the image and pause the video. *What is that?* It looks like a gigantic gray bucket.

"By the way, I was right." Nay sounds proud of herself.

"About what?"

"About Xu and Cece doing the dirty. Washington got a call from Cece while we were at this one bar and I swear that I heard Xu's voice on the line with her."

"How did you know that it was him? It's not like you know him or anything."

"Because Washington called the person Xu, okay? Maybe I don't speak Chinese but I get that much."

I change the subject. "What are you doing later today? It's my day off."

"Well, Washington and I were talking about hanging out more. He's pretty interesting."

"I bet he is."

"No, really. There's a lot that I can learn from him."

Nay's talking like Washington is some kind of wise monk rather than an ordinary guy with a facility for language and a penchant for bad wardrobe choices.

"Just be careful, okay, Nay?"

"Yes, Officer!"

My phone is running out of juice, so I plug it into the outlet beside my bed. I pull last night's program from where I left it on my nightstand, and reread both Cece's and Xu's bios. There, as a sidebar, is the brief story Kendra Prescott had written about the Stradivarius. "Cello of Secrets" is the headline. She writes that, constructed in the early 1700s in Italy, the instrument was taken over to China by Jesuit missionaries who performed classical music for royalty. One of the Chinese court members and generations of his family kept the cello safe and intact during various political turbulences in China's history—the family even defied the ban on Western instruments during the Cultural Revolution, hence their desire to keep their identity a secret. Hearing Xu perform as a teenager at a local competition, the family was inspired to present the Stradivarius, now valued at five million dollars, to him anonymously. Since Xu's uncle was a high-ranking official within the Communist Party, Xu was allowed to keep the instrument. There's also a quote in there from Xu saying, "I play for China."

Something about the story sounds off. Even though I just met Xu, I can't imagine him declaring, "I play for China." I return the program to the nightstand and get ready to start my day.

Once my bare feet hit the floor, Shippo is all over me.

He's right—it's true I've been neglecting him, and I figure that he can use a good walk. I slip into an old PPW T-shirt and sweatpants, put on my glasses and grab the dog leash.

It's warm today and I'm missing the few days of rain that we had back in February. My dad is all concerned about the drought and tells me that I need to take shorter showers to help in the conservation effort. Well, world, here we are—Shippo and I are members of the great unwashed, without one drop of wasted water.

When I turn the corner away from my house, it's like those Christmastime car commercials when a sedan—a gift from a husband, wife or parent—magically appears outside of someone's home. Except instead of having a big red bow around a new car, I find the Green Mile with a bunch of dead leaves on the roof. Pulling poor Shippo on his leash, I run up to it.

There are streaks of sap all over the car; those dead leaves aren't going anywhere without a good power washing. It's dirty inside, too; there are tons of balled-up wrappers from various fast-food chains all over. The thief's main dining criterion seems to have been food that can be purchased for less than a buck.

I curse myself for not having my phone with me. Not only that, I'm without my Glock. When it's so early, I don't think about carrying my gun around. In my experience, most criminal types are still in bed until way after noon. I try the door and it's locked; my keys are hanging on my living room wall.

Much to Shippo's disappointment, I cut our walk short. I need to get my keys, then make a call into the station.

I jog back to the house, only to find an older man looking

through the window screen to my living room. He's wearing jeans with a khaki shirt that looks like it could use a good wash and ironing. His hair is a mix of black, white and gray—the colors of a raccoon. When he turns, I see that he's white, or maybe Latino, with a heavy, untrimmed mustache. He could be a handyman, finding himself at the wrong house, or he could be a Peeping Tom.

"Can I help you?" I say, lowering my voice at least an octave. Shippo starts to bark furiously.

"Bacall!" he calls out. A small black poodle, unleashed, comes out of the bushes. She's a mini-projectile, heading straight for Shippo. As she gets closer, she emits a high-pitched screech. Shippo is not amused and unleashes more barks of his own. The old man scoops Bacall up before she torpedoes my dog.

"What the hell?" I cry out. "Leash your damn dog! And what are you doing on private property? You're trespassing."

"Ah, Ellie. Ellie Rush," he says.

I am so pissed that it takes me a minute to register that the old man knows my name. "I don't know you," I say.

"Puddy Fernandes," he says. "And this is Bacall."

Bacall is groomed as well—or should I say as badly—as her master. But then again, Shippo and I are not ones to talk.

"You don't know who I am," the man says when I fail to react to his name.

I let the heat of my anger cool down. Is this guy some kind of family friend or something I don't recognize? I don't want to say anything that I may possibly regret later.

Then he reports, "I'm your grandfather."

I hear the words, but they don't make any sense. "No, you're not," I say. I don't know what I pictured when I thought about my long-lost grandfather, but it's certainly not this guy. "Prove it."

"Your grandmother is Estel. She has the prettiest red hair and a mouth shaped like a heart."

Most of her former coworkers and friends call Lita by her nickname, Essie. Most people don't know her real name. But if he really knows her at all, it's also obviously been a while since this man has actually seen Lita. Lita now has hair the color of orange popsicles, thanks to some box dye that she uses. And she pretty much has to draw her lips on.

"Call your grandmother. Estel will tell you."

I ignore his directive. "What are you doing here? Are you the one who stole my car?"

"*Your* car? I don't think so. I bought that car from a Chevrolet dealer in Burbank in 1969. I don't believe that you were even alive then."

"It *is* mine. I have the pink slip to prove it. My grandmother gave it to me."

"Then why do I have this?" He pulls out a chain from his neck. Hanging around it is a rusty key, the same shape as the one I have on my key chain.

I'm starting to feel slightly nauseated. How can this man have an extra key to the Green Mile? Could anything he was saying be true?

"That wasn't the true color of the Skylark, you know," Fernandes tells me. "It was yellow like a canary bird. This here is one lousy paint job."

The Green Mile had been that same ugly green color for as long as I remember, but Fernandes's comment has a ring of truth to it. My little brother, Noah, scratched the sides with a hanger when he was about three years old, and I'd noticed the original yellow paint at that time. Lita had quickly covered over the scratch with touch-up paint. I was nine years old and had even helped her with it.

Fernandes keeps trying to offer more evidence that he is connected to our family. "Your grandmama has a birthmark on her thigh. It's a beaut—shaped like a pelican."

Ew. Like I would know that? I use this moment to check out my alleged grandfather more carefully. I hate to admit it, but I do sort of see a resemblance to my dad. They are about the same height, around five nine. Normal build. My dad's neck seems to bend forward more as he gets older, and Fernandes has the same type of posture. Dad has never had a mustache, but I know that he could easily grow one.

"Cute dog," Fernandes says.

Shippo growls in response. He doesn't care for either Fernandes or Bacall. I don't blame him, especially when the poodle starts her insane yapping.

I hesitate for a moment, unsure what to call my so-called bio-grandfather. Not Grandpa, for sure. Not Mr. Fernandes. Not Puddy (what kind of name is that, anyway?). I settle on not addressing him at all. "So, you're Latino," I say.

The man shook his head. "I'm Luzo. Portuguese blood."

"Portugal." So I may be not only part Japanese and Scottish, but also part Portuguese.

"Something wrong with Portugal?"

"No, of course not." My mind starts refashioning my elementary school family tree. Whereas there was once a branch that abruptly ended, now there's one that may stretch to Portugal.

"I heard that you're a cop."

I narrow my eyes. How does he know that?

"Rookie, right?"

It'll be good for Fernandes to know that I'm part of law enforcement. "Got out of the academy a little more than a year and a half ago."

"That's why I'm here. I want to help."

"Help what?"

"I want to stop the Old Lady Bandit. Before he kills anyone else."

I bend down and rub Shippo's head to hide the shock on my face. Old Lady Bandit? What kind of crazy coincidence is this? And why did he confidently refer to her as a *he*?

"Why would you know anything about that?"

"Let's just say that I've made some mistakes in my life when I was around your age. I've paid my debt to society; I can tell you that."

My stomach feels queasy. Whenever people say things like this, it means that they've been in jail. Does this mean I'm actually related to a felon?

"I live in San Bernardino now," Fernandes continues. "Getting my land legs back. Been at sea too long."

Is he speaking metaphorically? San Bernardino is a couple of hours inland, nowhere close to the water. "What, were you a sailor?"

"In a way. I was a crewman on container ships. Been to Latin America about forty-three times. China, at least twenty. Too old for all that now. Staying with a friend in San Bernardoo. That's when I saw the TV reports. I know this guy's MO. He's got his fingerprints all over these robberies. When I heard about this latest, with this security guard getting shot, I figured I had to do something. Got on the bus and looked up your grandmother."

I'm confused. Lita was in Puerto Rico until today. "You've talked to her already?"

He doesn't answer and continues to chatter about this guy he knows.

"How do you know him, again? And what's his name?"

"A guy I used to run around with. I know how he works. I know that he's the one behind those bank jobs."

Fernandes can sense my skepticism. I notice that he's managed to avoid my question about the guy's name.

"He has a certain style; let me say that. Wouldn't it make sense that the Old Lady Bandit is successful because he's done it before?"

He has a good point. "If you're so sure that it's him, why don't you talk to the detective in charge? I can give you his phone number."

"Ah, well, I don't feel that comfortable talking to the police."

What does he think that he's doing now?

Fernandes quickly clarifies, "I mean, I know that you're part of the LAPD. You can get me some inside information. So we can catch these guys."

"What, like vigilantes?" I smell manipulation, and I'm not going for it. "Listen, I really can't get too involved. There are policies in place."

Fernandes visibly sneers. "Maybe we're not really related, then. Because no granddaughter of mine would be worrying about some dang policies and all that when we're talking about people's lives."

That's a load of BS. "What was the guy's name again? I'll give it to the detective in charge."

"I didn't say." He then grins, revealing a brown front tooth.

What do I expect? It's not like they have teeth whitening in prison.

This guy—my maybe grandfather—is playing me. I don't want much to do with him right now. "Listen, I need my car back. I don't know how you found out where I was living or where the car was, but—"

"That's my car. I never said that Estel could give it away."

"I'm the legal owner."

"Then arrest me," he dares me. He then lifts Bacall onto his shoulder and makes his way down the street and around the corner, where the Green Mile is parked. The yapping continues until I hear the familiar slam of a car door and the rumble of an engine.

Shippo and I exchange looks. *No way,* I tell myself. *No way am I going to stand back and let this happen.*

"Oh, *querida*, it's so wonderful to see you." Lita gives me one of her famous wraparound hugs. "I just got in a few hours ago." She's squishy and soft, but I focus on what I'm here for. Even Shippo understands that we are here on a special mission and sits still on Lita's welcome mat.

I don't waste any time. "A man who claims that he's my grandfather stole the Skylark."

Her arms flop down to her sides. "I don't understand. Here, come in." Glancing outside, she ushers Shippo and me into her Spanish-style house in San Gabriel.

My hair is still damp from the two-minute shower that I took before driving over there in my rental. I did make time to swap my glasses for my contacts. Dealing with this requires clear-eyed vision. "This guy who claims to be Dad's bio-dad came and visited me today. He told me that you have a pelican birthmark on your thigh. And then he stole my car. Again."

Lita practically pushes me down in a chair in her living room and stands over me. "How did this happen?" Shippo, a disappointment of a guard dog, sniffs the edges of Lita's woven throw rug for who knows what.

"I don't know. My car was stolen right out of my driveway. No broken glass or anything. He had an extra key."

"That son of a bitch." Lita spits out the words as if they burn in her mouth. She then begins pacing around in a wobbly circle. "How did he know where you live?"

"So, is it true?" I challenge her. "He says his name is Puddy Fernandes. Is he really my grandfather?"

More crooked pacing. Shippo joins in, probably hoping this trick will win him a treat.

"Lita, I can't stand it anymore. Does any of this make sense to you?"

Lita takes a deep breath before speaking again. "I knew that he'd eventually surface. But how the hell did he find out about you? And how did he know that you had his car? And where you live?"

So there it is. This Puddy Fernandes is not a complete liar, at least not about the car.

"I don't understand this, Lita. Not one bit. How did this apparent stranger know that I was a cop? And why don't I know anything about him?"

Lita bites her bottom lip. Any evidence of relaxation from an exotic island getaway has been wiped out by this news. "You can't tell your father any of this. It'll crush him."

My grandmother gets up to make some tea, and I don't

hurry her. I know I'm not going to like what she's about to say, but I'm also curious as hell to find out.

She makes some of her South African bush tea. She makes it superstrong so it's practically bloodred. I don't really care for it that much, but I'm not going to refuse a mugful of it right now.

She holds her own steaming mug close to her face and I notice how freckled and wrinkled her hands are. Lita talks and lives like a much younger woman, younger even than my parents, so moments like this that show her age really catch me off guard.

She moistens her lips and begins. Her voice shakes uncharacteristically. She's stored this up for a long time. "He was so charming. Tall, dark and handsome with a handlebar mustache."

Handsome? My, how things have changed.

"I met him in a bar in North Hollywood. And he had this car, this beautiful car. He always had a thing for cars."

Like the Skylark, I think.

"It was just one of those magical, magical evenings. It was in the summertime. I remember because I was wearing a cotton sundress that was tight around the waist. He kept complimenting me about it. He was a gentleman, at least at first. Opened doors for me, all that. I was only twenty, so those things made a big impact." She takes a slow sip from her mug. "I wasn't a loose type of girl. I was a virgin before I met him. Can you believe it?"

I pray that Lita's not going to go into the details of her sex life. I'm still trying to erase from my mind the thought of that pelican-shaped birthmark Fernandes mentioned.

"He was in a respectable profession. Involved in the entertainment industry."

"What did he do?"

"He was a gaffer, you know, lighting electrician. He was originally from San Diego. Son of a Portuguese fisherman. Came up to Hollywood to escape that hard life on the sea. He was always good with his hands." Lita swallows. "My mother encouraged our relationship. She was impressed by him. Impressed by the car."

Lita doesn't talk a lot about her parents. I don't know anything about her father, but I know that she was raised by her single mother, just like she raised my dad alone. "She thought we'd get married. Those days, a girl had to be married by twenty-one or so, or she was viewed as an old maid, day-old leftovers. It was the early sixties, remember. Everything was going fine. But Puddy had this friend Ronnie. A bad influence, I'll tell you. He was the one who got Puddy in trouble."

"Ronnie what?" I say, too eagerly. This must be the guy connected to the Old Lady Bandit.

"Oh, I can't remember his last name. He was a makeup man, horror movies and TV shows. Talented, but Ronnie was into cards, always in debt. Puddy even loaned him some until he couldn't do it anymore. Then I heard that Ronnie went to the mob."

"You mean in Vegas?"

"No, we had our own Mafia over here in Los Angeles, believe it or not. Your LAPD chief back in the fifties, Parker, dismantled most of its power. But it still was around to some degree in the sixties. Enough for Ronnie to get into trouble."

I immediately think of Parker Center, the old police head-quarters where Aunt Cheryl used to work, though her office now is in a different building, all glass and sunny.

"I told Puddy to stay away from Ronnie. But he wouldn't listen to me. We began to fight. A lot. He pushed me down one time. He apologized afterward, but I never forgot."

I can't imagine anyone doing that to Lita. It makes me so angry that I wish Puddy were here so I could smack him.

"One day, Puddy comes to my house. He says he's been called away to some job out of state. Someplace where it will be hard for him to call. But he'll be back."

Lita rests her freckled hand on her forehead for a moment. "Then I found out that I was pregnant. I was desperate. I didn't know what to do. So I went to his apartment in Burbank. His place was all cleared out. The landlord told me that Puddy had been in the middle of packing when he was arrested."

She lifts her head. "I tried to find out what I could from the police. Looked through old newspapers. Finally I found a news story that said Puddy had been arrested as an accessory to a robbery in West Los Angeles. He was sentenced to seven years in prison."

So my fear was right. My grandfather was a jailbird.

"My mother was devastated. She made up stories about him to all our family friends. But when I finally had your father, I didn't include Puddy's name on the birth certificate. So your dad became a Rush like me instead of a Fernandes."

"Was that his real name? Puddy?"

"No, it was Pascoal, a real Portuguese name." Lita put her mug down. "It was rocky living with my mother. We fought all the time. But because of her being around, I was able to get my teaching credential while raising your dad. Even able to have somewhat of a social life—my mother always wanted me to get married.

"When my mother died—all too young—I started to tell people the truth, at least that I didn't know where Puddy was. I told your father that his father had been just an indiscretion of mine, but that I was so thankful for that relationship because it gave me him. I told him nothing about Puddy's arrest."

All the missing puzzle pieces to Dad's life seem to be coming together. For all these years, I thought that I was used to not knowing. But now, hearing this all from Lita, I saw that keeping those secrets hidden hadn't helped me personally—although maybe they had benefited me professionally. Since I knew nothing of this at the time, there'd been no reason to write up Fernandes's record in my LAPD application.

"In some ways, I think your father is like my mother. He always wants to accentuate the positive and all that. He's my sunshine."

"And Fernandes? You never saw him again?"

Lita shakes her head. "No. He did leave the Skylark for me. For us all."

"And you didn't know whether he was dead or alive."

"Well, I was curious. Then with all this Internet stuff in the 1990s . . ."

"You looked him up."

"Besides the robbery conviction, there was nothing. No record of Pascoal or Puddy Fernandes owning property.

Giving donations. Working anywhere. It's like he just disappeared."

"He told me that he worked on container ships. Was a crewman his whole life."

"Oh, he hated the ocean. And the water. That was his father's life. He was even allergic to seafood," Lita said, then mused, "Maybe he had no other options."

I nodded. I'm sure having a prison record hadn't helped his work prospects.

"I debated to tell you when you graduated high school. And then you were in college and before I knew it, you had graduated and were on your way to join the LAPD. Having a felon for a grandfather wouldn't help you, I figured. I didn't want you to have to answer for that. Puddy's run-in with the law was nothing to do with you."

"You know, Fernandes came to see me because he claims to know who is committing the Old Lady Bandit robberies."

"Don't believe him. Stay away from him. He can't be trusted."

"Well, that's what I told him. That I couldn't help him out."

"Good girl, *querida*."

We remain quiet for a few minutes as we watch Shippo play with a piece of loose string, probably from Lita's throw rug. This whole thing with the Old Lady Bandit is pretty serious. A conviction for first-degree murder with special circumstances could possibly mean the death penalty. Suddenly, I feel exhausted. This has been a lot to take in, and I need time to process how it will impact me personally. I'm a lot like Grandma Toma in that way. And this is sure a lot of new and a whole lot of personal. I look at my phone for the time. "I better get going."

"A date?" Color has returned to Lita's face.

"Some errands. And then dinner at my parents' tonight."

"Oh no, don't go. Make some excuse. Say that you got the flu."

"Why?"

"You shouldn't tell your parents about all this. Let some time pass."

"I'm not planning to, at least not tonight."

"*Querida*, you are just a pitiful liar. You'll spill about your grandfather."

"I'll just avoid talking about the car."

Lita shakes her pinkish orange locks. "No, no. I'm going with you."

"Lita, we weren't expecting you; you must be jet-lagged," my mother comments as we both enter my parents' house. Mom's face says it all: *And we'd rather not have you here.* But Lita doesn't have the Japanese "let me read your mind" gene. No, Lita is, in fact, quite oblivious to anyone's feelings except her own. And she loudly advocates for those feelings, which can be pretty cute or very annoying, depending on what kind of mood you are in. I'm still a bit shell-shocked, so I'm depending on Lita to keep the conversation going.

"I slept on the plane. And Puerto Rico is practically within the U.S., anyway."

She heads to the kitchen, and as her back is turned from us, Mom jabs me in the ribs and we pantomime a conversation.

Ow! I mouth.

Did you know that she was coming? she silently gestures.

No. I lie without saying a word.

"Oh, it smells just lovely in here." Lita takes a deep breath and opens the door of the hot oven to take a look. "What is that, chicken parmesan?"

"No, chicken marsala. Please, don't release the heat, Estel." Mom pushes the oven shut and darts me a dirty look.

"Here, I picked these up at the farmers' market in Pasadena." I place a bag of Asian pears on top of the kitchen island. The gift appeases Mom for a moment, until I see her eyes scan Lita's empty hands.

Grandma Toma then appears in the doorway. She's been living with my parents ever since she left some curry boiling on the stove while she was out, triggering the fire alarm and leading firefighters to break through her front door. "Hello, Ellie," she says and I give her a quick hug. She then looks at Lita. "I didn't know that you were coming." Grandma Toma can be a bit no-nonsense, while Lita gets great joy from nonsense.

"Oh, it's just been too long." Lita, who's about a foot taller, squeezes Grandma Toma toward her. Grandma Toma's face is smashed against Lita's ample chest, enveloped in flowy material, and she makes fish lips in her struggle to breathe. Finally released, Grandma Toma escapes to the opposite side of the kitchen.

Mom opens a cupboard and starts to take out some dishes. I assist by taking down some wineglasses from a high shelf of the china cabinet. I am going to need some wine to get through tonight.

"So, any leads about the car?" Mom immediately asks.

"Have you done something new with the kitchen?" Lita

interrupts. "I don't remember this being right here." She slaps the surface of the island.

"Ah, that's been there since we remodeled. Fifteen years ago."

"Oh, really? I guess I never noticed."

I pick out one of the red wines on display on the kitchen counter. They're all Two-Buck-Chucks that Mom purchased from Trader Joe's.

"Do you know how the Skylark was stolen?" Mom's not going to give up so easily.

"Wine, anyone?" I ask, taking out my parents' high-tech corkscrew from a drawer.

"Oh, yes, *querida*, for me," Lita says.

My younger brother, Noah, slides into the kitchen in his socks. "And yes, for me, too." He's only sixteen years old.

"I don't think so," I say. Noah is on a very short leash and needs to be restrained fairly often. Earlier this year he got busted by my mother, who is scarier than any DEA officer, for his adventures in pot smoking and growing. Perhaps he inherited some outlaw gene from Puddy? I quickly uncork the bottle and pour two very full glasses of wine for both Lita and me.

"My, my, my! All my favorite women together in one room," Dad exclaims as he walks into the kitchen. He's obviously just come home because he's still wearing his trademark blue Windbreaker, his personal work uniform. He gives both Lita and me hugs, and I offer him some of the two-dollar wine. He takes off his Windbreaker and hangs it in the hall closet, part of his Mr. Rogers–esque routine (except he never wears cardigans).

"Okay, what's going on?" Mom places her fists on her hips.

"We're just drinking some wine," I say and then drain a glassful. I know what's coming next.

"Every time I bring up the Skylark, you both change the subject."

"Oh, yes?" Lita says, practically batting her eyelashes. Lita operates on only two modes—flirty and nonflirty. Flirty is definitely not going to work on my mother.

"I want to know what's going on and I want to know now," my mother, the Grand Inquisitor, declares.

Grandma Toma's eyes brighten. Usually she's off watching her beloved college basketball in her room (my old room), which has the only TV set in the house. (Instead of watching television, my parents constantly listen to public radio, which drives my brother crazy.) But March Madness has ended and apparently Rush Madness has just started. Grandma Toma takes a front-row seat at the kitchen table.

"Is this about Grandpa?" Noah breaks in.

All of us—Mom, Dad, Lita and I—turn to my younger brother. "What?" we say in unison.

Noah sits on a barstool in front of the kitchen island, crunching on a pear.

"I met him at Lita's house when I was watering her plants. He told me not to say anything until Lita got back. Something about him wanting to surprise you. Oh, by the way, Lita, you owe me twenty bucks for keeping your plants alive."

A part of me wants to close my eyes so I can avoid witnessing what is to come, but a bigger part of me needs to watch it all happen.

"What. Is. Going. On?" Dad thunders. He usually has a

goofy grin on his face, his slightly crooked front teeth always visible. His mouth right now is a straight line. I can tell that he's pissed as hell.

Usually Mom's the enforcer, so I'm a little confused. Dad rarely loses his cool.

Noah's face, I swear, has turned gray. Right now he could be playing one of the zombies on *The Walking Dead*. It's one thing for Mom to be mad; we're all actually kind of used to it. It's comforting, in a weird sort of way. But seeing Dad mad means that something is definitely not right in the world.

Grandma Toma, who's a little hard of hearing, nudges Noah for assistance. "Now what's going on?"

"Mom, why don't you go watch some TV," my mother says, a little too abruptly.

Grandma Toma shrugs her shoulders and shuffles off in her house slippers.

"What is going on?" Dad repeats. His anger is aimed toward his mother, whose face is the same ashen color as Noah's.

"Noah's right. It's your father," she whispers.

"My sperm donor? Because I don't remember ever seeing a father in the house, although there've been plenty of men."

Uhh. That was a low blow. Not that Lita doesn't deserve it, but still. Dad never, ever goes there.

"What the hell, Mother? Why was he at your place and talking to my son? Why has he suddenly appeared after all this time? And why does my son know about this before I do?"

"I was out of the country. In Puerto Rico." Lita scrambles to explain. "I just found out that he was in town just today."

"He mentioned something about having been in jail," Noah blurts out.

"Beautiful. Just beautiful," Dad comments.

Mom, surprisingly, is silent. She looks as shocked as we are—maybe more so—that Dad is having a meltdown. Or maybe it's this new information discombobulating her, that we, specifically her husband and children, are genetically linked to a felon.

"He got out a while ago, actually," I can't help but add. "It was back in the sixties."

"You, too?" Dad looks betrayed. Yeah, I guess I'm Daddy's little girl.

"He came to me, Dad. He said that when he heard I was in the LAPD, he wanted to tell me that he thinks he may know who's behind the Old Lady Bandit bank robberies. Lita thinks it's this guy he used to run around with way back when." I don't mention anything about Fernandes also being responsible for my missing car. There's obviously only so much my father can take right now.

"I forbid you to talk to him!" Dad shouts, which is a plainly ridiculous thing for him to say. He then addresses Lita. "And I forbid you to talk to my daughter about this behind my back. This is just—just unacceptable." Dad opens the hall closet and pulls his blue Windbreaker back on.

"Gary—Gary—" Mom calls out. Before following him outside, she turns. "See what you've done," she says to all of us.

Hey, I'm an innocent victim, too, I think.

Meanwhile, Lita's looking completely defeated. Her gauzy, loose outfits usually give her a playful air, but right now she just looks deflated and bedraggled.

Grandma Toma reenters the kitchen. "Your chubby Indonesian friend is on TV," she announces and then shuffles back to her room.

"What?" I don't have any Indonesian friends. But both Noah and I run after Grandma Toma, while Lita stays in the kitchen alone with the wine bottle. We plop down on the couch in front of the large flat-screen television that overwhelms the room, including my old small twin bed in the corner.

The anchors have moved on to a story about the split of some reality show couple, so we rewind the DVR to watch the story from the beginning.

"Grand Avenue Fatality: Homicide or Accident?" reads the slug at the bottom of the screen. A reporter is on the scene at the Walt Disney Concert Hall. "Family members of a Boyle Heights gardener who passed away today claim that his death was no accident."

I gasp. *Poor Mr. Fuentes.*

"Did you know the guy?" Noah asks.

I shush Noah as I concentrate on the news segment. "Eduardo Fuentes died this afternoon at Los Angeles General Hospital after sustaining critical wounds from a fall down these stairs." The reporter then gestures to the stairs behind him. "His family says he was actually pushed by Fang Xu, the father of the highly acclaimed cellist Xu, who performed here at the hall yesterday."

The report then cuts to recorded footage of a middle-aged woman I recognize as Marta Delgado talking into multiple microphones. "My father was a dedicated worker his whole life. To be killed like this, for who knows what reason, is murder in our eyes. And the Chinese government is just protecting the man because his son is a famous musician."

Video cuts to last night's reception. First Xu on the stage with the USC professor, then Mr. Xu, standing near the translator, Washington Jeung, and Nay. Nay looks a little heavy in the shot; she's not going to be happy.

"That's Nay!" Noah exclaims. "I thought that she was Cambodian."

"She's from Lakewood," I answer back, shushing him.

"That's your friend, right? Likes to talk a lot?" Grandma Toma says.

"Yeah," I say. I wonder whether Nay has heard about Fuentes's death.

My phone immediately starts ringing. It's the private phone number of homicide detective Cortez Williams. The number that he once warned me to lose forever.

"Where's your friend, Nay Pram?" Cortez demands.

"What's going on?"

"We can't locate Xu or his father. We think that they are leaving via private jet for a foreign country. They can't leave California. Especially now."

I can finish Cortez's sentence. *Especially now that Eduardo Fuentes is dead*.

"The PR person at the hall says the Xus left last night with a translator, Washington Jeung, and that a reporter from the local college newspaper was with them. Nay Pram. Isn't that your friend?"

Unfortunately, I can't fully protect Nay. I've already burned too many bridges for that. "Yes, that's her. But she has nothing to do with Xu. She's involved with the translator. That's all."

"Do you know where she is?"

"Actually, I'm not sure."

"Well, if she's your friend, you better get in touch with her. If the translator knows where Xu and his father are, she may, too. She needs to tell us ASAP, okay?"

After I agree, Cortez starts to end the conversation.

"Wait," I call out. "Is there anything new in the Old Lady Bandit case?"

"Why are you asking?"

"I was just wondering."

"That's what I was worried about, Ellie. Your wondering is dangerous."

We say good-bye for real, and I feel like a fool. I don't know what to do with the information that Fernandes gave me. Actually, on second thought, what information? There's nothing concrete. No name. I don't even know how to reach Fernandes— only that he's out there somewhere driving my car.

I call Nay but I only get her voice mail. *Damn you, Nay,* I think to myself. I leave her a brief message telling her to call me.

I try texting her: *I need to talk to you.*

Nothing.

Then I remember. I use my Shippo Twitter account.

Shippo Wan Wan
@naypramreporter Where are you?

I wait. Then finally, a response.

Nay Pram
@ShippoWanWan WASSUP?

Shippo Wan Wan
@naypramreporter Do you know about Mr. Xu?

Nay Pram
@ShippoWanWan WHAT ABOUT HIM?

Shippo Wan Wan
@naypramreporter Just call me.

No response.

Shippo Wan Wan
@naypramreporter CALL ME!!!!

Shippo Wan Wan
@naypramreporter I'm not kidding!!!

Nay Pram
@ShippoWanWan OK. GIVE ME A SEC.

Shippo Wan Wan
@naypramreporter Now!!!

My phone immediately rings. It is, of course, Nay.

"What's going on, Ellie?" Nay says. "What's the big emergency? You know I don't like being addressed with exclamation marks." Background noise almost overwhelms Nay's voice. It's loud, like an engine, swooshing and then dissipating.

I'm not used to Nay getting mad at me. Usually it's the other way around, and I'm a little thrown off. "Where are you?"

"Saying bye-bye to the Xus. Well, at least the dad."

"Are you at LAX?"

"No, these people are swagger; they rent their own plane. Ellie, it's so cool! I'll tell you all about it later but my phone is almost dead."

I cut her off. "NAY. I need you to keep Mr. Xu there, okay? It's important. I don't know about Xu, but his father has to stay in this country. Talk to detectives."

She senses how freaked-out I am. "Chill, okay," she says. "Mr. Xu is around here, somewhere—" Nay's voice then cuts off. Her battery's probably dead and she never has her charger when she needs it.

Okay, Nay, I say to myself. *Van Nuys Airport, here I come.*

FIVE

I never drive into Van Nuys unless I really have to. I mean, what's in Van Nuys? It's a burned-out patch of ground, filled with generic mini-malls and curious light-industrial businesses. And, of course, the private airport. I knew of its existence, but have never gone to it until tonight.

Traffic on the 134 is actually not bad—it's the tail end of rush hour—but once I get on the 170, I'm basically at a standstill. The last time I was here was to go to Tillman Reclamation Plant in Van Nuys, which recycles wastewater; you know, the water in our toilet bowls after we flush. It was for Mother's Day one year because, believe it or not, it happens that the wastewater recycling plant also has one of the most gorgeous Japanese gardens I've ever seen in LA. My father was so jazzed, he kept repeating, "Can you believe this thing of beauty is here, a product of recycled wastewater?" My mother and Grandma Toma, the actual Japanese and the honored guests, were less impressed. Grandma Toma kept sniffing and saying, "Something stinks."

Mother's Day is this weekend, and it's bound to be awkward. Usually we have a brunch at my parents' house. To be fair, Mom ends up doing a lot of the work, but then, the day is also for Grandma Toma and Lita. Grandma hates crowds and waiting, so to keep the peace, it's easier to just do the celebration at home. I do make what I can—usually coffee cake, fruit salad and freshly squeezed orange juice—and Dad makes his famous frittatas. Noah even gets in on the action, and in recent years has broken out our old espresso machine to make custom cappuccinos and lattes with not only coffee but matcha tea.

My phone vibrates with a text from Noah. Although I know that I shouldn't be on my phone while driving, we're not moving, so I read it: *dad & mom R home now. won't talk to Lita. she left.*

Fantastic, I think. *Friggin' fantastic.*

Since traffic's still stalled and I'm on my phone anyway, I Google the private airport. All sorts of information appears. I pride myself on knowing a lot about LA, but I didn't know that the modest Van Nuys Airport is one of the world's busiest general aviation airports despite not having a main terminal. More like fixed-based operators, or individual hangars with private carriers. It's also apparently about seven hundred and thirty acres in size, which means it's going to be hard for me to figure out Nay's exact location.

Once cars start moving, I switch from Google to GPS and let Mildred—that's the voice of my GPS—guide me to the general vicinity of the airport. I get off at Sherman Way and travel west. This neighborhood is pretty much what you'd expect in an area where people, especially men, fly in and out. Strip clubs and fast food. What happens in Van Nuys stays in Van Nuys.

It's dark now and practically everything looks the same. There's a gate around the perimeter of the landing field with a mishmash of aviation-related businesses around it. I'm not wearing my uniform, but I have a police Windbreaker in my trunk. Correction: in the Green Mile's trunk. The car that I don't have. *Crap.*

I'm really in a bad mood right now, and I try to steady my mind. *Don't think about your grandfather. Think back to your conversation with Nay.* I remember the sound of a helicopter. I pull over and Google "helicopter tours" and "Van Nuys." Only a couple of places come up. The one with the highest Yelp review rankings says it's the place to go for night tours.

I drive as quickly as I can but I'm really out of my element; I don't recognize a thing. I see a company that grows sod. What is that doing here in Van Nuys?

A few single-engine airplanes fly overhead, so I know that I'm close to the runway. And then I see it. A building advertising helicopter rides. The lights are still on inside. Next to it is another nondescript two-story structure, some sort of charter airline company. Could definitely be one that the Xus are using. I find a parking spot; the lot is pretty much empty aside from a handful of cars. The closest one is a white Chevrolet. I shine my pocket flashlight through the window into the vehicle. On the floor of the back section is a folder and papers. I recognize the logo. It's the press packet from the Eastern Overtures concert.

Even though I haven't seen Nay, I suspect that she's in

the area. It's enough. I call Cortez and leave my location on his voice mail.

There's a heavy gate in between the two buildings with a sign warning against any unauthorized persons entering the landing strip. Even against the night sky I can see the curved outlines of old-fashioned airplane hangars. I don't feel like I'm in modern-day Los Angeles right now. It's like I stepped back in time. Or I'm in the Midwest—or at least how I picture the Midwest, with tons of open space.

I pull open the heavy glass door and see a ticket counter, just like any airline. And beyond that is a simple waiting area, where Nay is seated by herself on a plastic chair.

"My phone died." Her useless Android is still in her hand. "Why are you here, anyway?"

"Where is everyone?"

"Mr. Xu went to the bathroom. But then he was taking too damn long, so Washington went to check on him."

"Dammit. They probably took off."

"I really don't think that he meant to push that guy down the stairs, El. I think it was an accident. Both of us think that."

"You mean you and that Lincoln guy—"

"Washington!"

"Whatever, you don't know him. You just met him. He could be in on this whole thing with the Xus."

"In on what?"

"I don't know." I'm totally frustrated and I'm not quite sure what I'm saying. "It's just not smart to trust strangers. You don't have the best track record with men."

"That's harsh." Nay's voice takes on a coldness that I've rarely heard. "Ms. Perfect. Ms. Protector of the Public."

"Don't go there—"

"No, let's go there. You and Benjamin were together for two years, so that makes you a solid judge of character? And I'm what? A skank?"

"I didn't say that. Don't put words in my mouth." Nay and I have never exchanged words like this, and our fight seems surreal. This is a bad dream, right? Except it isn't. "Didn't you see the news reports? This is turning into an international incident."

"Don't tell me. You called him. Mr. Yummy. I suppose he wants to talk to me."

"I had to keep him posted," I admit. "Cortez and his partner will probably be here at any minute. I can take you home if we leave right now."

She shakes her head. "I'm a journalist. I'm not scared of any cops," she says.

A man comes from around the counter. "Sorry, miss, but we just got notification from the police that we need to cancel this flight," he tells Nay. He doesn't seem to notice that his two passengers are missing.

The flight crew is now unloading the luggage from the plane. The last piece of luggage catches my eye: a bright purple cello case with a splash of silver logo. I can make out the abstract design better now. It's definitely the outline of some kind of bird with nine heads.

More than what's on the case, I'm interested in what is inside. Why would the Xus abandon a five-million-dollar cello? A cello that one man already nearly died over? The cello that Mr. Xu was fighting to retrieve? The cello Kendra Prescott was hassling the police about?

No one's here yet, so I go over to the purple case.

I snap it open to reveal a honey-hued cello. Is it the same one that Xu was playing last night at the concert? Beats me. It looks like any other cello, as far as I can tell. Since I don't know when I'll get the opportunity again, I start taking a healthy number of photos of this cello with my phone. Nay starts taking pictures of me taking photos—for what purpose, who knows?

"I'm going to take off," I tell Nay after I'm finished. I really don't want to be around when Cortez and Garibaldi get here. I'll be pushed aside again, and it'll be too embarrassing for that to happen in front of Nay. "Are you sure that you won't come with me?"

She shakes her head. "No, thanks. I have a job to do. I'm a big girl; I don't need you. In fact, get out of here."

Her words sting. We've been through heartbreaks, all-nighters, dictatorial professors and probably hundreds of bowls of ramen.

I feel shaken, down to my *corazón*, my heart of hearts, my *kokoro*. Nay is the sister that I never had but always wanted. Sure, she's a bit wild, but it's true—I'm too vanilla sometimes even for my own taste.

But Nay turns her back on me, and I have to hustle. As I get into Kermit, without Nay, I see Cortez parking his car on the other side of the lot. I freeze, but he has no idea that I'm driving this Hyundai. Cortez's partner, Garibaldi, gets out of the passenger's side door, and for a moment, I consider running back inside the charter plane terminal to flail my arms around Nay and tell them to back off of her. Yet I don't. Nay made her choice.

As I drive back home, I barely notice what freeways I

travel. Sometimes in LA, you go into automatic driving mode when your thoughts are heavy. And my thoughts are superheavy right now.

It's not until I'm back home and practically in bed that I officially receive the breakup text from Nay at midnight: *THINK ITS BETTER IF WE DONT TALK FOR A WHILE*.

I hold my phone still, just staring at the text until the screen finally goes dark. *What the hell happened tonight?* I wonder. I drove all the way to Van Nuys to help her. Or was it to help myself?

BFF breakups are ten times worse than boyfriend breakups. Boyfriends can usually be replaced, sooner or later. But a best girlfriend? Those are hard to come by. Me and Nay took a good two years before we transitioned from friends to best friends.

With Nay cutting me loose, I feel anchorless, untethered. I'm not used to being completely alone. Over the past four years, I had Benjamin and Nay. Now I have neither.

I wake up the next day with a migraine. By the time I get in to work, my head is throbbing in spite of the two TYLENOL Extra Strength capsules.

I sit in our roll call. My CO, Tim Cherniss, is leading our session. Cherniss is so squeaky clean and straight that some officers find him difficult to listen to. He hardly ever cracks jokes, and when he does, they're usually the kind you might tell your kid or nephew, not a roomful of cops.

"As I'm sure you're all aware by now, a seventy-year-old

Hispanic male, Eduardo Fuentes, passed away at LA County General yesterday. Injuries sustained from a fatal fall at the concert hall. He was one of the contract gardeners there."

"What garden?" one of the officers asks.

There's a garden upstairs, idiot, I think. Nobody explains it to him because they don't know, either. Cherniss ignores the comment and continues. "Ever since the media reports last night, we've received some anonymous calls. Detectives will be following up with interviews of all musicians and staff members. Rush, Jaffarian, you two will patrol the area to make sure there are no disturbances."

"What's this all about?" one of the senior members of our team asks.

"I'm not privy to the details—we have a job to do, and we'll do it."

Anonymous calls, I think to myself. It does sound suspicious. Could Fuentes's attempt to take the cello be connected to something bigger?

Detectives have already arrived by the time Officer Armine Jaffarian and I arrive. I station myself and my bike in front of the stairs, while Armine takes the corner.

The artists' entrance is connected to the elevator in the parking lot. But since they don't want anyone walking through the upstairs garden, now the musicians have to get off at ground level and walk to the front of the hall. The elevator that opens up to the sidewalk is encased in a glass box. There's a door that locks from the outside, to protect the musicians from the riffraff, I guess.

The musicians look like ordinary people casually dressed in jeans, T-shirts, knit tops—except for the instrument cases they're all carrying. One man, with a case the size of a big backpack, wears a leather jacket over a black Who T-shirt, definitely evoking more of a rocker image than that of a classical musician.

Most people have already arrived when I hear some deafening rap music coming from a black BMW. Cece is in the driver's seat. The pink-streaked violist makes a wide turn into the street leading to the parking lot; then, a few minutes later, I see her reappear on ground level in the glassed artists' entrance. Her viola case in hand, she pushes open the door to the sidewalk and jogs to the hall entrance. She's wearing an orange peasant dress cinched at the waist and large sunglasses—and a huge smile on her face. *Do you not realize that someone died yesterday from a fall that occurred a few feet away?* I want to shake the yellow crime scene tape in her face.

I feel like everything is getting under my skin today. I stop some European tourists from going up the stairs, and I guess I'm pretty harsh with them, because Armine calls me on it later after she goes across the street to buy us a couple of hot dogs from a street vendor by the court building. "What's going on with you, Ellie? Man problems?" she asks, handing me a hot dog. She's put mustard, onion and relish on it—just how I like it. We've worked as partners enough times to know each other's preferences. For example, I know she's a café Americano woman and that she takes her dog with only ketchup.

I lift my hot dog from its cardboard holder and take a bite. It's not bad for courthouse street food.

"No, actually, girlfriend problems," I say as I'm chewing. I don't even care if it's rude.

"Girlfriend? But I thought . . . Oh."

"No, I'm not gay—"

"It's okay. It really is."

Armine, who has a husband and two kids, probably doesn't have a lot of time for female friends. But when you're my age, you're nothing without your homegirls. I don't bother to convince Armine that she's getting the wrong idea about me. She's constantly peppering me with questions about my love life anyway. Maybe now she'll stop.

We return to our stations. Through the glass of the hall lobby, I can see Cortez and Garibaldi talking to the PR flak. She's still wearing her hair back in a ponytail, except this one is a bit messier than the one the other night.

Boyd and Azusa, patrol officers from our station who've been assisting with interviews, come out and greet me.

"What's all this about the anonymous leads?" I ask them.

Boyd's not going to offer me anything. All Azusa says is, "Nobody really knows anything."

About what?

"Well, gotta go type up our reports. If we had iPads or the newest laptops like the school district, we'd be done by now," complains Boyd. "I've rewritten this damn thing three times already." Throwing away a page of his notebook in the trash, he walks over to the patrol car parked along the curb.

I get what he's saying. When I was first hired, I was shocked to see how shoddy the equipment and facilities are that we patrol officers have to work with. It's a completely different world at the new LAPD headquarters, though, where my aunt and Cortez are stationed.

"They're not giving up anything," I tell Armine as I ride over to her. "No idea what this new anonymous information is."

"Does it matter?" Armine asks. "It's not like we are detectives or anything. It's like the sergeant says—we just do our job and that's that."

Armine has two kids and a husband who's out of work. For her, the LAPD is a steady gig. A job. But I didn't go through the academy for just a job. I want to make a difference. Our division is going through the motions to uncover the truth, but I'm starting to wonder how committed we really are.

After work, I stop by Osaka's but don't see anyone I know other than the waitstaff and line cooks. I feel so out of it, I can hardly believe it when Kermit takes me to the edges of MacArthur Park, to Rickie's apartment.

He's outside and wearing a beanie, which has flattened his Mohawk and makes him look like any other Filipino twentysomething now.

"No Osaka's tonight?"

He shakes his head. "Trash day tomorrow. Gotta do some diving. You can come with me."

I realize I'm pretty desperate, but am I desperate enough to raid trash cans for the sake of Rickie's company?

"It's legal, you know, if that's what you're worried about."

I know that it's legal. *Abandonment of property*—isn't that what the proper term is? Once you throw something out, it's public domain.

I extend my arms. "I'm in my uniform. Can't have someone take a photo of me and post it on the Internet."

"Well, here you go." Rickie peels off his black trench coat. He's wearing short cargo pants, and I can see one of his tattoos, a character from his favorite comic book series,

Love and Rockets, on the side of his left calf. After removing a pair of rubber gloves from the pocket, he tosses the coat to me. "There's another pair in the other pocket."

The trench coat fails to cover my bare legs—I definitely look like a female flasher. But in the neighborhood that we'll be wandering in, it's better to be mistaken for a sexual deviant than an LAPD cop. "I'll go with you, but I'm not getting inside any garbage bins."

"Suit yourself."

We go on foot, Rickie pushing an abandoned shopping cart from the local drugstore. So incredibly embarrassing. We walk down an alley on the side of a mini-mall, one of the hundreds that exist in the area. I pretend that I'm going undercover as a homeless woman—that's the only way I'm going to get through this.

"How did you learn all that stuff about the legal precedence?" I have to admit that I'm at least a little impressed about his know-how.

"Meetup group."

"There's a Meetup group for Dumpster diving?"

"There's Meetups for everything."

He's right. Mom used meetup.com to find a group of fiftysomething breast cancer survivors who wanted to start running marathons *and* master the art of making macaroons. Believe it or not, turns out there were a bunch of them.

"So what's up?" he asks.

I almost stumble on a broken piece of sidewalk.

"You must be pretty distressed to hang out with me by my lonesome."

I can't BS Rickie, and it's actually a relief. I tell him everything about Fuentes, Xu, Mr. Xu, Nay and her man of the day, Washington Jeung. What I keep to myself is the stuff about my long-lost grandfather.

"It's not like Nay to blow me off," I tell him. We've had our fights, but they're usually over practically before they start.

"She's taking this journalism thing seriously."

"She just started at the *Citrus*. It's not like she's Christiane Amanpour."

"It's like when you joined the academy, you totally disappeared. You kind of blew her—well, all of us—off."

I want to deny it, but I can't argue with the truth. Instead, I change the subject. "What's going on with Benjamin, anyway?"

Rickie shakes his head. "Dunno. Talk about being MIA."

"Is he doing okay in school? Is it money?"

"He's all right on both counts, far as I know. If things get real bad, he has his family."

It's true—the Chois are a tight-knit family. They're nice people, and Benjamin's sister, Sally Choi, is a defense lawyer. Truth is, crime does pay, at least for the attorneys. They can afford to help him out if he needs it.

"Here, watch my cart," Rickie says as he begins to climb up a Dumpster. So gross. Fortunately, he doesn't actually jump into the garbage; he stands on a metal bar connected to the outside of the container, then bends straight down to begin his hunt.

I'm impressed how flexible he is. Who needs yoga?

A plastic garbage bag is opened, and empty fast-food cups—the straws still poking out from the lids—tumble out into the alley.

"You know you're making a mess?"

"Going to arrest me for littering?"

More garbage, smears of barbecue sauce on plastic plates, half-bitten sandwiches, tangles of Chinese noodles. I feel like throwing up after seeing this hodgepodge of multicultural food.

Rickie retrieves a grocery store salad, its packaging still intact. He looks at the expiration date and then tosses it into the cart.

"Ew, Rickie, you're not actually going to eat that?" I'm aghast.

"Expires today. It looks fine, no brown lettuce. Do you know how much perfectly good food Americans waste?"

I stay quiet, feeling chastised. I can imagine, based on my own habits. Throwing out the rotting vegetables and fruit in my refrigerator is a weekly ritual of mine. I always go to the store thinking that I'm going to eat healthy, but then just end up doing takeout while the good-for-me food goes bad.

We hit a couple more Dumpsters, adding two unopened bags of tortillas and an untouched roasted chicken, wrapped in an aluminum bag, to our shopping cart. Since Rickie now has dinner, we search for miscellaneous treasures down a residential side street dotted with small houses and apartment buildings.

Since it's garbage day tomorrow, the city-issued Army green containers are all out on the street. The recyclables, of course, have already been picked over. Rickie leaves those for the homeless and semipro scavengers anyway.

We walk past an apartment where pieces of furniture have been hauled out onto the dead grass by the sidewalk.

"Oh, lookee what I found!" Rickie crows. It's a red retro-looking chair.

"That's actually pretty nice," I admit.

"You want it? You need some color to punch up your place."

I walk carefully around it, half expecting a rodent to run out from underneath its round cushion.

"It's not going to bite you. It's perfectly fine." Rickie's gloved hand gives the chair a good shake and it rotates back and forth. "Oh, snap, it swings. Cool. You've got to take this, El."

"Why don't you go for it?"

"Are you kiddin' me? My roommates will kick me out on my ass if I bring in anything more from the streets. My stash for eBay and craigslist sales is already taking up most of the apartment."

A truck full of flattened cardboard boxes and assorted broken furniture parks in front of the driveway beside us. The driver also spies the red chair and starts to get out of his truck.

"Look, we have some competition." Rickie wipes his forehead with the back of his gloved hand. "What do you say?"

I lift the chair on top of the shopping cart. Luckily, it's light; less than thirty pounds. With that, I've officially become a Dumpster diver.

I forgot how fun it can be to spend time with Rickie. There's a reason for his eccentricities, I know. His family is crazy big—between his older stepsisters and stepbrothers, there may even be as many as twenty of them. Like a runt in a large litter, Rickie's always had to fight for every scrap of food or clothing. He's street-smart and City Hall–smart. He has a passion for local politics, and his knowledge has come in handy when needed. It's just that he's so damn high-maintenance.

He helps load the red chair into Kermit. "Ugh," he says. "This car is a disservice to that awesome chair. See what treasures you can find in the trash."

A switch flips on in my mind. *Treasures and trash.* The page that Boyd had thrown in the trash can. A public trash can. On a public street.

"Hey, have you done any trash diving in downtown?" I ask Rickie.

"What do you have in mind?"

I drive Rickie to Grand Avenue. With the red chair in the rear, he's like a rolled-up pill bug in the passenger seat. Luckily, the drive is short, barely ten minutes.

Since too many people might recognize me on this block, I ask—well, plead—with Rickie to do the dirty work. I promise him some carne asada tacos from a local food truck, which seals the deal.

"Downtown's a different deal than MacArthur Park," he says before he leaves the car. "Requires more stealth." He takes the trench coat back from me and drapes it over his body. Rickie is tall, over six feet, but he somehow manages to blend in with the other artistic night wanderers on Grand Avenue. Once he's at the trash can, he descends over it like a gigantic crow and then returns to the Hyundai, stinkier and a few pounds fatter with a plastic bag of trash.

"Dang, did you have to take the whole thing?" I quickly drive away, checking my rearview mirror for any of my law enforcement colleagues.

"What, did you want me to dump it all on the sidewalk?" Rickie takes a small flashlight from his pocket and holds it in his mouth as he paws through the contents in the trash bag. "Aha!" He plucks out a ball of lined paper and uncrumples it in his gloved hands, bits of food falling into the car. I try not to gag. He attempts to read the note: "'I asked Mr. Bikel if he had heard of any . . .' This is real bad handwriting."

"Go on, Rickie."

"Okay, something, something . . ."

At the next light, I snatch the note from his hands. Sure enough, it's Boyd's boxy handwriting.

I asked Mr. Bikel if he had heard of any stories of persons wanting to steal Xu's cello. He replied in the negative. Mr. Bikel was quite hostile and claimed that Mr. Fuentes would never participate in anything illegal. Mr. Bikel apparantly was a friend of Eduardo Fuentes.

It's no wonder that Boyd had thrown this draft of his report away. The little he's written here is too wordy and confusing. And he also misspelled the word *apparently*.

"Ellie, green light." Rickie nudges my elbow. "Good stuff in the note?"

"Not bad."

"Anything you'd like to share, Officer? After all, I am your partner in crime."

I give Rickie an eye roll.

"Hey, I could have been arrested for what I did. The evidence is still on me." He shakes the trash bag for effect, spreading all that pleasant-smelling goodness inside my rental car.

"I thought it was all legal. Abandonment of property and all that."

"Well, the city could claim ownership. Who knows when you get the government all involved."

"Well," I say, "I know that I need to find out who Mr. Bikel is."

"Okay, whatever. Doesn't sound that exciting."

"Thanks, Rickie," I tell him when I reach his apartment after stopping to get the tacos—now already devoured. "You really helped me out. I appreciate it." His shirt is covered in wet spots from God knows what, so I forgo a hug and just wave good-bye as he gets out of the rental car.

Driving home with the red chair in my backseat, I pass by my neighborhood Catholic church. I'm friends with the priest, Father Kwame. Although I can't even call myself a lapsed Catholic, I'm a product of their private school education. Even more important, I do believe that God is out there; I'm just not quite sure how to label Him; although calling God a "He" comes more easily than a "She" (maybe a result of my mother-daughter issues?).

I park Kermit outside along the curb and walk across the sidewalk, up the stairs to the small attached office where Father Kwame also lives. I press down on a button on the intercom and in a few seconds hear his familiar comforting voice. I identify myself and then the door swings open.

"Ellie, it's so good to see you. It's been a while. A couple of months?"

Father Kwame doesn't ask me if I want to come in. He

assumes it. I walk inside and he follows me into his living room, which is the closest thing I've seen to a parlor in twenty-first-century Southern California.

He goes into the kitchen to brew some tea—again, it's just what Father Kwame does, so I don't even bother to tell him not to.

He brings the tea in ceramic cups on a tray. After he settles down in his easy chair with his teacup, he finally asks, "How are you doing?"

"Crappy," I say. Father Kwame's not your typical Catholic priest. At least not like any other one I've ever met before. First of all, he prefers listening to talking or sermonizing. And he doesn't seem to mind if you say something a little off-color or rude. In fact, he says that he prefers to hear someone's true heart, not something prettied up or manufactured. So I give him my current truth. I tell him about Nay, the situation with my grandfather, and the death of Eduardo Fuentes. Even though in some ways it's the least personal to me, the passing of the gardener has affected me the most.

"I really feel bad for his family. He seemed like a man who was well loved, who people looked up to. I only spoke to him for a few minutes, but he was really kind."

"Maybe you can write his family a letter."

"No, that would be overstepping. This is still an active investigation. The family might be able to turn around and use my letter as evidence that Mr. Fuentes hadn't been doing anything wrong. In fact, I actually doubt that he was. But the thing is, I have no proof."

"Will you go to his funeral?"

"I don't even know when or where it might be." I've only

ever been to one funeral, Grandpa Toma's, and I was still in elementary school at the time. Besides, he was cremated, so all we had to do was bow to a photo of him in his fishing vest.

"It wouldn't be too difficult to find out," Father Kwame says.

Dammit. He would have to be a voice of reason. *Ellie,* I tell myself, *you're a cop. You have to get used to seeing dead bodies.* "You're right," I say. "Do you mind if I look it up now?" I pull my phone out of my pocket.

"Of course not. Your portable computer, yes?"

I check the website of the Spanish-language newspaper *La Opinión* first; there's nothing there. I wonder whether there hasn't been enough time for the family to make arrangements yet.

The story does quote a pastor at an East Los Angeles church where Eduardo Fuentes was a member. I show Father Kwame the name of the church. Templo Arbol de Vida. The Temple of the Tree of Life.

"It sounds Pentecostal," Father Kwame says. "Those churches often use phrases like 'river of life' in their names."

Once I hear that the church may be within the Pentecostal denomination, I really don't want to go to the funeral. What if they start speaking in tongues or something? I won't know what to do.

"You may have been the last person he ever talked to," Father Kwame reminds me gently.

"I'm pretty sure that I was." I study Father Kwame over my now-cold tea. "You think that I owe it to him to go?"

Father Kwame shakes his head. "No, he's already passed. He doesn't care anymore. But I do think that you owe it to yourself to attend. To pay your last respects to his family. And if you need someone else to accompany you . . ."

"You'll be my plus-one."

Father Kwame smiles. "You betcha."

When I get home, I strip off my uniform and stuff it into my washer. It's one of those tiny ones with an attached dryer above. However small those appliances are, they are a hundred percent better than my last apartment, which had no washers or dryers. Going to the Laundromat at ten o'clock at night in Los Angeles is no fun, I'm telling you. Definitely did my wash with my Glock around my waist.

After tossing Shippo a bully stick, I pull a pint of salted caramel ice cream from my freezer and a spoon from my kitchen drawer. Plopping down on my bed, I look over the *Don Quixote* concert program while licking spoonfuls of ice cream. Shippo mimics me by chewing his treat. Like owner, like dog.

I turn to the back of the program where all the musicians are listed and look for the name "Bikel." I easily find an Oliver Bikel under the category of "Contrabassoonist." I take out my phone from my pocket and Google the name, and an image of the musician who was wearing the Who T-shirt at the concert hall comes up. I think that he might be the same guy sitting in the back row of the orchestra during the Brahms performance. There's a brief bio, too. In addition to all of his musical accomplishments, it says that he's "an avid amateur gardener." Maybe that's why the Mr. Bikel mentioned in Boyd's handwritten report was so emphatic about Eduardo Fuentes. It could be that he knew him as more than just a laborer who worked at the concert hall. Were Fuentes and the classical musician unlikely friends?

Even though people talk about how LA is some kind of melting pot, the truth is that we pretty much stick close to people like us. Is Bikel an exception or is there another reason why he came to Fuentes's strong defense?

SIX

I have my earbuds in as I leave Kermit at home and ride the Gold Line to work the next morning. It's not even eight o'clock on Saturday. My phone rings; it's my mother. We haven't spoken since the fiasco at my parents' house, but it doesn't surprise me that it's her. Who else would call me so early? "I'm calling to inform you that your father and I will be out of town tomorrow." My mother sounds very businesslike, a secretary instead of a family member.

"But tomorrow's Mother's Day." And also my day off.

"We were thinking that under the circumstances, it would be better to take a break from family activities."

"Dad's that pissed? It's not our fault that this Puddy Fernandes suddenly appeared in our life. We're the victims, too."

Mom doesn't say anything for a moment. "That's his name? Puddy Fernandes?"

"Well, I guess his legal name is Pascoal Fernandes. So Dad, Noah and I are part Portuguese."

"Don't say that. You're mostly Japanese."

"No, Mom, I'm only half."

"But in terms of your values, your upbringing."

"I think that we got some fine values from Dad and Lita."

"Hmpf."

"Anyway, isn't that who you are really mad at—Lita?" I try to keep my voice level so not to attract attention from the other train passengers.

"She shouldn't have kept all those secrets from your father. For fifty years!"

"So now you're going to punish me and Noah for what Lita's done? That's not fair. And Grandma Toma, what about her?"

"We were thinking about taking her with us."

"Mom, that's not cool. Lita's going to be really hurt." Not to mention, it means Noah and I will have to entertain her by ourselves on Sunday. "I know that it's none of my business, but I think Dad should meet Fernandes. Just to get it over with."

"I'm surprised that you would say that. Lita already confessed to Dad that he was the one who took your car. You're a police officer. He's a common criminal, a hood."

A *hood*? I haven't heard that word used since my high school staged *West Side Story*. "So what, Mom? So we're not a perfect, upstanding family? Is that so bad?"

Mom doesn't answer and then hangs up the phone.

Even though there's no sound coming in through my earbuds anymore, I don't bother listening to music. I need the silence, the space, to process what is happening to my family and me. Dad is like Lita (and her mom, I guess) in that he always tries to see the positive side in everything and everyone. Whenever my mother wanted to discipline me, he'd always advocate for talking it out instead. Every drawing, every disastrous craft project, was a masterpiece. When I failed to get two serves over the net in our high school championship volleyball game, Dad claimed that we lost the game due to bad refereeing.

Up to now, he'd only ever described his mom, Lita, in the most loving terms: Numero Uno Mama, Best Mother Alive, Ms. Fierce. She has three mugs that say "World's Best Mom," because Dad keeps forgetting that he's already given her one before. Lita says that she'll never tire of receiving mugs with that message. (Grandma Toma, on the other hand, would complain, "We already have enough mugs in this house. What am I going to do with this one?")

Now these two positive forces in my life can't be in the same room. I admit that I've always taken both Dad and Lita for granted. For them to be at odds with each other makes me feel as if a crack has started to expand in my family life. I hope it can be fixed, but wonder if there will always be a mark where the break was.

Today, Johnny and I are assigned to patrol Grand Park. Grand Park used to be just a place near the courthouses and parking lots that my family just drove past during the weekends to get to Grand Central or Little Tokyo. A few fountains, some dying grass, nothing to write home about. Then, a few years ago, a transformation began to happen. The lawns became lush; walkways rolled out; neon pink chairs moved in. A narrow fenced-in dog park was even created for all the beautified dogs of downtown LA. Exercise classes are held on the main lawn, and now that a two-bit reality show star has started attending the yoga class, for some reason a higher-up thinks it will be good to have some nominal LAPD presence nearby. (I'm not even familiar with the cable channel that airs the show. The series is called something like the *Real Divorcées of Bunker Hill* or something like that.) Well, two bicycle cops are as nominal as you can get.

Everyone and everything around here still seems hung-over from the Cinco de Mayo celebration on Olvera Street last week. Instead of couples or groups of people, there are just a few solitary people wearing shades out walking their dogs. Aside from the yoga class, the liveliest presence here are the park's trademark pink chairs.

Johnny doesn't seem to mind this assignment. In fact, he spends an inordinate amount of time watching the Real Divorcée. Dressed in a halter top and the tightest pair of yoga pants I've ever seen, she makes sure that her butt sticks out as far as it can as she assumes the positions of downward dog, then cat and cow. Her every action is being recorded by two video cameramen and a super bored-looking woman in her forties who's probably the producer. If she's this bored with the subject matter, I gotta think that certainly doesn't seem promising for the future of the show.

My phone vibrates and I sneak a look. It's Nay. I tell Johnny that I'm going to check out the other side of the park and, entranced by Real Divorcée's Booty, he barely acknowledges having heard me.

Once I'm far enough away, I call Nay back, but only get her voice mail.

I text: *Hey, you called?*

No response.

I wait a few minutes and then text again. *You okay?*

Finally I get a reply: *SORRY BUTT-CALLED BY ACCI-DENT. SUPER BUSY. ON DEADLINE.*

On deadline? Since when is Nay worried about deadlines?

I know being on the *Squeeze* staff is a big deal for Nay. She has dreams to be the next Lisa Ling. But she's never put friendship on the back burner. I know I have, though, especially when I was at the academy. Maybe now I'm getting the karma that I deserve.

I'm not going to get any updates on the Xus from Nay, so I consider my other alternative. The embodiment of hotness, Cortez Williams. I don't want to call him, but it feels like my only option. I clear my throat. "Hi," I say when he answers. "It's Ellie."

"Hey, Ellie." Cortez sounds like himself, like back when we first were getting to know each other. "Thanks again for the heads-up on that charter flight. We were able to pick up Mr. Xu. He was heading for a hotel that was just around the corner. We've investigated and determined that the Fuentes incident was an accident. So it's all over."

"Does the Fuentes family know?"

"We let them know this afternoon."

"How did they take it?"

"Well, you know. They are pretty upset. But, according to all accounts, Fuentes was attempting to steal the cello. Mr. Xu pushed back and unfortunately . . ."

"But why would he even try something like that? There was no getaway car. He'd just be running down Grand Avenue carrying this huge multimillion-dollar instrument? He was a pretty old man; he wouldn't be able to get too far. It doesn't make sense." *And what about Bikel's statement?* I don't mention that out loud, though, since I'm not supposed to know about it.

"Criminals often do things that don't make sense."

But he wasn't a criminal, I think to myself. No record. That much I had checked on my own. "Okay, but if the cello is that big a deal, then why did Mr. Xu—and, for that matter, Xu himself—just abandon it at the airport? Mr. Xu said it was worth five million dollars, but he leaves it to the baggage handlers? I'd have that cello checked out, if I were you. And not just by the place that Kendra Prescott recommended."

Cortez doesn't saying anything. He probably knows it's a good idea, but doesn't want to admit he didn't think of it first himself.

"Where is the cello, anyway?"

"We're waiting for Xu, the musician, to claim it. Fang Xu wanted to take it with him, but legally it belongs to his son."

"Anyway, I'm really calling about my friend Nay Pram. Did you interview her that night?"

"Yeah, just some basic stuff. Garibaldi handled it. It was obvious that she didn't know much. Didn't she tell you about it?"

"Well, we kinda had a falling-out. I haven't seen her since Thursday. She's been putting me off. Guess she's been busy researching and writing her articles."

"Those things happen, Ellie. Hard to be friends with civilians. Sometimes they don't understand and you don't understand them."

There's a click on the line and Cortez has another call

coming in. After we end the conversation, I feel like everybody has something important to do. Everybody except me.

Johnny rides toward me and brakes a few feet away. "I got her number," he reports.

"Whose number?"

"The reality show girl. Chale Robertson."

"The Bunker Hill divorcée? Johnny, isn't she a little old for you?" I'm all for men dating older women, but Johnny usually prefers his dates a few years out of high school.

"She still looks young. And she's into biking. Like seriously into it."

"Just watch out that you don't end up on her reality show. Captain Randle won't like it."

Johnny's not listening to me. He's already texting something sweet and charming to the divorcée. While he does get tongue-tied at times, there's nothing wrong with his thumbs.

A little while later, Johnny gets called to join a group gathered around the Los Angeles Central Library. It's some kind of protest about funding cuts. I, on the other hand, am supposed to go back to the station to complete some paperwork.

Before I leave, my phone begins to vibrate in my pocket. It's Google Alerts, notifying me of a post on an East Los Angeles mortuary. It's a listing of Eduardo Fuentes's funeral at his church, Templo Arbol de Vida. I quickly read the notice, which is all in Spanish. It's tonight at seven o'clock.

I make a quick call to the Catholic church in Highland Park. Father Kwame's there and available. Despite my reservations, I guess I'm going to a funeral tonight.

Once I return to the station, I park my bike on the wall

with the others and check the air pressure in my tires. I accidentally rub some dirt and dead leaves from my wheel onto the side of my shorts. It's all going into the wash, anyway.

As I'm leaving, I run into the patrol officers Boyd and Azusa. "Hey, Rush, want to get some drinks with us? We're going to Grand Star."

I haven't been to the Chinatown hangout in months. "No, thanks. I can't tonight."

"Hot date, huh?" Boyd says.

"Yeah, something like that." I don't tell them the date is for a funeral, which I'll be attending with a Catholic priest. Just permanently stamp "Loser" on my forehead, okay?

Father Kwame is waiting for me outside of the Templo Arbol de Vida church, which actually is a former bungalow in East Los Angeles, on a residential street just off of Whittier Boulevard. I'm a little late—I went to my place after work to change into a simple black dress—but judging from the other people gathered outside, the funeral hasn't started yet.

As we walk in, I accidentally brush against the knee of an Asian man in an ill-fitting suit, sitting in the last row.

"Oh, I'm sorry," I immediately say.

He glares at me.

Wow, Mr. Cranky, I said I was sorry. And why is your knee sticking out into the aisle, as if you're ready to bolt at any minute?

Father Kwame and I sit in the second row from the back in front of the mad-dogging man. From our seats, I can't see the family, though I spot a couple of blond heads in the fourth row. Everyone else here seems to be Latino. Not just

Latino, but all Spanish-speaking. Luckily, that's not an issue for us, since Father Kwame, who can speak several languages, and I both speak Spanish.

The walls that probably once divided rooms in the house have been torn down to accommodate an open sanctuary that can probably fit one hundred and fifty people, tops. There's a row of windows toward the front, all now covered with a thick velvet curtain. Three acoustic musicians sing in Spanish beside a gigantic cross made from what looks like driftwood. The song's about what you'd expect in a Christian church: God, Jesus, blood.

I brace myself for talk of burning bushes, or anything paranormal, but it's pretty much like other Protestant services I've been to. Unlike Catholic mass, there are no robes, incense, or wafers—which is fine with me.

The minister is about my dad's age, with a mustache and thinning hair. He's taken off his jacket and wears a striped tie with his shirt. Even though he's not close enough for me to know, I feel sure he'd smell musky clean, no flowery cologne, but something straightforward. And safe.

The religious stuff doesn't interest me as much as what the minister says about Eduardo Fuentes's personal history. He was from a small town in the middle of Mexico and came here when he was thirty, then became a naturalized citizen in the 1990s. That was when he was able to call over his nephew Raul Jesus, his sister's son, to the United States. Eduardo and his late wife, Cristina, had only one child, their daughter, Marta, and three grandsons. When Marta's name is mentioned, a sob breaks out from the front row. No doubt from Marta herself.

Eduardo was one of the founding members of this church,

the minister says. An elder. I figure that's why people keep pressing into the church, filling every space in the pews and even the folding chairs that have been placed in the back. Father Kwame and I are sandwiched between women who bring out fans to cool themselves. They obviously knew there's no air-conditioning in the small building. I wish I'd known, too.

The guitarists then get up onstage again, and a line is formed to view the body in the open casket. I gulp. I am less than thrilled.

The last row goes first, and the cranky old Asian man pulls on his suit jacket, as if that will make him more presentable as he stands in line. He's short, only about five two if even that. He ducks his head toward the body, and when he turns around, his eyes look kind of moist. His face is weathered and dark. He looks like a man who has spent time in the sun, like Fuentes. Maybe they were in the same line of work.

The row of family members—I recognize RJ and Marta from the hospital—rise and give the old man hugs. He seems a little taken aback.

We're up next and I take a deep breath. I take a few steps forward and look down in the casket. It's lined with white, puffy material, which makes Mr. Fuentes seem like he's lying on a cloud. He's wearing a suit and his face looks stiff and waxy, not wrinkly and smiley like he was when we talked about the Gracias sage, the purplish flower that he'd been in the middle of planting at the concert hall garden. I expected to feel sad, but I actually feel nothing. This is not the man whose hand I held on to while he tried to mouth his last word.

I turn to the relatives sitting in the front row of the church. Eduardo's daughter, tears pooling down her face, studies me for a moment. "At the hospital," she murmurs. "Police." She then takes a deep breath; I fear that she's going to let out a scream of grief. Instead, she leans forward. *Is she going to be sick?* I wonder. No, it's not vomit—she intentionally spits on my shoes. They are not fancy shoes; I got them for barely forty bucks at Nordstrom Rack for events. But still.

"My father was not trying to steal that cello. How dare the police close his case!" she says to me in a voice loud enough for everyone to hear. The words, *police* and *policía*, can be heard throughout the crowd.

I'm stunned, and even Father Kwame, who's rarely taken aback, looks disturbed. RJ, the nephew, quickly stands up. "You better leave," he says.

Father Kwame carefully guides me through the crowd of mourners, who all give me dirty looks as I pass by. Once we're outside, Father Kwame asks me if I'm okay.

"I'm all right," I tell him. "I've been spit on before." Now that my initial surprise has passed, I'm feeling nonchalant about it. Like I'm some sort of LAPD *veterana*, even though I'm barely out of probation.

"Where did you park? I will walk you to your car."

I don't need Father Kwame to protect me, but I accept his fatherly care. I feel a stab of self-pity over not having my father around as my personal cheerleader. It wasn't like I'd intentionally invited Puddy Fernandes into my life—he'd barreled in, and took my car with him. If I'd a say in the matter, yeah, I wouldn't have engaged in any kind of conversation with him. But that's not how it went down. My dad needs to understand that.

I hope he does soon.

When we're about a block away from my car, I hear someone call out, "Officer!"

I turn around. It's Wendy Tomlinson, the gardener who witnessed Mr. Xu push Fuentes down the stairs. Instead of khaki pants, she's wearing a dress. And of all people, she's with Oliver Bikel, the contrabassoonist. The two blondes in the crowd.

"Hello," I say, wondering whether they saw my little incident with Fuentes's daughter.

"I wanted to see if it was true," she says. We stand underneath a streetlamp and everyone's face looks a bit ghostly. "Are the police really not going to charge Fang Xu with anything?"

I want to say, *No and it totally sucks. Something's off, but I'm not sure what it is.* But instead I just shove my hands in the pockets of my dress. "Yeah, I guess they've determined that Mr. Xu was defending himself against a potential robber."

"That's bullshit." Bikel's voice is much higher than I expected. I guess I'd just assumed it would sound deep, like a contrabassoon. "I told the police that there's no way Eduardo would do such a thing."

Another person walks toward us on the sidewalk. The short, cranky Asian man who was in front of us in the receiving line.

"Mr. Arai, you've worked with Eduardo before," Wendy says to him. "Don't you think it's crazy that the police think he was trying to steal that cello?"

The old man moistens his lips. He obviously doesn't want to stand around and talk about Eduardo Fuentes outside his funeral.

"He'zu not kind of guy to make trouble," he finally offers. His accent is heavy. He sounds like some of Grandma Toma's relatives who have lived some years in Japan.

"See," Wendy says. "This man has worked with Eduardo for, what—"

"Thirty yearsu."

"He should know," adds Oliver.

"Really," I say.

"Yeah, straight as knife." The man then slices the air like he's simulating a karate chop. I think that the expression is straight as an arrow, but I get the general gist.

He excuses himself and we make way for him to pass by.

"I think that you guys got this all wrong," Wendy says as Father Kwame and I also keep proceeding to my car. "This is no way to ruin the reputation of an honest man."

Standing in front of Kermit, Father Kwame clears his throat, as if he is struggling to find something encouraging to say. But no words can lighten this situation. In these people's eyes, the police are scum and there's no convincing them otherwise.

SEVEN

On Sunday, despite my arguments, Mom and Dad decide to go through with their separate Mother's Day excursion with the Good Mother, Grandma Toma, leaving Noah, Shippo and me to celebrate with Lita on our own. This is going to be awkward.

We haven't made any reservations and none of our favorite eating spots has any openings. "How about McDonald's? They have a senior special or something. Old people are always hanging out at the McDonald's in South Pasadena," Noah suggests as the two of us brainstorm last-minute ideas at my dining room table while we wait for Lita to arrive at my house.

"We are not taking Lita to McDonald's for Mother's Day."

"Then what?"

"I suppose I can whip something up in the kitchen," I say.

"Since when did you start whipping things up?" my brother asks doubtfully.

I go into my tiny kitchen and try to summon my inner Rachael Ray. Can I make a three-course meal in thirty minutes, all with a smile on my face? Yeah, right. At least Lita's low-maintenance. My usual coffee cake and fresh-squeezed orange juice should be okay. I'll just fry up some bacon to go along with it, and it'll be fine. Everything is better with bacon.

Soon my house is smelling entirely of bacon. Noah's on a mission to "harvest" my neighbor's oranges for some juice. Anything that hangs over the wall is mine, I tell Noah. That's the law.

"If you say so," he replies, taking a Trader Joe's bag with him outside. Shippo, his tail wagging, is only too happy to act as his accomplice.

We are still prepping when Lita walks in without even knocking or ringing the doorbell.

"Happy Mother's Day, Lita!" I call out when I notice her. She seems subdued. She's probably bummed that her only son isn't celebrating the day with her.

"Oh, that looks *deliciosa*." She compliments the coffee cake that I've just taken out of the oven, but her eyes have lost their usual sparkle.

"Dad will come around," I say to her, putting my arm around her and squeezing her shoulder.

"I don't know. This is the first time he's ever stopped talking to me. I sent him a letter, apologizing and revealing everything I know. I even came clean on the Skylark, that Puddy was the one who stole it."

We sit around the table and squeeze the orange halves. I've held off from buying an expensive electric blender. Instead, I have one plastic juicer, which we let Noah use, while Lita and I just use our hands to extract a few drops of juice from each half. Luckily, my brother has managed to fill the Trader Joe's bag with oranges, so we have a pretty big stash.

There's a knock on the door. I frown. I'm not expecting anyone. Shippo barks ferociously, the way he gets when he doesn't like the person on the other side of the door. I look through the peephole. *Oh my God, no.*

"What are you doing here?" I open the door just enough to talk to Puddy Fernandes.

"I'm here to talk to the mother of my child. I know she's here. She won't open the door to me at her place. She almost ran me over with her car the other day."

"This is not a good time."

"Who is it, Ellie?" Lita asks from the kitchen, her hands dripping with juice.

"Uh—" Turning for one minute, I lose control of the door. It swings open, revealing Puddy Fernandes, who's wearing the exact same clothes as he was on Thursday. Based on how he smells, he's been sleeping in them, too.

"Estel, my girl." His arms are outstretched, revealing underarm sweat marks on his shirt. Following him is his torpedo of a dog, Bacall.

"Don't you 'my girl' me, you son of a bitch." And then Lita pulls back her right arm to unleash the most amazing punch I have ever seen in person.

Fernandes's head snaps back and he immediately clutches the bridge of his nose. Shippo starts barking like crazy again, setting off high-pitched yaps from Bacall. I position myself to intervene, but Fernandes lets out a crazy laugh that sounds like Shippo coughing up grass. "You haven't lost it, have you?" he says, his voice sounding a bit nasal from the pressure he's placing on his injured nose. He then lets go and smells his fingers. "Mmmm, oranges." A line of blood streams from his left nostril.

Noah's eyes are as big as saucers while I push Fernandes into a chair and try to administer some first aid. I get a washcloth from my linen closet and toss it to Noah. "Get some ice cubes," I tell him. "And soak this in cold water."

I push Fernandes's head back—not as gently as I probably should—and wipe blood from his upper lip with a tissue. Up close, he smells even worse. Noah hands me the damp washcloth with a couple of ice cubes, which I press against his nose.

"Is it broken?" Lita asks. I'm not sure whether she's concerned or hopeful.

The nose doesn't look crooked, but it's definitely swelling up.

"Can't let anything happen to these good looks here." Fernandes smiles widely, exposing all his brown teeth. Lita grimaces.

"You'll have to go to a doctor tomorrow after the swelling has gone down," I tell him. "The bleeding has stopped, so that's a good sign, at least."

Noah pours Fernandes some fresh orange juice, which he accepts gratefully. "Haven't had a drink so delicious in decades," Fernandes says, after taking a small sip. "On a container ship, everything is usually freeze-dried or frozen."

"Are we supposed to feel sorry for you because you haven't had a chance to drink fresh orange juice?" Lita asks.

"Why all the hate? Is this what I get after all these years?"

"Puddy, I don't see hide nor hair of you in fifty years and

now you show up out of the blue and I'm supposed to be happy about it?"

"Well, if I had known that I was a father and a grandfather, I would've tracked you down. I had to hear that from this boy." Fernandes nods his head toward Noah.

Lita turns to glare at Noah.

"All I said was the Skylark used to be our grandfather's," Noah says weakly.

Usually my brother acts all chill, but this family stress has brought out his younger self. I realize he's the one who must've given Fernandes my address in the first place.

"No, Noah, I take responsibility for all of this *mess*," says Lita. It's clear that by *mess*, she's referring to Fernandes.

"Listen, I'm just here as a Good Samaritan. A good soul." Leaving his rough-and-tumble sailor speech behind for a moment, Fernandes talks as if he were reciting a page out of *Don Quixote*. His nose is now all red.

Lita looks unconvinced. For that matter, so am I.

"Ronnie killed someone. An innocent person. I've maybe done wrong, but I've never hurt anyone. I just want him stopped."

"How do you know that he's behind the Old Lady Bandit?" Lita asks. My question exactly.

"Can you get me a photo of the Bandit from your computer thingermajigger?" Fernandes asks.

I go into the bedroom and get my laptop from inside my dresser. My Glock is nestled right beside it. I think twice about getting my gun out, too, but since Noah's here, I decide against it.

I bring out my laptop and go online to find news clips showing security camera footage of the Old Lady Bandit.

There are some other criminals with the same nickname, but ours in LA is the easiest to find. I click on some links that include video still images.

The Old Lady Bandit looks like she could easily play an evil witch in a production of *Snow White* or *Sleeping Beauty*. She's hunched over, with a scarf around her head. Deep wrinkles on her forehead, drooping cheeks and bags under her eyes.

Upon seeing the photographs, Fernandes gets super-excited. "See, there, that makeup technique? That's Ronnie's technique. I'd know it anywhere."

I zoom the images to full screen to get a better idea of what he's talking about.

"It's collodion. Cellulose nitrate, real flammable stuff. Nowadays, it's all latex, but that's what they used back in the sixties. Look at the forehead and the way the cheeks fall down, like rotting fruit. That's Ronnie's handiwork. I'm sure of it."

Both Noah and I squint at the screen, while Lita sits back with her arms folded.

"I'm telling you, that's his signature."

"From fifty years ago?" Lita says.

"Listen, I've been waiting for this moment for that weasel to emerge from his miserable hole. He ruined my life. After being in the slammer, I couldn't get a regular job. Had to go out to sea."

"You ruined your own life. You didn't have to chase him like a dog going after a bone in the first place. You were a grown man."

Fernandes's swollen nose makes him look comical, like a sad clown. "I had a future. I could have made it in the industry.

And I could have made it as a father." He starts to sniffle. "May I use your bathroom?"

"It's through the bedroom," I tell him, a little embarrassed. Even though my new place is bigger, I don't care for the awkward layout, like how the only way to reach the bathroom is by going through my bedroom.

After Fernandes goes into the bathroom, I ask Lita, "What do you think?"

"I think he's lying. There's something he's not telling us."

I think Lita is right, but I have to admit that Fernandes's vulnerability does have its charms. I can feel myself softening toward him.

Shippo starts barking again at the front door.

Now what? I think. I open the door without checking the peephole. My parents are standing on the welcome mat.

"Mom, Dad," I say, more as an announcement than a greeting. They both pile into the house. Grandma Toma is immediately behind them, and so is Aunt Cheryl. *Oh crap,* I think.

"Hola, queridos," Lita murmurs, but doesn't get up from her seat.

Noah covers his face with his hands.

"So this is your new place," Aunt Cheryl says, doing a quick survey of my humble abode.

"It's bigger than her other place, if you can believe it." Mom is the master of insulting me while complimenting me at the same time.

Grandma Toma immediately plops herself down in my new red chair (which Rickie was right about; it really adds a nice something to the room), and starts spinning around in it.

"That's a nice vintage piece." Aunt Cheryl zeroes in on

the chair. "I think it's designer. Where did you find it?" She's a fan of all those home-renovation cable shows.

Before I can answer, the toilet flushes and I see Mom silently counting the people in my living room.

I close my eyes.

"These low-flow toilets don't really do their job, do they?" Fernandes walks out, rubbing his hands on the sides of his pants. "Oh, hey, when did the parade arrive?"

Fernandes and my father lock eyes and the resemblance is unmistakable, even with Puddy's swollen nose. Dad could be Fernandes in twenty years if he stopped brushing his teeth and hair right now.

Dad doesn't need anyone to connect the dots for him. "This. Is. Unacceptable," he declares to no one in particular. Maybe the entire universe.

Grandma Toma stops spinning in the Dumpster chair.

"Ah, everyone," I say, because being a good hostess means always introducing your guests, right? "This is Puddy Fernandes. And this is everyone."

"Is this Gary's father?" Grandma Toma spells it out.

Aunt Cheryl steps forward. "I'm Deputy Chief Cheryl Toma of the LAPD," she says. "And I'm going to arrest you for grand theft auto."

I'm not quite sure whether Aunt Cheryl is serious or not, but I decide to play along.

"It's my car," Fernandes says quietly.

She tells him to sit in the living room chair, which he does without argument. I pick up Bacall and put her in his lap because that's the only way his insane poodle will keep quiet. Shippo, satisfied that the dog is out of his line of vision, retreats to his dog bed with a huff.

"What happened to your nose?" Aunt Cheryl finally asks.

"I punched him," Lita declares.

I expect some reaction from Dad, but there's none.

Nobody follows up Lita's answer with a *why*. I guess we all figure she had her reasons.

"The car is mine," Fernandes repeats.

Lita, like Aunt Cheryl, goes on the offensive. "It's not your car. You left it to me. And I gave it to Ellie."

"How did you transfer ownership? You must have forged my signature."

"Puddy, it was fifty years ago."

As Lita and Puddy continue their squabbling, my mother begins to wipe off all the sticky orange juice and pulp on the table. I've forgotten all about the bacon and the coffee cake that have been cooling on the stove. I cut the cake into thick slices and place them on our makeshift interrogation table.

"You baked this for too long," Mom says, but I notice that doesn't prevent her from picking at a slice.

Dad, meanwhile, situates himself in the corner of the room. I'm kind of surprised that he's even stayed inside. Grandma Toma has sunk into the Dumpster chair. I'm going to have to check the springs. Noah has a blank look, as if he's staring into space, but I know he's hanging on to every word.

"Well, whether or not my name is officially on the car anymore, I still have a key."

"You're not the legal owner, sir." A vein begins to bulge out on Aunt Cheryl's forehead, a sure sign that she's becoming exasperated. "And the car was parked on private property. Why didn't you check with the resident regarding whether it would be all right to remove it from her driveway?"

"Ah, well—" Fernandes looks my way. I can sense some kind of psycho story brewing in his mind. He places the wet washcloth back on his injured nose. It's so bizarre to see this unkempt man—my grandfather—sitting across from my perfectly groomed aunt. Then I remember what Fernandes told us, that he has inside information that could potentially help us apprehend a bank robber wanted for murder.

"I might be willing to drop the charges," I say, "as long as Mr. Fernandes cooperates."

"Cooperates with what?" Fernandes's voice is a bit muffled by the washcloth.

"He has a lead about the Old Lady Bandit. He says that he may know who is committing all those bank robberies," I declare.

Aunt Cheryl, like all female Tomas, has a good poker face. (I'm obviously a Rush in that regard, but I'm working on it.) Right now she looks bored out of her mind, but I know that the more expressionless she seems, the more excited she may actually be. "Well," she says, "that could change the situation. If your information pans out, I could put in a good word for you with the DA."

Fernandes finally lowers the washcloth. He attempts to breathe in and out of his nostrils, which are narrowing by the minute from the swelling. "I'm going to need some assurances that anything I say will help me gain immunity from any charges."

"Mr. Fernandes, you are not in a position to make deals." Aunt Cheryl won't budge.

Fernandes lowers his eyes in defeat. "Okay. I'm here as a Good Samaritan anyway." He sighs. "His name back then was Ronald Sullivan. He could be going by other names now; I dunno. We worked together on movies. He was the head makeup artist, and I was the gaffer. But he was hooked on the horses, always needed money. I had nothing really to do with that bank robbery back in the sixties. I mean, I helped him with his makeup. That was about it. We made him look about fifty years older. About the age that we are now." He laughs, but no one laughs with him. Instead, Lita frowns. Noah is listening intently; this is much more entertaining than any video game. My parents, on the other hand, are stone-faced. I don't know what they're thinking.

Fernandes pets his poodle as he remembers. "Somebody ratted us out days later. It didn't matter how much I denied being involved. Had a horrible lawyer. Did my time, five years. When I got out, nobody would hire me. My mother had died during that time, so I took up my daddy's profession. The sea. Fifty years of seasickness.

"Ronnie, on the other hand, was having a good ole time in Vegas, last I heard. Doing makeup for shows or something. But that was about a decade ago."

Fernandes's whole body seems to have shrunk in the chair. He seems much older than Lita, although they must be close to the same age. "I did all that Internet search stuff. Nothing came of it. Thought maybe that he might be dead. That is, until I saw that video on television."

I bring out my laptop and find the page featuring the stills of the Old Lady Bandit.

"That's his handiwork. I can recognize it anywhere. He may not be the guy underneath that makeup, but Ronnie applied it. I bet my life on it."

Aunt Cheryl writes this all down in a notebook that she always carries in her purse. She tears out some blank pages.

"Okay, Mr. Fernandes. I want you to write down everything you just told us. And give us your contact information."

Fernandes hesitates for a moment and then picks up the pen that my aunt has also handed to him. My mother and I take some dirty plates into the kitchen while Dad stays in his corner, just staring at his bio-dad. Apparently this all has grown tiresome for Grandma Toma, however, because she's fast asleep in the red chair.

"You need to do something to freshen up this place, Ellie," my mother tells me as we start to wash the dishes. "Plus, the inside of your refrigerator is just filthy."

Uh, Mom, I've been a little busy. Didn't you just witness what's happening in my living room right now? I hear Shippo's ball being bounced on my hardwood floor. At least he has Noah to keep him company.

Mom washes and I dry. Some things never change. I wonder what Mom is thinking. *Aren't you freaked-out?* I think. *I certainly am. In just one week not only have I met my grandfather for the first time; I'm also finding out that he may have crucial information about an open murder and robbery investigation.*

"You are free to go, Mr. Fernandes," we hear Aunt Cheryl say. Both Mom and I step back into the living room. "But leave the keys to the car."

"But it's my car."

"The pink slip is in my niece's name," Aunt Cheryl says definitively. I guess she's been paying attention. "I'll call you a taxi and pay for wherever you need to go. Within reason, of course." Aunt Cheryl then excuses herself and says that she'll wait for Fernandes on the sidewalk.

Forgetting about Bacall on his lap, Fernandes rises to his

feet. Bacall jumps down onto the floor and looks at Shippo, thinks twice, and wanders to the front door.

Addressing my father, Fernandes begins to speak. If this were a Western movie, he'd be holding a hat in his hands. "I erred. Made some big mistakes. But you have to know that I went by your mother's house after I got out of jail. I saw you then from a distance, but I had no idea that you could be mine. There was another man there with you and your mother." Knowing Lita's track record, it didn't surprise me that there might have been another man around the house.

"Look at you now. A beautiful wife. Two smart kids. You're some kind of engineer, I hear. It's all due to your mother. But now I can go through life knowing that something good came out of me. I know that you don't want to have nothing to do with me, and that's okay. I'm proud to call you son. Anyone would be."

Fernandes rubs his graying mustache before digging out his car key and placing it on my living room table. Lita is as still as a statue. Only her eyes blink, faster than usual.

I give him the washcloth filled with ice to take with him. "It's okay. I don't have any matching towels to go with it, anyway."

Fernandes stands still in front of the doorway, registering all of our faces before he leaves, then closes the door behind him.

"Wow," Noah says from the floor, rubbing Shippo's belly while he lies on his doggy bed. "That was intense."

None of us says anything for a while. Dad looks like he doesn't know what to do. Finally, he says, "Happy Mother's Day, Mamita."

And then Lita bursts into tears.

For the most part, our family is not the crying type. Grandma Toma doesn't cry. Noah doesn't cry. Mom doesn't cry and neither does Dad. And Aunt Cheryl definitely doesn't cry. So to see Lita like this is, well, a bit awkward. Noah keeps petting Shippo as if it's the most fascinating thing he could be doing right now. Mom gets up, starts to walk over to Lita, and then backtracks. Dad is frozen in his spot. I begin to make an attempt to console her, but it's Grandma Toma who surprises me. She rouses herself and shuffles over in her Clarks Mary Jane shoes and wraps her arms around Lita's neck. "It must have been hard for you to be on your own all these years," she says, her forehead resting on Lita's. She does this for only about two seconds but it almost feels like we have been visited by the Dalai Lama.

Mom starts blinking her eyes hard and fast. Noah makes a face, like, *Can you believe this?* Even Shippo is mesmerized and watches silently from his doggy bed.

Dad clears his throat. "Caroline, c'mon, we better get going," he says. Mom is only too happy to comply.

Lita attempts to give Grandma Toma a good-bye hug, but is sidestepped and instead ends up wrapping her arms around air. Grandma Toma is already out the door. Everything seems to have returned to normal, and Noah heaves a sigh in relief.

"I guess I'll just go home with them," Noah says, careful not to make eye contact with Lita.

Gee, thanks, Noah.

This whole encounter with Fernandes and Dad has apparently taken a toll on Lita, however, because she announces that she'll be leaving, too.

"Thank you for this beautiful Mother's Day brunch," she

says to me. "Everything was exquisite. You definitely have your mother's touch."

I go out on the porch and watch as my parents, Noah, Grandma Toma and Aunt Cheryl all squeeze into Dad's Honda hybrid. A hybrid yellow taxi is waiting on the curve as Fernandes and his dog get into the backseat. Lita, on the other hand, is in the driver's seat of her yellow Cadillac, the Wild Rose.

My first Mother's Day get-together in my own place. A complete fiasco, but it actually went a lot better than I might've expected, under the circumstances.

I pick up my car keys and get ready to call the Green Mile back home. Shippo joins me as we walk to where Fernandes said he'd parked the car around the corner.

"What the hell did he do to you?" I mutter as I reexamine the Skylark. Shippo starts licking something sticky on the bottom of the driver's-side door.

"No!" I pull at his leash. "You need a bath, Green Mile."

Shippo is always game for an expedition, no matter how mundane. So our trip to the car wash is a literal tail wagger. I wish that I could be so content.

We go to one of those cheap car washes, located on the side of a gas station. I'm placing my ticket in the kiosk when my phone rings. It's my long-lost ex-boyfriend. Benjamin Choi.

"Where are you?" he asks as the machine's tracks move the Green Mile forward into the bay. Water shoots out from the top and sides and I can't see much through the windshield.

"Car wash."

"Oh," he says.

I feel my face flush. We actually did it in a car wash one time. "Anyway," I prompt him to change the subject, "where have *you* been?" The mechanical arms position themselves over the car. Squirts of soap and then the scrubs of brushes. Shippo is captivated by the sounds and cleaning foam on the windows. Then more water again, followed by a quick but intense blow-dry.

Benjamin is silent for a moment. "I've been wanting to tell you. My mom was diagnosed with cancer."

"Hold on." The green light goes on at the end of the wash and I ease the car from neutral to drive. I park on the side of the station by two large vacuum cleaners.

"Benjamin—" I say. My voice sounds tender, more tender than it's been in months. "I'm so sorry. What kind?"

"Ovarian."

"What stage?"

"Third."

I curse. Loud. And long.

"I know, I know. It really sucks," he says, explaining that she had a hysterectomy that day.

We're both quiet for a moment. Benjamin knows I understand. Which, I realize, is probably why he's been wanting to talk to me in the first place.

"Tell me how I can help. I can run errands. Bring food."

"Ellie, you can't cook."

"But I have money."

"Don't worry about it. But this helps. Just talking to you."

"Have you told anyone else yet? I mean, other than relatives."

Benjamin is silent, so I know he hasn't. Except for me.

"I remember when I first found out my mom had cancer," I tell him. "I couldn't believe it. I mean, she was supposed to always be around for me."

It was before college and the Fearsome Foursome. It had been around the time that my college applications were due. My high school friends hadn't known how to deal with it. So, for the worst months—the months of operations and chemotherapy—I felt alone. Noah was still in elementary school, so most of the babysitting duties were on me. He was the one who would ask me, as we watched Mom's hair fall out and heard her throwing up in the master bathroom, *Is Mom going to die?* So, at seventeen, I had to put on a fake happy face and say, "What, you idiot? Mom's not going to die. She's going to be torturing us forever." My mother put on a brave face because she didn't want it to affect my grades or my essays. But how could it not? I'd had good grades, had considered applying to Ivy League schools or maybe Stanford or Berkeley, but I changed my mind when all that was going on. Both my parents argued with me, but I wouldn't back down. Pan Pacific West, a reputable liberal arts school only a few miles away, was good enough. Noah didn't say anything at the time, but I know that he was relieved to hear I'd be sticking around. He was only ten years old at the time.

"I'm glad that we can still talk," Benjamin says now. "After everything."

"Listen, when all is said and done"—I take a deep, deep breath—"we are friends, Benjamin. Nothing is going to change that."

"Oh, the family's all here. I gotta go," he says.

"Tell your mom Happy Mother's Day, for me, okay? And that I know that she'll pull through this."

"Thanks, El." Benjamin's voice cracks and then our conversation ends.

I sit in the Green Mile for a while, next to the vacuum hoses, curved like elephant trunks.

In terms of my love life, there's my pre-Benjamin phase and my just plain Benjamin phase. During my pre-Benjamin, I dated my share of guys in high school. Nothing hot and heavy. Dances, football games, group events. But I noticed a trend: when I wasn't that interested, it seemed that they always were. I had that conversation several times. *You know, let's just be friends. I value our friendship too much to mess with it.* Blah, blah, blah.

I hated those talks most because they were lies. It wasn't that I deeply valued my friendship with these guys; it was that I didn't like them in that way. I couldn't imagine myself kissing them (yuck!), holding their hands, or having their arms around me. Absolutely no chemistry.

On the flip side, I did have my share of unrequited crushes. You know, the kind when your whole body flushes when you see *that guy*? Your body temperature goes up about fifty degrees. You imagine kissing their face, their lips, their neck, and having them ravish you. Unfortunately, or maybe fortunately, that's as far as any of those ever went. Just in my head.

With Benjamin, though, there had been immediate attraction on both sides for once. I was into his casual messy style. The longish hair. The slight afternoon shadow—well, as much as a Korean guy could have—on his unshaven face. He didn't talk a lot. He was perfectly comfortable with moments of silence, and I became comfortable with them, too. We didn't have to entertain each other, be on our best behavior. I could burp and fart and wear no makeup. He honestly didn't care. I loved how easy our relationship was, at least until I graduated early and entered the Police Academy. Then it became . . . less easy. More moments of nagging, on both our parts, accusations, arguments. A whole lot of drama. Our breakup had been messy, but after all that drama, in a way it was a real relief by the end.

I finally shake myself out of my reverie and start to clean out the interior of the car. I throw away all the balled-up fast-food wrappers and containers. I attempt to suck out all the dirt with the gas station's vacuum cleaner, and a strange rattling noise emanates from the hose. I turn off the vacuum and take a closer look at the backseat floor. There are a bunch of rusty screws all over the place. *What the heck?* What was Fernandes doing in here?

Whatever. This day has been too complicated already, and I'm in the mood for a simple reward. I feel an urge for sugar. Pure sugar. After I finish vacuuming, I go into the car wash and get a big bag of gummy bears. I go back to the Green Mile and eat every single dang one.

EIGHT

The next day, I'm at the station all day. Since I've gotten a reputation for being able to write and edit police reports, Captain Randle has tapped me to go through some other officers' reports that need work. Arresting suspects is only part of our job; we also need convictions. Of course, those are the responsibility of the DA's office, but we don't want a shoddy report to be the reason why a perp gets off on a charge.

We learned things at the academy I hadn't expected. Sure, there's firearms training and all the physical stuff, including getting tased (hurts like hell when you get zapped, but when it's over, it's like it never happened. Pepper spray, now, that's altogether different; the burning sensation can last for a couple of days). Also on our academy training schedule were Spanish and report writing classes (both of which I aced). My ability to craft solid reports, understandable to a regular layperson on a jury, is being talked about. So much so that even veteran detectives have asked me to proofread what they've written.

A little before noon, I get a call. Not on my personal phone, but at the station.

"Hello, Ellie."

I can recognize that voice anywhere. "Ah, hi, Aunt Cheryl. I mean, Chief Toma."

"I was hoping to see you. Time for lunch?"

I've stacked some finished files on Captain Randle's desk. He won't refuse me a lunch break.

"Ah, sure." I expect her to suggest the Metro Club, a fancy-schmancy place where the city's power brokers hang out. Not too excited about that prospect because I always feel like a dork there in my bicycle shorts and messy bun.

She surprises me by suggesting the Japanese garden at the community center in Little Tokyo. "I'll pick up a couple of bentos," she tells me. "Broiled salmon okay?"

I bike over to the center and carry my bicycle down the stairs of the building. I've always called this place my "secret garden" because I first visited it with my parents after I read Frances Hodgson Burnett's book about the poor little rich girl who discovers a secret garden in her uncle's house. Except instead of roses, this garden has sculpted pine trees and a stream that travels down three terraces.

Since it's located at basement level, the garden is not readily visible. Only locals, or visitors who have read about it online, know where it is, and around lunchtime on a weekday, it's absolutely empty except for my aunt, who's sitting in the shade by a bamboo grove. The plastic bento boxes are laid on napkins. Aunt Cheryl, in fact, is also sitting on a napkin and there's one spread out for me, too.

"How much do I owe you?" I go for my wallet in my shorts and Aunt Cheryl waves me off. "Don't be ridiculous."

The man-made stream and pond glisten in the distance. We eat in silence for a while, our disposable wooden chopsticks digging into sections of the grilled salmon, stewed carrots and taro, crunchy bright yellow pickled daikon and sticky rice decorated with black sesame seeds.

"I wanted to talk to you about Pascoal Fernandes," Aunt Cheryl finally says. Our clandestine location for lunch suddenly makes sense. My mysterious grandfather is not only my secret; he's also hers.

I swallow a mouthful of food.

"He gave me a phone number and address in San Bernardino, but the man who lives there says that he hasn't heard from him in more than a week. The taxi on Mother's Day dropped Fernandes off on a corner in North Hollywood, but there's nothing really there."

"You mean you don't know where he is."

Aunt Cheryl nods. "I've been doing some independent research. Pascoal Fernandes was arrested in 1964 for being an accessory to a bank robbery in North Hollywood. He was sentenced to seven years in prison, got out in five. But other than that, nothing. Not even a traffic ticket over the past fifty years."

"Well, he did say that he's been in and out of the country, working on a container ship."

"Do you believe what he says? This man, a convicted felon, who just appeared out of nowhere?"

I hadn't really thought about that.

"If he was working on a ship, what kind of ship was it? What was it transporting? Are you getting my drift, Ellie?"

"Are you saying that he might be a pirate or something?"

"Maybe nothing so extreme. It's just that we don't know. I've done all I can on my end without raising suspicions. I can't keep accessing records like this without cause. I need your help, Ellie. I need you to find him. Because Pascoal Fernandes is as much your problem as mine."

"How is he your problem at all? You don't have anything to do with Fernandes," I protest. "It's not like you're a blood relative or anything."

"He's still connected to me, whether I like it or not. He's connected to me. My critics look for anything that can be used to undermine my credibility. News that my brother-in-law's father is a convicted felon could be dangerous ammo in the wrong hands. I just want to find out what I'm up against. Before they do."

I ball up a napkin in my fist.

"Do you get what I'm saying, Ellie?"

I do, but I'm not happy about it. After my meal with Aunt Cheryl, I tell myself to avoid having work lunches with her in the future. Nothing good really comes from them, only more stress. What can I possibly find out about Puddy Fernandes that Aunt Cheryl hasn't found out already? She's the assistant chief and had ties to the FBI fingerprint database and LAPD mug shot files. What more can I bring to the mix?

The next day, I ride my personal bike to work; not something I do often, but I have extra energy to burn off. Sometimes it's good for me to see things as a regular civilian bicyclist does: like how cars get ridiculously close and how drivers even sometimes yell obscenities for no reason, just mad at the world, I guess. My bike is old, from high school. I'm not like Johnny with the latest bicycles—he has more than a dozen, including BMX racing and mountain bikes. He brags that he's spent more than twenty grand on his bicycles. I just think to myself, *Dude, you could have put a down payment on a condo with that much dough.*

I'm doing outreach today with various tenants' groups, and I meet with Mrs. Clark, whom I've known since I first started my job with the Bicycle Coordination Unit. She thought she was getting a raw deal when I was first assigned to her group, but although it's taken a good six months, she's gotten used to me. And I, to her. She's prickly, but I've grown fond of her, and she gets that I care about her, her grandchildren, her neighborhood. She used to always wear her hair relaxed, but she's gone natural and wears it in a halo of salt-and-pepper ringlets. It becomes her, and I tell her so when I enter her home, just a few blocks east of Staples Center.

Her bungalow is similar to ones in Eagle Rock and Pasadena. It has a sturdy porch outside, and inside are plenty of built-ins like dish cabinets and bookcases, lined with photos everywhere. There are photos in standing frames on the fireplace mantel and shelves. Photos arranged underneath various oval and rectangular cutouts. Photo magnets on her refrigerator door. Framed photos hung in the doorway. Most of the photos are of her grandchildren and late husband. Very few are of her daughter, although a prominent one does feature the daughter, her children and their father. A much, much happier time.

The LAPD is a cosponsor for an upcoming health and children's fair that will be taking place at a local community center. Although Mrs. Clark has been able to get tons of sponsors, nobody wants to actually help plan the thing.

"It's the first one," I tell her, remembering other outreach events I've helped launch. "Maybe people just need to find out what it's all about."

"Nobody wants to work together unless something bad happens. Then everyone gets riled up."

We plan to pass out children's fingerprint identification kits to families, but it turns out that some parents are resistant to participate. All of the reluctant ones happen to be Spanish-speaking, so we jump to the conclusion that they may suspect the information will be used against them in some way.

"I'm actually trying to learn some Spanish," Mrs. Clark tells me.

I'm surprised. She's been the most vocal complainant about things like store signs that are only in Spanish.

"You know, Spanish was my major in college," I tell her. "I can recommend some good language books if you want."

"No need. I'm not much of a book person. I've been watching Spanish TV. Actually the Lakers were so bad this season that they looked better on the Spanish channel. Hey, I'm even starting to watch soccer!"

We both laugh and her granddaughter walks into the living room from her nap. There are creases on her face and her eyelashes are clumped together from wake-up tears. I remember how when I first met her, she was so scared of me in my uniform, with my holster and my club. Now she views me like an aunt or older sister and stumbles toward me to give me a hug. *This is how it should be,* I think.

After leaving Mrs. Clark, I visit a couple more tenant representatives and attend a neighborhood meeting at a school. Teenagers like my bike. They often want to ride it, but I have to tell them they can't. The last thing I need is someone circulating a cell phone photo of a kid with a possible gang affiliation on an LAPD bike. Officer Marc Haines, who's now working with Media Relations, would definitely be on my case for that.

Throughout the day, I check my phone. Benjamin's mother is still in ICU. Mrs. Choi has always been sweet to me, always giving me little gifts of candy and cakes. After living in Brazil for a couple of decades, her Portuguese is better than her English, so our conversations were usually a mix of Spanish and Portuguese. Now, finding out that I'm actually part Portuguese, I wish that I had learned more of the language from her.

The weather has been beautiful, so even after I get home, I keep riding up Figueroa to York and then east through South Pasadena. South Pasadena reminds me of a real-life Stars Hollow from the TV show *Gilmore Girls*. There are trees everywhere, old ones with leaves the size of outstretched hands. It's a place where at Halloween people put pumpkins and scarecrows out on their front porches, where they have Fourth of July parades with old cars, and a weekly farmers' market near the library. No wonder Mom wants me to live here.

When I reach Old Pasadena, I slow down. There are a lot more pedestrians here. All ages, but mostly soccer moms wearing outfits taken from their daughters' closets, or young people about my age. Old Pasadena is so cool, with its preserved and rehabbed old vintage buildings. There are intricate, unique moldings near the roofs of structures—better than a mall from the seventies. Unfortunately, most of the businesses are still the same ones you'll find in any mall.

So much for uniqueness. At least you can shop while feeling the warmth of direct sunshine instead of interior fluorescent lights.

I lock my bike on a rack next to a two-story building. Adjacent to it is a nine-level structure that most passersby wouldn't think twice about. But some real estate people are banking that this corner of Old Pasadena will become the heart of Silicon Eastside. One of my PPW classmates, Supachai Sperber, has a corner office on the top floor. Supachai is already a millionaire—actually, a billionaire. Supachai was raised in Bangkok, with a Thai mother and Jewish American father. He went to a boarding school in San Marino (I hadn't even known until then that we had boarding schools in LA!) before enrolling in PPW when he was sixteen years old. He graduated in three years, same time as me, but even younger; he was only nineteen. He didn't waste any time before launching his own company, SupaSper, Inc., which specializes in computer facial recognition. He got his billion (mostly in stock options, but still) from selling it to some social media site.

Supachai, ironically, is now all about Internet privacy and preventing companies from following our Internet surfing. He feels guilty about contributing to mass surveillance, and now spends most of his time trying to help regular people, especially millennials like us, hide our digital footprints. So those ill-advised photographs with plastic red cups—gone. Racy videos with your ex—gone. Information about your shoe purchases—gone. Supachai tells me if I don't want to be trailed by businesses, I should turn off my smartphone when I'm not using it. I forget to, but then, I don't have a ton of apps anyway.

He calls his new company "SupaSpies" and even has "Supachai Sperber, Head Secret Agent," on his glass door. (I guess if you have a billion dollars, you can call yourself anything you want.) I know Supachai is a night owl, so I'd banked on still finding him at his office after six o'clock at night. The workday has probably just begun for this head secret agent.

"Ellie Rush, it's been ages!" The door opens automatically when I arrive, thanks to Supachai's robot secretary. Supachai already knows it's me from the security camera mounted at the top of his doorway. "What's it been, five months? Not since my New Year's Eve party?"

Supachai is famous for his rooftop party on December 31. The biggest challenge is getting to it, since the streets are closed to vehicles and clogged with Rose Parade campers. Nay convinced me to go with her this year. I'd planned to hole up at home and feel sorry for myself—I'd just split with Benjamin.

Supachai's office is an incubator of creative ideas (and perhaps bacteria, the latter from the half-empty cups and take-out containers on the edges of tables). He's hung a bunch of found objects—a single tennis shoe, a rusty hamster cage, a child's drawing—from his ceiling. In one corner are wads of chewed gum à la Cal Poly San Luis Obispo's Bubblegum Alley, where students created 3-D gum graffiti on the walls of a narrow walkway. He's also taped about a hundred fortune cookie messages together lengthwise to serve as a decorative garland.

"You seem busy," I say.

He shrugs. "What do you need?"

"Can't I just be making a social call?"

"You're not that type of girl, Ellie."

"What, I'm not social?"

"You're not the type to visit someone without a reason."

That makes me sound like an opportunist. I frown.

"No, I like that about you," Supachai insists. "You're a purpose-driven person. And we need a lot more of you types out in the world."

Whatever. I hate it when Supachai gets philosophical. It makes him sound like a total jerk.

"I need to find out what someone has been doing for the past several decades," I tell him. "And where he might be now."

"You know I don't do that stuff anymore." I stay quiet and Supachai sighs. "Okay, who?"

I give him the name. I spell out the first name for him. "P-A-S-C-O-A-L. He's also known as Puddy. And it's Fernandes with an 'S.'"

"Pascoal Fernandes," he says as he types on my laptop. "Only about fifteen thousand hits on Google. Pretty common name in Portugal and all over the U.S."

"Well, he's in his seventies. And from San Diego."

"That's a start."

"He has a record. Was arrested for bank robbery in North Hollywood in 1964."

"Now you're talking." Supachai is typing all this in. "You got a photo?"

"I don't. But I might be able to get one."

"No worries. This may be enough."

"I need to find out what's he's been doing for the past fifty years. I mean, he claims that he's been on a boat."

"Military?"

"Container shipping."

"Ooh. That's a tough one. Those guys are like hobos, you know, the ones who used to ride on railroad cars. That'll be a challenge, but I might be able to dig out some kind of employment records. Any other aliases? A cell phone number? E-mail address?"

"Nope. I guess he's been off the grid for a while."

"I'll try," he says.

"Thank you, Supachai. And you know—"

"This will all be on the QT." He nods. "Anything else?"

I swallow. Supachai has me pretty figured out.

"Any idea on how I can find Nay?"

"What's going on? You two are usually like the Little Twin Stars," he says, referring to the Sanrio cartoon angels.

"The angels have split up." Or, should I say, are taking a break from each other. "I really can't get into it now. I just want to make sure she's okay."

Supachai tells me that research will take a bit longer. I reconsider what I'm asking. "You know what? Forget about the Nay thing, okay? I owe you one."

"Drinks at Eastside Luv," Supachai says. He loves exploring East LA but doesn't like to do it on his own.

I get up to leave and the robot secretary instantly opens the door for me.

"Hey," Supachai calls out, "do you still see Benjamin?" He knows we broke up, but he's in the dark about the details. Supachai is close to all his exes—there were quite a few at his New Year's party.

"Yeah, we still keep in touch." I don't mention anything about his mom's cancer and surgery.

"Tell him hi for me, okay?"

I nod. As it happens, I'll be seeing Benjamin tonight, but we probably won't be talking about Supachai Sperber.

St. Vincent's Hospital is east of Little Tokyo, on Alvarado and Third streets, and walking distance from the Original Tommy's, the meanest, tastiest chili burgers on the West Coast. I've never been to this hospital before, but it's not large, so I'm easily able to find the waiting room on the floor for ICU patients.

"Ellie!" Benjamin's four-year-old niece, Camila, comes running toward me. I didn't think that they let kids that young in a hospital, but I'm so happy to see her. I give her a quick hug and ruffle her brown hair. I have missed her.

She has the smoothest skin, and adorable tadpole eyes, which she obviously gets from her mother's side. Camila's dad is white, like mine. We *hapas* have to stick together.

"Benjamin's Ellie is here," Sally, Benjamin's sister, calls out to other members of the Choi family sitting together on padded chairs. Mr. Choi nods hello to me as he eats. I see Korean sushi, marinated bean sprouts and spinach, sliced apples—they seemed well provided for, but I offer the Subway sandwiches that I purchased to the mix.

Benjamin immediately gets up and takes the plastic bags from me.

"How is she?" I ask.

"Good. They're moving her from ICU to a regular room."

"That's great news." I'm so relieved. "I got you jalapeño potato chips, too," I say. Benjamin is addicted to them.

He hands the bags off to his sister, then leads me to an old woman with beautiful skin and snowy hair sitting in one of the larger chairs. "Ellie, I want you to meet my grandmother."

"Oh," I say, a little flustered. His grandmother is direct from Korea. I don't know whether I should bow or offer my hand, so I do neither. "Hello."

There's an exchange of Korean back-and-forth. I wonder what they're saying.

"Konnichiwa," she finally says to me.

"Sorry, she doesn't get that you're a hundred percent American," Benjamin murmurs in my ear.

"It's okay," I tell him. "I'm hoping for the best for your daughter," I say to his grandmother, and Benjamin translates.

Her eyes get watery and she grabs for my hands. She holds them tight and I squeeze hard, too. Sometimes it's better not to use words.

Finally, I let go and let her get back to her eating as she murmurs something in Korean back to me.

Benjamin has already started to unroll a sandwich. "Thanks for these," he says.

"Sorry it's not fancier."

"No, it's perfect. And you got me the jalapeño potato chips. I love these."

I smile, but not too widely. We're not back together again.

"So what did the surgeon say?" I know the drill.

"They were able to get the cancer out."

All of it? I'm wondering.

"There was some in her lymph nodes. But it seemed isolated. They removed those spots, too."

Anything in the lymph nodes is not a good sign. It means that the cancer could have spread to other parts of the body.

But you can't think about that, or it will make you crazy. Odds are Mrs. Choi will have to have chemo or radiation.

"Once she's all moved in, Dad and a few of us will be able to see her."

"I'm so glad that she's doing okay," I say. "You all must be exhausted."

Benjamin pushes hair away from his face. "How's everything? Work?"

For Benjamin to be asking me about work means that he's trying hard to be a good friend. He hates that I'm a cop; in fact, that's a big reason behind why we aren't together anymore.

"You know, same ole, same ole." No need to get into details. "By the way, you haven't heard from Nay, have you?"

"She sent me a text last week. Claimed that I was being jerk for not responding to her text. I just didn't want to deal with all that. Why? Is there something going on?"

I don't want to burden Benjamin with our drama, so I downplay it. "She's just been busy with school."

A slight frown line forms in between Ben's eyebrows. A part of him doesn't believe me. He knows me too well.

"Anyway, I'll be thinking about your mom," I tell him. I don't say anything about praying for her because I know Benjamin doesn't believe in it. We hug just for a second, and when we let go, I see a bunch of Benjamin's relatives, including Camila and Sally, smile at us as if they are in on a secret.

I leave the hospital glad that I could be there for Benjamin. A couple of months ago, I wouldn't have been in the same place.

When I get into the Green Mile, the phone rings and I pick up without looking who's calling.

"Yeah," I say.

"Ellie? It's me," says Cortez. "I'm just getting off and figured that you'd still be awake. Want to get some coffee?"

I first met Detective Cortez Williams at a crime scene in Chinatown, but in spite of the sad circumstances, I did feel a spark of chemistry. He's got, as Nay would say, a "yummy" body, at least as much as I can tell from his dress shirts and tailored pants. He's barely thirty and already a homicide detective. Despite being seven years older, he likes listening to me. I'm not used to older people asking for my opinions.

We never really date-dated. I guess we went out a couple of times—enough for a couple of kisses. Then everything fell apart even before it began.

I have no idea why Cortez wants to see me tonight. Instead of going out for coffee, though, I tell him to stop by my house. I know what message I'm sending, but I'm wiped out. Plus, truthfully, I wouldn't mind a little action. It's been a while since any man has touched these lips.

I rush home and quickly take care of the dirty dishes in the sink and the clothes strewn on the couch. I haven't gotten around to sweeping the floor when there's a knock at the door. I usher Shippo into the bedroom and close the door. Cortez adores dogs, but I don't want anything to distract him from, well, me.

I check the peephole, then open the door. Cortez has loosened his tie. I can see the curve of his white T-shirt underneath his tangerine-colored dress shirt. Don't ask me why I find that sexy, but I do.

"When did you get your car back?" He gestures to the driveway where the Green Mile is leaking oil again.

"Oh, that," I say. "Forgot to tell you. It's a long story."

"I have time." Cortez wanders about my living room, checking out my Mexican-painted mirror on the wall, the framed posters, the Japanese doll. I've put new things up since I've moved. "Your new place is bigger. Better neighborhood, too."

"Tell my mother that, okay? She's still freaked-out that I'm living here and not in South Pas or Pasadena."

"How is your mother, by the way?"

Cortez has met my mom a couple of times. She was pretty suspicious of him at first, but she didn't know that Benjamin and I had broken up. The last time they met was at Aunt Cheryl's award ceremony, and by then Mom had gone completely Team Cortez.

"She's okay. We've had some family drama recently."

"Family *is* drama," he replies and smiles. I feel better already.

I offer him some beer, wine, coffee or water. He goes with the beer, which makes me happy that I just stocked my refrigerator with a selection of local craft beers from Eagle Rock. I give him a Manifesto, while I opt for the low-alcohol one, Solidarity. I still want to be able to think straight.

He sits on my couch and pops open the cap with a bottle opener on the table. He takes a swig from his bottle, and I take one from mine. This feels chill, perfectly natural. An evening after work. Then Cortez explains why he's here. "It's the Old Lady Bandit case. She hit another bank today, around closing time."

"Oh." I feel like an idiot for not paying more attention to

what's been going on. But in my own defense, I've been at the hospital, where it feels like the whole world sits still.

"Your aunt had a lead for us. A guy called Puddy Fernandes. Do you know who he is?"

"Ah. Well." I totally don't know what to say. Aunt Cheryl obviously didn't bother to reveal that Puddy is, well, kind of, sort of, family.

I've lied—well, withheld the truth—from Cortez before, and that's what almost led to our relationship getting wrecked forever. I don't want to risk it again, even at the expense of airing our dirty laundry.

"He's kind of . . . my grandfather."

"What?!" Cortez puts his beer bottle on my coffee table. I've definitely got his attention. He's shocked but also a little amused.

"Look, he's basically just a sperm donor, more than anything else. Until the other day, I'd never even heard his name, let alone met him before in my life. Neither had my dad, for that matter." I tighten my grip on my beer. It's already almost room temperature. "He's the one who took my car. Was the original owner from the sixties. He still had a key."

"So Chief Cheryl Toma has some skeletons in her closet." Cortez is just enjoying this way too much. "No wonder she hasn't been revealing how she came up with him. I guess she doesn't want it coming out that she's related to a convict."

"Well, he's not one of her blood relatives." I rush to Aunt Cheryl's defense. "He's not even technically related to her by marriage, since he never married my grandmother." While I, on the other hand, have a good dose of Puddy Fernandes in my DNA.

"He was a bank robber. Saw his record."

I frown. "Listen, the guy did his time. He's just trying to help."

"Ellie, in my experience, no one 'just wants to help.' I've learned that everyone who comes forward has an agenda, an angle. You have to consider what he'll get out of informing on another person."

Cortez is usually more upbeat than most other homicide detectives I've met, so I'm surprised that he sounds so jaded, and I resent that he's talking to me like I'm completely green. Sure, I've recently come off probation, but still.

"You can't tell anyone else about Aunt Cheryl's connection to Fernandes. Especially Garibaldi," I tell Cortez.

"No, I wouldn't tell him anything like this," he agrees. "I'm the lead on the Bandit case, anyway, so no worries."

"Did you find any information on Ronald Sullivan?"

Cortez shakes his head. "Last thing on record was that he was working for a casino in Reno. But that was about ten years ago. It's like he's disappeared off the face of the planet."

"No wife or kids?"

"Not on record. There's a nephew, though, with a record of his own."

"How old is he?"

Cortez narrows his eyes. "Ellie, your information about Pascoal Fernandes is enough. You don't need to get involved."

You had literally nothing until I got involved, I think to myself. *Why don't I get the props that I deserve?*

"That's interesting about your aunt, though." Cortez takes another swig of his beer, while I have long since abandoned mine. It's started to taste bitter from the content of our conversation.

"What do you mean?"

"Maybe what they are saying is true."

"What are they saying?"

"That she's getting pretty cozy with Councilman Beachum."

My worst fear realized.

"You know that he's planning to run for mayor, right? It would be a good alliance for your aunt."

"What, do you think that she'd prostitute herself to become police chief?"

"Your words, not mine."

"Maybe you should be out there catching the Old Lady Bandit instead of talking smack about your superiors, who, by the way, seem to be out getting more leads than you detectives are." I'm not sure why I'm being so defensive. It's not like Aunt Cheryl needs defenders, especially not a peon like me. But I'm pissed.

"Whoa, whoa, I'm not saying *I* started those rumors."

"No, but you actively listened to it and are now spreading stories about what you heard."

"Hey, I'm sorry. Really I am."

"Is that it? Is that all you came for? To pump me for information about my aunt?" My emotions rush out of me before I can really think. "Well, mission accomplished. I think that you better leave now." I immediately regret what I've said, but there's no taking it back. Cortez is already heading for the door.

NINE

I feel raw and vulnerable after Cortez leaves. Shippo senses my mood, and doesn't beg for any extra late-night treats. He gets in a tight circle inside his doggy bed, his snout hidden from view. His eyes remain on me. Waiting for what, I don't know.

When I've worked with neighborhood associations, some person—usually someone pretty old or pretty young— inevitably asks me, "Why are you cops such assholes?"

It's a no-win question. If I explain what kind of pressure we are under, it's like I'm admitting that we are jerks. If I get defensive, I'm just living proof of their accusations.

I do ask myself another question, however: Why do we police officers turn on one another? And why is someone like my aunt Cheryl such a threat to other cops? I want to work here at the LAPD for a very long time, and to see how my aunt is treated gives me a clue about how I might be received as a supervisor in the future.

At the next morning's roll call, Sergeant Jorge Mendez, our bicycle liaison, is there to discuss the Cyclists/LAPD Task Force's efforts to reduce bike thefts. Jorge, who pronounces his first name the *gabacho* way—"George"—is really all-American. He's born and raised in East LA. When I was going through my bicycle training, he took me riding down Whittier Boulevard, the heart of the barrio. He has a squeaky-clean look; even his forehead is shiny. I try not to fixate on that as he talks about the latest crime statistics affecting bike riders.

While most other crimes rates in LA have gone down, bicycle thefts have gone up—in some areas, as much as a crazy two hundred percent. We are supposed to distribute community alert flyers at neighborhood meetings, as well as give workshops on how to properly lock up bicycles. There are even DIY tips for those who don't have much cash for pricey bike locks: wrap an old bike chain in an inner tube and lock that to the bike frame. Or even place a business card inside the frame or write your name and contact info on the rim strip. Bikes can be someone's sole mode of transportation. I understand how desirable a sturdy bike can be.

"You doing any bike baits?" someone asks.

Apparently the San Francisco Police Department has a devoted anti–bike theft unit. They have special bikes with GPS tracking units that are used in sting operations. The officer in charge even has an active Twitter feed where he sometimes posts mug shots of criminals caught in the act. That's a good use of social media, I guess. It's hard to figure out how and when to employ things like Twitter in law enforcement.

Jorge either doesn't hear or chooses not to answer the question about bike baits. Traffic enforcement is what the department is working on, so it's more about giving citations to both drivers and bicyclists for reckless traffic offenses. This doesn't make us very popular with anybody, but what can I say—it's our job.

After Jorge's presentation, we are given our assignments. I'm with Mac today and we're assigned to patrol PPW. I'm surprised. Mac and I are rarely paired together, which has been fine with me. Mac gets on my nerves, and vice versa. What lessens the blow is that I'll be at my alma mater. Patrolling PPW always soothes me, and I could use a big dose of calm right now.

Graduation is coming up in a few weeks, and it's good for the students to know that there's a police presence on campus, just in case they're thinking about any protests or stunts that would put PPW in a bad light. The graduation speaker whom the administration has selected is a cable television executive (actually I think he produces that *Real Divorcées* show), so I've heard from Rickie that the female graduates plan to wear sashes that read, REAL WOMYN, NOT REALITY WOMEN, and turn their backs to him as he speaks. Pretty nonviolent.

While we're on patrol, I pray that Mac doesn't mention anything about my aunt. She is his Public Enemy Number One, and I'm ready to bite his head off if he disses her.

We ride down Figueroa Street. Mac's riding as fast as he can, as if he's trying to lose me. But no such luck. I'm at least ten years younger than him, and can match him pedal to pedal.

Once we arrive at the corner of campus, Mac abruptly stops. I come close to crashing into him, but am able to swerve to the side into some grass. Thank God there are no students walking near us.

"You cover the north; I'll do the south. Meet up at twelve hundred," he says. In other words, noon.

Normally, I wouldn't passively go along with what Mac says. He's been with the department much longer than me, and he likes to throw his weight around, but technically we are both P2s. Today is different, though. "Okay," I say and take off. North is where the student center and services are located. Like the *Citrus Squeeze* newsroom.

I tell myself that going to the newspaper is part of our patrol, because who knows what could be happening at the student center, right?

I take my bike into the *Citrus Squeeze* offices. In front of the reception desk are stacks of today's issue, unwanted like wilting lettuce. It's amazing that the *Squeeze*, which does have a digital edition, still comes out in print, while a lot of "real" newspapers don't. The only reason students even pick it up is to have something to sit on so they don't get grass stains from the lawn.

"Hey, Ellie. How are you?" Stanford Botifoll is one of those nerdy short guys whose brain is so big it's probably the heaviest part of his body. He wears gigantic black-rimmed glasses that shouldn't work, but actually make him look cool, since they're totally in style these days. When I was a senior and he was a freshman, we were in the same political science class and we had to debate different sides of getting involved in the Gulf War. I'm not too proud to admit that he beat me hands down.

"Hey, Stanford." I slip off my helmet and hang it by its straps on my bike handle. "Last issues of the year, yeah?"

"It's been a madhouse," he says, although the newsroom is completely empty. "We're just putting today's issue to bed."

"So, where's Nay?" I say as casually as possible.

"She's out on assignment."

"Since when do you have assignments? You're a school newspaper that ranks the best earbuds and delivery pizza."

"Don't be that way." Stanford actually looks hurt. "The local public radio station is actually considering her for a summer internship."

Really? I'm shocked. Shocked that Nay's journalistic star has risen so fast and shocked that she hasn't told me anything about it.

"You know, we've wanted to do a story on you. 'PPW Student Goes Jump Street.' "

"Yeah, I've seen the articles you've done on the LAPD." Recently there was a series of Instagram photos showing police brutality with the hashtag #mylapd on the *Squeeze*'s online edition.

"What did the LAPD expect when they went on social media? Photos of cops helping old ladies across the street?"

"Listen, the NYPD started that Twitter stuff, not us. I don't even have a Twitter account."

"Noticed that. I tried to friend you on Facebook, but couldn't find you."

Another reason not to have a Facebook account, I say to myself. I sure don't need the editor of the *Citrus Squeeze* following my every move.

"We always want to get the other side, too."

Yeah, right. I must be wearing my skepticism on my face, because Stanford then adds, "You know, we're up for a National Pacemaker Award for our series on student debt after graduation."

Uh, I think, *am I supposed to be impressed?* I know, I

shouldn't be so cynical, but now that I'm on the other side of law enforcement, I see how many times the media gets stuff all wrong.

He notices that I look completely unimpressed. I notice a smear on his right lens.

"The Pacemaker is the Pulitzer Prize of student journalism."

The newspaper's phone rings and there's no one else to answer the call. Stanford is only too happy to end our conversation to attend to it. He sits at a desk with his back turned to me, so I lean my bike against a cubicle and quickly look at the large computer screen display with a full-page layout for today's issues.

"China Nabs Another in Graft Scandal," the headline on page two reads. The *Squeeze* usually places world news on the second page. It's almost always stories from wire services like the Associated Press. But this article has an actual *Squeeze* byline from Nay Pram.

There's no dateline identifying where the writer is reporting from for the story, so I'm assuming that Nay's not actually in China. But how can she report on such a story here in Los Angeles? Maybe Washington Jeung has become an important news source.

"Can I help you with anything else?" Stanford is apparently done with his call and stares at me looking at his page in progress. His chin rests on his folded arms as he leans over the four-foot-high cubicle wall.

My face flushes pink. Caught in the act! "Ah, no," I say. I quickly walk around to my bike and guide it forward, as if there's something pressing I need to respond to.

"I'm interning at the *LA Weekly* this summer," he calls

out before I'm no longer within earshot. "Anytime you want to be interviewed."

Yeah, right. Don't hold your breath on that one.

Once I'm back outside, I give silent props to Nay. She's really doing it—investigative journalism—with China, of all things, as her topic. I begin to think about Xu again. His cello. Although I never attended any student performances while I was at PPW, I know that our music department is world-class.

I ride down a curved, paved walkway through the middle of north campus. PPW is pretty old, at least for LA, and buildings have been added as time went by. So instead of a consistent look with brick buildings, like USC or UCLA, PPW has a smattering of structures from a bunch of different eras. The most modern one is the Science Building, which has been created out of opaque glass and metal. Most classical is the Arts Building with its steeped roof and Victorian adornments. The basement windows are always open and you can usually hear voices singing opera and musical instruments at practice.

I go into the Arts Building and study the board that lists professors and their office numbers. The classical music professor is Professor Adele Horst, and her office is right here on the first floor, room 137.

I knock in the open doorway of her office, my bike at my side.

Professor Horst is a thin, birdlike woman. She's wearing bronze bangles on her fragile wrists, and studies me over her reading glasses, whose chunky frames are clear plastic. "You know that my wallet was stolen a month ago," she says. From her accent, I'm guessing she's Eastern European, maybe German.

"Oh, I'm not here about that," I say. "I'm a former PPW student."

"You didn't finish?" she says, insinuating that no PPW graduate would then turn around and become a cop. The disdain in her voice is obvious. It's very familiar, especially in the Rush house.

"Actually, I graduated in three years."

I get her attention. "And how can I help you, Officer?"

"I wanted to ask you about cellos."

"That question is quite general."

I ask whether I can come into her office and she nods yes. I position my bike so it's still visible from inside the professor's office; then I pull out my phone and quickly find the photos of Xu's cello. I place my phone in front of her. "I wanted to ask you specifically about this one. Does it seem particularly valuable?" *Worth five million dollars?*

She grimaces. "What a stupid question. I have to see the instrument in person. I can't come to any conclusions based on a photo taken on an iPhone."

I was afraid of that, but I had to try. Perhaps seeing my disappointed look (I really need to work on my Toma poker face), she relents a little. "I can't tell you if it's valuable, but I don't think this one is terribly old, however."

"You don't?" I think back to Kendra Prescott's article. Didn't she say that Xu's Stradivarius was from the 1700s?

"Instruments of a certain age usually have marks on them. Certain imperfections. Remnants of their past. Where the musician's body touched the cello. I don't see those marks in this photo. In terms of the general craftsmanship, you need to check the purfling, the details on the scroll. All of those details have to be examined carefully. The color. The grain.

And even then sometimes it's quite impossible to tell. The Chinese have even made it more difficult now that they are using European wood."

My ears perk up. "The Chinese are making cellos?"

"And violins and violas. The works. Their craftsmanship in the past has been deplorable. Using wood that was too young. But they've improved immensely. The sounds coming out of those Chinese-made instruments are actually—I hate to admit—quite comparable to much older instruments crafted in Europe. But they are still not exactly the same."

"And the price?"

"A third or even less. It's no wonder why they've become so popular. There's even a sales office here in Los Angeles for the best of those factories. I have directed students there, if they are in need of a cheap instrument," she admits.

I want to get to the subject of Xu, so I ask Professor Horst whether she knows him.

"Oh, him," she says. "His technique is a mess. So emotional. But his country loves him. And so does ours."

All righty, then. Based on her dismissive attitude, I'm assuming the professor skipped out on Xu's concert last Wednesday.

"The Chinese, they are just musical babies," she sniffs.

I'm shocked that Professor Horst would say something so derogatory, especially to me. I'm half-Japanese, but I could have just as easily been half-Chinese.

"Because of their country's Cultural Revolution, they were closed to Western music," she goes on. "Now the young people are eating it up. It represents freedom to them."

Well, judging from the audience at Xu's concert, American concertgoers could use an injection of youth, I think.

Instead, I ask Professor Horst whether she's familiar with a violist named Cece Lin.

Professor Horst's bracelets jangle as she lifts her arms in enthusiasm. "Cece Lin! Now, *she* was something. She could have been a master soloist. But instead she decides to stop touring and stay in LA. Why? Why would such a talent do that with her gift?"

"She's still with the Philharmonic," I say.

"She's just whiling away her time. She's not venturing out, challenging herself. She's among dozens of other musicians, blending in."

"So you know her?"

"Of course. Everyone in the music scene knows of Cece Lin ever since she joined the conservancy in Philadelphia. She must have been only nineteen years old." The professor folds her arms. "It was her and Xu—the stars from Asia."

I stay quiet as the professor warms to her topic.

"Then, out of the blue, Cece announces that she won't pursue a career as a soloist, and she chains herself to the Philharmonic! I'm sure that she broke her parents' hearts."

Professor Horst then looks me in the eye. Hers are the bluest blue, and I can easily picture those same eyes in the face of a much younger person. "I tell my female students this—always have your eyes on the prize."

I don't ask her what the prize may be. Fame and money?

My radio squawks. It's Mac, wondering where I am. He says I need to go back to Central Division. That's a little unusual. I reply back to him and wonder what's going on. *Is it an emergency, or is it something I've done?*

I thank Professor Horst for her time and pedal back to

the station as fast as I can. It's warm today, and my hair becomes damp with sweat from my helmet.

I'm guiding my bike inside when I hear, "Where have you been?" Tim Cherniss's smooth chin juts out. My CO is obviously not happy.

"Patrolling PPW," I tell him. Like I was assigned to do. Kind of.

"Got an e-mail message from Rampart," he tells me. "The Chinese Consulate contacted them. Seems like a student reporter was harassing their security guard this morning and they want more bike units patrolling that neighborhood."

I'm preparing myself to ride out west. Then Cherniss drops the bomb. "She identified herself as being with PPW. Steinlight mentioned that one of your friends, a Nay Pram, has been pretty insistent about receiving information about the Xu case."

I try to keep my heartbeat steady. I can't let my CO see how nervous I am. "And?"

"Do you know anything about this?"

"No," I say emphatically. Because I really don't.

"Rush, you have a history of sticking your nose into areas where it shouldn't be."

"Sergeant, I don't know anything. Anyway, did they get a name? Photograph?" God, I hope that they don't have security footage.

Cherniss doesn't respond.

"Then why do you think it was Nay? It is the Chinese government, you know."

Cherniss's face softens. He's probably the type to think that Chinese spies are lurking at every corner, and I feel a little bit guilty exploiting that. "Sorry, Rush. Had to do due diligence."

After he walks away, my body feels limp. I take a deep

breath. I immediately go into the ladies' room and start texting Nay in one of the stalls. *Were you at the Chinese Consulate today?*

No response. What else is new?

As I leave the restroom, my phone begins ringing. It's not Nay, however. It's a call from my parents' house.

I answer. They usually don't call during the workday unless it's an emergency.

"You have to come home," Noah says.

"What's going on?"

"Dad's lost it."

"What are you talking about?"

"He wants to quit his job, pack us up and travel in an RV."

"What?" I can't believe what Noah's saying.

"Ellie, he wants to homeschool me in the RV my junior year!"

No wonder my brother sounds so desperate. "I'll be there as soon as I can."

Luckily, I have the Green Mile today, so I go straight to my parents' house after work.

Noah answers the door before I even get a chance to knock. "Took you long enough," he says.

Dad is lying on the couch surrounded by color brochures all featuring RVs. He's practically blanketed by issues of various magazines. *MotorHome. RV Life. Trailer Life. Gypsy Journal. Highways.* I had no idea. It's almost like RVing is some kind of religion.

"What's all this?" I ask.

"Ellie!" Dad sits up, almost sliding off the couch in his sea of glossy paper. "Did you hear? We're going to go RVing for a year."

Mom enters the room, wearing her usual tracksuit. "Hello, Ellie," she greets me, sounding subdued.

"Caroline, look at this one." Dad pulls out a brochure for a crazy black RV that looks like one of those rock-band tour buses. Inside of the RV I see photos of granite-topped sinks and leather couches. Heck, it looks nicer than the rooms of my apartment. Way nicer.

"Top of the line. I figure we can go to all the national parks. Presidential libraries. This will be a great education for Noah. Instead of reading about it, he can experience it!"

Noah grimaces.

"Mom, you think this is a good idea?" I ask.

Mom says nothing.

Grandma Toma walks in the room, her hair in rollers and covered in a clear cap decorated with faint flowers. "Well, I'm not going to live in a house on wheels," she announces.

"Dorothy, look. This is not a camper. It's spacious. It has beds."

"Listen, I lived through the camps, living cramped together in the same room as my parents, my brothers and sisters. I did it once. I'm not going to do it again."

We all remain quiet. For Grandma Toma to play the internment camp card means serious business.

"Well, if you don't want to come with us, I guess you'll have to stay at a retirement home, then," Dad says.

"Fine by me. At least I know Cheryl and Ellie will come visit me," Grandma Toma retorts.

At the mention of Aunt Cheryl, Mom gets visibly agitated. She never wants to be outdone by her older sister. She lets out a mock cry. "Gary, I'm not going to abandon my mother in a retirement home. Maybe just picking up and leaving isn't the best thing. Noah is doing so well in school now, and he may do the Academic Decathlon next year."

"I'm not—" Noah begins, and Mom shoots him a dirty look. She's been nagging him to join his private school's Academic Decathlon team, which he has been adamantly refusing. Now she's got him in a full nelson. *You join the Academic Decathlon team, and I'll make sure that we won't be spending Christmas in Kansas looking at one of the world's largest balls of twine.*

"Oh, yeah, yeah," Noah quickly rebounds. "I have been thinking of doing the Academic Decathlon. It'll be a once-in-a-lifetime opportunity." Damn, when he puts his mind to it, Noah can lay it on thick.

"What do you think, Ellie? Do you think that this is a bad idea?" Dad asks.

What I really think, Dad, is that you are freaking out about Puddy Fernandes. I'm not going to say anything about that, though, because I'm freaking out inside, too. I'm just keeping it bottled up, deep, deep inside. Instead, I say, "How about you start off small? Take an RV trip this summer. You could go to see Mount Rushmore."

It's almost as if the whole household lets out a collective sigh of relief.

"I can stay home for that one," Grandma Toma says. "I don't need to see the faces of a bunch of old *hakujin* men on a side of a mountain."

"Maybe Ellie can come with us, too," says Noah. I turn to give him a look. Why does he want to punish me? I'm trying to do him a favor.

"I'll stay with Grandma Toma while you guys are all gone," I suggest sweetly.

"Perfect! It's settled. An RV trip to Mount Rushmore this summer," Dad says.

Mom and Noah still don't look that pleased, but they know the alternative could have been a hundred times worse.

While I'm at my parents' house, I use their laptop and Wi-Fi. I can't help myself—I start to Google "China" and "violin/cello manufacturers."

A bunch of websites come up, some in Chinese characters. I scroll down the pages until I see something in English. "Phoenix Instruments," the link reads, with a location in Arcadia. That sounds familiar.

I click on the link. It's an elegant website, full of photos of beautiful string instruments, their hourglass shapes both refined and, yeah, a little sexy. There's a slight variation in the colors of the wood. Some of the violins, violas and cellos are a rich maple syrup color; others, more on the reddish side like cherrywood. The website images are supereffective. They make me feel like taking up the cello, even though I'm fully aware from my karaoke outings and brief lessons in both piano and guitar that I'm completely tone-deaf.

The logo on the website banner catches my eye. It's a bird with multiple heads. I've seen that image before. I click on a button about the company's purpose and mission:

Phoenix Instruments prides itself on providing the very best in violins, violas, and cellos for the beginner to the most advanced musician. Using the best aged wood from Europe, PI guarantees quality in sound. Founded by Chuncheng Wang, PI has as its logo a predecessor of the Chinese phoenix, which is a symbol of Wang's home province, Hubei. Besides a factory in Hubei, PI has a sales office in the U.S.

The English is a bit awkward, but I get its general gist. Hubei . . . Where have I seen that name before? Phoenix Instruments in Arcadia—wasn't that where the flak, Kendra Prescott, had recommended that the cello be appraised?

"Are you thinking of learning a string instrument?" My mother is looking over my shoulder at the screen. "I tried to steer you toward the violin, but you said it was for sissies."

Hey, that was when I was in the sixth grade, and already feeling pressured to get some extracurricular activities under my belt to beef up my future college application. *Excuse me for having had an adolescent mini-rebellion.* "I went to the Xu concert," I tell her.

"You did? Your father and I were thinking of going, but it was sold out."

"You actually saw him live?" Noah also gets in the conversation.

What? I'm surprised Noah even knows who Xu is, let alone that he sounds impressed that I've been to his concert.

"He and this Parisian rapper just released a single together." Noah pushes himself onto my seat and starts to type a new URL on my webpage.

He directs us to a music video on YouTube.

The rapper is a woman. She's super dark-skinned, almost blue-black, with a shaved head upon which she's wearing a white feather Mohawk, and she's dressed in a skintight leather bodysuit. As she raps in French, the video shows Xu, wearing a plain white T-shirt and jeans, responding with a punctuated rhythm on his cello. English subtitles are provided at the bottom of the screen: YOU CLOSE OUR EYES AND SAY IT'S FOR OUR OWN GOOD. THE DRAGON OF DEATH COMES AND WHEN THE SMOKE CLEARS, NO HOPE REMAINS.

"The melody's cool," I say, and I mean it. Not sure about the translated lyrics; it sounds better in French, though I do appreciate seeing Xu in a more contemporary musical context.

"That Xu is very photogenic." His physical charms are not lost on my mother.

"It's pronounced 'Chew,' Mom." My brother, the sophisticate.

"I know this song," Dad joins in. He starts to sing it in terrible French, causing Noah to hurriedly click the pause button.

"You get the idea," Noah says to me.

"Dad, how come you know this song?" I say.

"Bono produced it. It's against cultural repression. Xu was sending a message to his country, and they're not happy about it. I heard all about it on public radio."

Both my father and younger brother seem to know more about Xu than I do. *Oh, Ms. Sherlock,* I tell myself, *you still have a ways to go.*

TEN

The next day is my day off. That Phoenix Instruments sales office is on my mind. Why would Kendra Prescott recommend a Chinese string instrument manufacturer to appraise the value of a cello that had purportedly been built in the 1700s in Italy?

I leave a voice mail message for her at the music hall. "Please call me," I say. "I have a question for you." I know that I am putting my nose where it doesn't belong, like Tim Cherniss said, but this bugs me. Seriously.

I get caught up with some bills, paying a big chunk of my income toward my student loan. I have to admit it's a bit painful. Although I got a great education, my mother is right that I didn't need a bachelor's degree to be a cop. But if I hadn't gone to PPW, I wouldn't have met Nay, Rickie, Benjamin, or any of my other friends from college. I can't imagine life without them.

I murmur a prayer for Benjamin's mother and, while I'm at it, for Nay, too. Not having her around reminds me how dependent I am on her. I'm ashamed to admit that, yes, I do sometimes feel slightly superior to my friends: I'm the organized one, the good one, the one who got all As, who turned in her assignments on time, the responsible one with a real job. My face and heart burn to realize how lousy I've become inside. I'm pretty good at covering it all up, but I still hope no one else has noticed.

I attempt to clean my house, throwing away most everything from the vegetable drawer in my refrigerator. I feel bad doing that, especially after my outing with Rickie. Maybe I couldn't have fed a starving family in Africa with everything I've wasted, but it would have kept Rickie happy for at least a couple of meals.

Shippo watches me intently from his doggy bed. I've already fed him, but he's always ready for any handouts. *You ain't gettin' any.* I stare back into his eyes. *No spoiled pups in this house.* That's a lie, of course, but I try to stay firm.

There's nothing like housework to exhaust me. I lie on my bed and reach for Xu's concert program, which is still on my nightstand. Leafing through it, I stop at his bio and read it over. There it is. Hubei. Xu is from Hubei Province. I think back to his cello case, the abstract nine-headed bird. It's the same creature I saw on Phoenix Instruments' logo.

I pick up the phone. No call back from Kendra. I can't just wait around like this.

I sit up abruptly, causing Shippo to also sit up in his doggy bed. He thinks that we're going somewhere, and he's right. I get up and fasten the fanny pack with my Glock in it around my middle. When I go to retrieve Shippo's leash, he comes running to the living room. "Ever consider playing the cello, Shippo?"

There's no good way to get to Arcadia on the freeway from my house, so we take the back streets, but at least with the windows wide-open, both Shippo and I can get some fresh air—well, as fresh as the air in LA can be.

Phoenix Instruments' sales office is a narrow sliver of a building in between a fancy sandwich lunch spot and a bona fide music store that offers lessons for children. In spite of its small size, it's easy to find on a major street off Santa Anita Boulevard.

The area is safe, so I tie up Shippo to a metal newsstand next to the office door. Whenever I would leave Shippo outside like this in a public place, Benjamin would get furious at me, saying that he could be vulnerable to dog thieves. *Are fat Chihuahua mixes in large demand?* I'd think. (Never out loud, of course. I would never dis Shippo like that.) Since Benjamin and I are no longer together, I'm reverting back to my old ways.

When I enter, I realize that the Phoenix Instruments space is narrow but deep, shaped like a lane in a bowling alley. Instruments are displayed against one side of the wall.

An Asian man, probably in his forties, welcomes me at the small counter in the front. "Hello, how can I help you?" He wears a navy blue polo shirt with the Phoenix Instruments logo over its left pocket.

"Just looking," I murmur, keeping my head down.

I walk around the small showroom, going from violin to viola to cello, trying to look like I know what I'm doing. I'm interested only in the cellos, of course, so I take extra time with the three cellos on display. They seem pretty much identical to me and no different from any other cello I've ever seen. I pluck the strings like a guitar just to test out the sound. Yup, it works.

"Would you like to play one?" The salesman brings out a bow.

I shake my head. That would be disastrous.

"How much is the most expensive one?" My question definitely sounds strange out loud, but the salesman doesn't react. Perhaps he's gotten that question before.

"About five thousand," he tells me.

"I'm actually interested in a very specific instrument. This one." I show the salesman the photo of Xu's cello in its case, and I swear the man turns two shades paler.

"Ah, well, that's a fine cello, but it's not ours."

"How can you tell?"

"I can just tell. This is my business. My father founded this company."

"Your father is Chuncheng Wang?"

The son seems disturbed that I know so much about Phoenix Instruments, even though that information's right on their website.

"Do you know whose cello this is?" I ask.

"No, why would I?" This guy is a terrible liar.

"It's Xu's. You might have heard of him."

"Oh, Xu. Sure. Everyone knows Xu."

"Especially you. Because your company made this cello for him."

"Impossible. His cello is from Europe. A Stradivarius. A line dating back to the seventeen hundreds."

As if. "Aren't you tired of covering for him? Don't you want everyone to know that your cello—a cello made in your Hubei Province—is the one that's making such beautiful sounds?"

Noises from the back room. I thought that we were alone, but there's a third person in the narrow sales office. Mr. Xu makes his appearance from the back.

So this is his hideout. He looks terrible. His hair is greasy and plastered down on his head. He hasn't shaved. His clothes don't fit him right; they're too big and too informal. Must be the salesman's.

Mr. Xu says something to me in Chinese.

I shake my head. *I don't understand.*

The salesman says something back to Mr. Xu. Probably, *This girl is an American barbarian. Or worse yet, a Japanese.* I know that older Chinese, like older Koreans, aren't too fond of Japan and probably rightly so.

Mr. Xu's face is drawn as he murmurs something to the salesman. He's no longer speaking in the same excited tone as he did when I first encountered him at the foot of the concert hall stairs.

Wang translates: "He wants to know if you know where his son is."

I'm surprised by the question. So Xu has honestly disappeared?

I shake my head again.

"He wants you to know that he didn't lie about the man trying to steal that cello."

Why should I believe you? I think. *If you didn't keep up the charade that the cello was worth anything in the first place, no one would have tried to steal it.*

Just then, I glance outside through the glass door and suddenly panic: Shippo is gone!

Leaving the two men without explanation, I run out of the store. *No, no, please God, not my dog.* I swear at myself for being so careless. I'm going to be punished for not heeding my ex-boyfriend's warnings.

"Shippo!" I yell out down the street. Could he somehow have gotten loose? He's a little crafty sometimes, but he's no Houdini. I definitely double-knotted the leash.

A few shoppers carrying bags watch me as I frenetically run down the street. "You see a Chihuahua mix? Off-white?"

They say no, sad, empathetic looks on their faces.

Santa Anita Boulevard is busy, with a lot of traffic. If Shippo attempted to cross that street, he would most likely be squashed.

Tears spring to my eyes. I never intended to get a dog, especially not right when I joined the Police Academy. I had just moved into my first rental house, was minding my own business, when I spied a dirt-soaked, flea-bitten mongrel walking on the streets around Thanksgiving. Benjamin and I had washed him down in my backyard and this cute, smiley Chihuahua mutt with a curlicue tail emerged. We were that close to taking him to the local shelter, but opted instead to post signs featuring the homeless dog's goofy grin. Nobody responded to our posters. My rental had a doggy door, which we both saw as a sign. The dog quickly made himself at home. Grandma Toma was the one who said, "he has a funny *shippo*," meaning *tail* in Japanese. That clinched it. Shippo, it was.

I scan the intersection. There's a library across the way with lots of green grass. Shippo is a sucker for grass.

I hurriedly push the walk button and then dash across the street when the light turns green.

"Shippo!" I call out. No sign of any dog.

I see some Asian kids carrying about their weight in books. "You guys see a little white dog?" I ask them.

Their parents and schoolteachers must have repeatedly told them not to speak to strangers because none of them answer me.

I take a deep breath. Shippo is going to be fine. He's a smart dog. He'll probably go back to where I left him.

I cross the intersection back to the music store. Before I've reached the curb, I see Shippo—in the arms of Washington Jeung.

I immediately take Shippo and bury my face in his fat folds. *You stupid, silly, wonderful dog. Don't you ever do that to your mama again!*

The leash is still firmly around his neck. I don't understand how he could have gotten loose. And then it hits me.

"You took him!" I say to Washington, feeling the heat of anger rise to my face. I put Shippo down on the sidewalk and hang on to his leash. "What the hell? Why did you do that?"

"I wanted to get you away from Mr. Wang and Mr. Xu. So we can talk more privately." Washington Jeung is dressed casually in a T-shirt and shorts. I don't know what he does for fun, but it's certainly not lying out at the beach. He's super pale.

"So talk."

"What's the latest on the Eduardo Fuentes case?" he asks.

"The police aren't interested in Mr. Xu anymore. He can go home and nobody will stop him."

Washington's chest expands with air and then he lets out a long sigh. Why does he seem so relieved? "He's not going anywhere until he finds his son. Do you have any idea where he could be?"

"You all have more insight into that than I do. Maybe Cece can tell you."

"That's not going to happen," he murmurs.

"What?" I hug Shippo closer to my chest.

"Nothing. What about your friend? Nay Pram? What has she told you?"

The way Washington is talking, it's obvious that he hasn't seen Nay for a while.

"Why don't you tell me?"

"I know that she tells you everything. You're like sisters, right?"

I don't respond. His comment, however, does warm my heart. Maybe Nay hasn't written me off like I think she has.

"She doesn't understand the whole story," he says.

I keep quiet, hoping that he'll reveal the story to me.

He studies my face for a moment. "You don't know anything," he then declares. He's more discerning than I give him credit for.

He shakes his head and then leans down to pet Shippo good-bye. "She used me, you know," he says before he leaves down the main street. Shippo, being the gigolo he is, whimpers and pulls his leash to romp after his new friend. I try to resist his efforts. What kind of magic does Washington have over my dog? Giving up, I let Shippo follow Washington's smell. But as mysteriously as he appeared, Washington Jeung is gone.

When I try the door of the Phoenix Instruments office, it doesn't budge. Taped on the locked door is a handwritten sign, misspelled: *Closed, due to family emrgency.*

I'm almost home when my phone rings. This time I actually stop the car at the curb before I answer. It's a 213 number. Downtown LA.

"Hello," I answer.

"Who is this again? Your message wasn't that clear on voice mail."

I recognize the voice immediately. "Kendra, this is Ellie Rush. Officer Rush with the LAPD Bicycle Coordination Unit."

"Oh yeah, the bicycle cop." Kendra's voice loses the tone of formality that it had before. "How can I help you?"

"Well, it's about Xu's cello."

"He's already completed his concert here."

"I know. I was just wondering why you recommended Phoenix Instruments as the appraiser of the cello. Just seemed a little strange, being a Chinese company and all."

"Ah, well. Mr. Xu insisted on it. He said that they would understand the true value of the instrument."

Aha, I think. *Fang Xu insisted on it, did he?*

"Is there anything else?" she asks impatiently.

"No," I say and thank her for her time.

Shippo, who's been belted into the Skylark through a special harness, sits beside me, panting. Some drool has dripped from his open mouth onto the vinyl seat, but I don't care.

"Did you hear that, Shippo?" I say to my passenger, rubbing him behind his ears. "I think that your mama is starting to connect some dots."

ELEVEN

I usually don't get into work early, but I do today. I leave my car and bike at home and take the Gold Line in. I even get a good seat by the window. I love the stretch where we are above the 110 freeway, above the train yard. We seem to be flying. I've been feeling like that lately, like the ground beneath me cannot be trusted. Why has Nay been avoiding me? She's obviously finished with Washington Jeung.

I make the transfer to the Red Line at Union Station, distracted by the enticing scent of gigantic pretzels being baked and tossed in sugar and cinnamon at a shop in the station. I get off at Pershing Square and walk through the Jewelry District and then the outskirts of the produce and flower markets.

I'm in a pretty good mood, all things considered. That is, until I hear what's being said in the room where we have roll call.

Mac is talking to a group of officers, all men, of course. Some have Starbucks cups; others hold Styrofoam ones filled with the brown liquid the station calls coffee. "She'll probably have all of us acting as her personal coolies, I'm tellin' you. So before you know it, you'll be pulling her rickshaw. She wants to be chief someday."

My presence is a conversation killer. Before, I wasn't sure how many people knew that I was the niece of the assistant chief, but by their actions, I get a definitive answer. All of them. The men scatter like cockroaches. I'm upset to see Johnny among the pests. From all the times that we've worked together, I thought that he would be on my side.

It's just Mac and me left facing off with each other.

"Stop spreading lies," I say to him.

"You know they're not lies. She's your aunt; you know how she is."

It's one thing for Mac to have personal issues with my aunt. It's quite another for him to spread his crap around the squad room, a place where I also work.

"Just because you're feeling sexually inferior, don't put that on a female cop." I can't believe I just said that.

Mac desperately wants to chew me out. Yell obscenities. Maybe even shove me. But he would be in beaucoup trouble if he tried that. He knows it and I know it. And he knows that I know it.

Just then Cherniss enters the room. "Good, glad I caught both of you here. I'm planning to send the two of you to patrol the Public Practice program at the Music Center and Grand Park today."

"I'm not going anywhere with her!" Mac says, storming out. I'm actually relieved—now that he's thrown a tantrum,

I can be the one who's all Zen and Buddha-like. Believe it or not, seeing Mac's outburst gives me a sense of power, knowing that he caved in under the pressure. Usually it's me who gets all emotional. That he lost it right now reveals his Achilles' heel.

"What happened?"

I shrug my shoulders. Put on a mysterious Mona Lisa smile.

"Are you feeling all right, Rush?" is all the response I get. Cherniss says that he's going to sit down with both of us to talk about our issues, but in the meantime he assigns me with Armine for today.

After our roll call, Armine and I get our bikes from the wall rack.

As soon as we're outside, fastening our helmets, Armine asks, "What is going on, Ellie?"

"What do you mean?" I'm trying to maintain my cool demeanor, but I think that my upper lip is starting to tremble.

"Everyone in the squad room was whispering about you and Mac. They say you guys are having a feud or something."

"It's a one-way feud. He has a problem with me."

Armine gets on her bike and I get on mine. "I heard about your aunt. I didn't know that you were related to one of the deputy chiefs. You could have told me."

"I didn't want any preferential treatment. I want to earn my way up."

"You're still young." Armine then sighs. I hate that kind of sigh. My mother does it constantly. "No sense in being too proud. You'll find that we need all the help that we can get."

* * *

The Public Practice program is taking place at both the Music Center and Grand Park, so Armine and I decide to split up, with me taking the north side by the Music Center fountains.

Public Practice is a totally cool idea—amateur musicians apply to practice in public around the centers of music in downtown Los Angeles. Benjamin actually submitted his online application last year to practice his guitar. He didn't get accepted, and we both thought it was because a guitar is so commonplace. A didgeridoo, a long aboriginal instrument made out of bamboo, on the other hand, is not so common. A heavyset African American man, who looks anything but aboriginal, blows into his bamboo pipe on the edge of the fountain. The organizers have placed a sandwich sign that reads PRIVATE PRACTICE in front of him. The sign is also a self-introduction. It says that the didgeridoo player's name is Jervey; he's a writer and English professor at USC. He got into the aboriginal instrument when he badly fractured his leg and had a lot of time on his hands. A friend gave him the didgeridoo as a semijoke; I guess the joke is on the friend because Jervey sounds pretty darn good as he places his mouth on the end of the large reed and blows. The sound is bouncy and repetitive; I feel like I could be in the Australian outback, watching kangaroos jump by.

On another corner I actually do see a guitar player, a woman about my mother's age. Lois is a banker who picked up the guitar after her daughter left for college. She first started playing once a week and now does it five times a week because it relaxes her after work. Lois is definitely a beginner, but seems determined. I see why Benjamin wasn't accepted. You have to be willing to be swept away by your passion. No cool stoicism here.

After work, I stop by Osaka's, somehow expecting the Fearsome Foursome to all magically be there, intact. I recognize a couple of girls who were active with one of PPW's sororities. They've graduated now, and they look gainfully employed in their suits and ID lanyards hanging from their necks.

I don't expect that they would remember me. I stayed away from the Greek scene; I was known among jocks and Asian American circles. But one of them calls out to me. "Hey, didn't you go to PPW?"

She has freckles all over her cheeks and on the bridge of her nose. She's cute, really cute. She wears her straight blond hair back in a headband.

"Yeah," I say, in no mood for small talk. I've changed into my street clothes, and I look a bit rumpled. My hair is mussed up and frizzy. I'm wearing jeans and a knit shirt, compliments of Target.

"You played on the volleyball team," the taller, brunette one says. Her voice is low and steady; she's the quiet one of the pair. "My brother was on the men's team."

She tells me his name and I remember him. He looks like her, tall and lean with wavy brown hair.

"So what are you doing now?" the brunette, who tells me her name is Emily, asks.

"I work for the LAPD," I tell them.

"Oh, wow, communications?" the blonde—Hailey—interjects.

"No, patrol. I'm with the bicycle unit."

"You have got to be kidding me."

I brace for the awkward looks, the mocking comments. But the girls seem interested.

"You mean, you have a gun and everything?" Hailey asks.

"Yup."

"That is so wild."

"Hailey and I both work at City Hall in city planning. We should get together sometime," Emily says.

"Have you been to the Edison? Coolest bar ever," Hailey comments.

"Haven't made it over there yet," I tell them.

"We're planning to go over there now," Emily says.

Hailey gives me a once-over. "They do have a dress code. No jeans," she adds apologetically.

"Another time." I smile. Although I do have a couple of skirts and dresses hanging in my closet, my wardrobe is pretty jeans-centric.

We exchange contact information and even business cards (how important are we?) and bend over our phones, plugging in one another's numbers.

The two girls, their squishy handbags in the crook of their arms, then wave good-bye and leave the crowded ramen house. I notice the eyes of a number of men follow their exit, probably imagining what could have been. I know that I should be happy that I'm making new friends, but to be honest, interacting with them just makes me miss Nay all the more.

* * *

I don't even bother ordering anything at Osaka's. There's no wait for a counter spot, but I don't feel like eating alone. I instead go down the street to Fugetsudo, a Japanese confectionery shop that's around a hundred and ten years old, according to a sign proudly showcased out front announcing that milestone, along with some old black-and-white photos to establish their history.

When I say confectionery, I mean *manju*, sweet cakes usually filled with red bean, as well as mochi, steamed sweet rice that's pounded and sometimes flavored and colored. There's a pretty white one with pink and green stripes called *suama*. Some cooks have experimented with more contemporary ingredients like peanut butter and chocolate. I get a *suama*, Aunt Cheryl's favorite, and a peanut butter one, mine.

"Aunt Cheryl, are you still at work?" I ask on my cell phone. Carrying my little white paper bag of sweets, I walk down First Street toward her office.

"Working late," she answers.

"I'm nearby, and I have mochi, the striped kind you like."

It doesn't take much to entice her. "Come on up."

Since Fugetsudo is only two blocks away from headquarters, I reach her office in a few minutes. Her administrative assistant has gone for the day, so it's only the two of us, chewing on mochi around her glass table.

"How are things at work?" she asks in between chews.

I'm sure not going to mention anything about what happened with Mac. Aunt Cheryl is the main reason that he is out to get me, anyway. "Fine," I say, "although it's too bad that they couldn't figure out why Eduardo Fuentes was after

Xu's cello. I went to his funeral, you know. He seemed like a nice man."

"Well, nice men sometimes do not-so-nice things. That whole case is a royal headache."

"What do you mean? I thought it was closed."

"Xu and his father are missing, and the Chinese government is not happy about it. They want them back immediately. Apparently they fear for their safety."

"Really?"

"Yes. They even took the cello that was being held in storage for Xu."

I'm confused. Why would the government be interested in Xu's cello? Would officials there care that it was a fake?

"I actually saw Fang Xu yesterday," I tell my aunt, "on my day off."

On Aunt Cheryl's otherwise flawless face, lines deepen above the bridge of her nose. "Why didn't you tell me?" She is annoyed.

"I didn't know that we were keeping tabs on him." It's not like any of the detectives, Cortez included, is sharing information with me.

"Where is he?"

"He was in this office building for Phoenix Instruments. It's over in Arcadia."

"He's staying there?"

"Well, he was up until yesterday afternoon." I find the address on my phone and e-mail Aunt Cheryl a link. "I doubt he's there now."

Aunt Cheryl's phone beeps with probably my e-mail message.

"I don't think that he knows where Xu is."

"The Chinese authorities are more interested in the father, Fang Xu," my aunt tells me as she strokes her phone screen to presumably check the address for Phoenix Instruments. "The father is more their target than the son."

I wipe my mouth with one of the napkins in the paper bag.

"I also found out some information about Ron Sullivan," Aunt Cheryl then announces.

"You found him?"

"No, but I know more about his relationship with Pascoal Fernandes." She rises and pulls out two cold bottles of water from her mini-refrigerator. After offering me one, she opens the other and takes a sip.

"Yeah, they were coworkers on the same movies." I recall what my grandfather had told me. "Ron had gambling debts; he was the one who got Puddy to help him rob that bank."

"Well, according to an old detective that I was able to track down, that's not what happened."

"What do you mean?"

"Your grandfather was actually the mastermind."

"What?"

"Yeah, he was the one who orchestrated the heist. Ron Sullivan actually testified against Fernandes in the trial back in 1964."

"I don't understand."

"Puddy was the actual brains. He saw Ron's skill as a makeup artist and thought of exploiting it as a way to rob banks."

"I don't get it. So why is Fernandes in town?"

"Retribution, perhaps. Maybe he wants in on the action. No luck in finding him?"

I shake my head. "Maybe we should have let him hang

on to the Skylark. At least then we would have known what he was driving."

"True," Aunt Cheryl says. "Who would have known that old beater would be worth something?"

Her diss of the Skylark stings for a second, but I let it slide. The more important thing I need to focus on is what she's telling me about Fernandes. And it's not anything a granddaughter wants to hear.

TWELVE

So, Puddy Fernandes is a liar. Why should I be surprised? Dad certainly didn't pick up that gene, but could be it skipped a generation and now maybe has touched Noah. How about me? Although I'm known to be a terrible liar, maybe that's not my true self. Maybe I'm the biggest liar of all, because I can't even see the lies I tell myself.

I look down at Shippo, who sits at my feet beside the couch. "You know me, right, Shippo? I can't fake anything with you."

He tilts his head at me, and I know he's probably thinking, *Is it time to eat?*

At work the next day, Johnny and I are assigned to Chinatown. There's a funeral for a prominent Chinese leader at the Baptist church not far from the 110 freeway. Apparently some of the elders were present during a shooting at a church funeral back in the eighties, and they don't want to tempt fate by not having some armed officers at the sanctuary. Bike cops will be less intrusive than officers in black-and-whites.

I stand at the back door, while Johnny is at the front. He's started to attend neighborhood meetings with a Chinese-speaking officer, so he's been able to cultivate some good relationships with both merchants and residents. Johnny's clean-shaven (he couldn't grow a beard even if he wanted to) and nonintimidating. People think that he listens well since he doesn't say much, though that's mostly because of his speech impediment.

The funeral goes long and I'm dying of boredom. Most of it is in Chinese, and it seems the so-called mourners are bored, too, because they're all talking to one another during the pastor's eulogy. It's like a weird black comedy with the family members weeping in front but the others all chatting about whatever in the back. Once it's over, sans any kind of violence, I go around to the front of the sanctuary.

"Gotta run. I got a lunch thing at Philippe's. I'm late," Johnny tells me before riding off.

What the—? I think. *Did he just ditch me?* We usually eat lunch together, so now I'm feeling dissed and at loose ends. Where am I going to eat? Nearby is Eat Chego's, a brick-and-mortar branch of the Kogi Korean-Mexican taco truck enterprise, but the line is at least eight feet long.

I backtrack on Hill Street past a small hospital. While I wait at the intersection, I see a man dressed in scrubs hasten to lock up his bike on a rack. He does it all wrong, at least according to the Cycling Task Force's flyer, threading his lock through only the front tire. He runs inside the hospital before I can stop him.

The bike is pink, with a big metal basket on the back—not that there's anything wrong with a guy riding a pink bike; you just don't see it that often. It's kind of weird how there's a whole color guys aren't supposed to like. When Noah was in grade school, he always wanted to be the pink Power Ranger. My parents didn't care, but it bothered the headmaster of his private school when he declared pink to be his favorite color during an assembly.

Anyway, Johnny's mention of Philippe's has got me hungering for one of their French dip sandwiches. The restaurant claims to have invented the French dip (slices of beef, lamb, turkey or ham on a crunchy French roll with au jus to dip it in on the side in a little container. Yes, a vegetarian's nightmare). It's a simple place—coffee for forty-five cents, believe it or not—with plain, polished long tables and wood shavings on the floor. It's my family's go-to place to eat before Dodger games. (Of course, we also eat Dodger dogs at the stadium, too.)

Anyway, it's a free country, right? If I feel like eating at Philippe's, with or without a formal invitation from Officer Johnny Mayhew, I can. I could even choose to sit with him and his date at one of the eatery's communal tables. I lock up my bike next to his on the rack outside and saunter in, expecting to see him in a cozy spot with a female. As it turns out, he is not only with a woman—the Bunker Hill Divorcée herself, Chale Robertson—but he's also sitting with Cortez Williams, and next to Cortez is a woman I don't know. What is Cortez doing with Johnny, and more important, what is he doing with this woman?

She looks to be a little older than me, which makes her a little younger than Cortez, and she's got a great tan, but not the old-lady skin-cancer kind. She's naturally bronze, no need for artificial bronzer, damn her. Her light brown hair has plenty of blond highlights and brushes against sun-kissed shoulders. I know that her shoulders are sun-kissed, because I can plainly see them exposed in her tank top.

Johnny's right cheek is full of food. He waves me down with a napkin. "Hey, Ellie, over here!"

My annoyance ratchets down. Based on his enthusiasm, he obviously didn't have a grand plan to leave me high and dry at the Chinese funeral; he just had people to meet.

Cortez shifts his weight on the bench as I approach. "Hello, Ellie," he says.

"Hi." I wait for an introduction to the woman beside him, and surprisingly, it's Chale who offers it. "This is Misty. She's with the Venice police bicycle unit," she says, gesturing with a hand whose nails are even bejeweled.

"And this is Officer Ellie Rush. She's with the downtown BCU," Cortez says.

"We work together," Johnny manages with his mouth full.

"Wow, we should get together sometime." Misty says *wow* with great enthusiasm and earnestness. "We girls have to support each other."

Yeah, we girls. Wow.

"Hey, maybe Ellie can be part of this, too," she says to the others, as if an idea has suddenly crossed her mind.

A part of what?

Chale explains that the Venice and Central bicycle units are going to be featured on an episode of *Divorcées of Bunker Hill*.

I don't get it, and I guess my lack of understanding is plain on my face.

"Okay, my purse is going to get stolen in Bunker Hill and

then Misty is going to find it on a street entertainer on the boardwalk in Venice," Chale says. "I'm going to rush over there"—she smiles slyly—"in my designer bikini, of course—and it's hooray, LAPD!"

So much for the *reality* in reality TV.

Johnny just nods, devouring the other half of his French dip.

"Ellie, would you like something? I can order for you," Cortez says.

"Oh, yes, Cortez, get Ellie a sandwich." Misty gently nudges Cortez, like they're an old married couple.

"Come on, sit down," Chale insists.

"I'm okay," I say, even though my stomach is growling. The purse-theft episode sounds totally lame. "Are you sure that the captain . . . ?"

"He thinks it's great. So does Officer Haines with Media Relations," Cortez tells me.

Haines would, I think.

"Cortez will have a role, too," Misty says. "He'll be the one giving the public service announcement at the end."

What public service announcement? "Beware of reality stars in bikinis with large designer handbags"? "I'm surprised that you have time for this, Cortez," I finally say. "With the Old Lady Bandit investigation and everything."

Cortez immediately registers my sarcasm; I'm not sure about Johnny, who's in both French dip and Chale heaven.

"I didn't know you were assigned to that case," Misty says to Cortez.

Uh-oh, do I detect a lack of communication here?

"Well, I have to go. I have to get back to *work*." I'm good at piling on guilt. I've learned from the best: my mother.

I turn to the exit, and hear some quick good-byes behind me. I go back to the rack to retrieve my bicycle and start riding north on Alameda to burn off some steam. I know I'm being ridiculous. Cortez owes me nothing. No explanations. We are not dating. We are not girlfriend and boyfriend. Yet I felt a sharp pang of jealousy when I saw him sitting there with that woman. Another bike cop. A prettier and nicer bike cop than me.

I curse myself. I hate when I feel and act this way. When we were dating, Benjamin always told me I got so crazy insecure over nothing. I want to stop feeling inferior. I mean, hey, I graduated from college in three years. Got through the Police Academy. I'm working as a cop. I should be proud of myself. Stand tall. But it's hard for me to change. I can't just wave a magic wand and make myself feel better.

I pass a low-budget hotel that some of my friends from San Francisco have stayed at. The hotel itself is fine, but the rest of the area here is pretty industrial. I pedal past the Chinatown Gold Line train station, painted in bright red, green, orange and yellow, and adorned with—what else?—dragons. Across the way is Homegirl Café, a "second-chance" eatery that trains former convicts and gang members. I'm tempted to stop by to at least pick up a shortbread cookie, but I'm not in a mood to stand in line.

Before I know it, I'm practically out of Chinatown. I'm next to an old factory that maybe once manufactured noodles or embroidery thread. There's a beat-up van parked at the curb, its side door open. I see a man wearing a torn T-shirt guide a bicycle from the van into the back of the building. It's not just any kind of bicycle: it's a pink one with a big metal basket on the back, now missing a front tire. It's the same exact one that I saw in front of the hospital earlier. The roll-up door is then quickly lowered by another man from the outside. He spots me and acts weird, slamming the van's side door shut and running to the driver's-side door. Before I can stop him, he gets in and drives away.

I radio in that I may have located a piece of stolen property. The bicycle didn't look like it was worth that much, so it's not going to fall into grand theft or anything like that. There's a regular metal door next to the roll-up. I bang on the door's surface with the back of my club. In spite of the noise, no one lets me in.

I ride to the front of the building. It's a storefront selling big, plush stuffed animals, the kind offered as prizes at carnivals. The woman behind the counter is talking on a cell phone and makes a face when I enter on my bike. Walking toward me from the back storeroom is the same Asian guy in the torn T-shirt. He didn't go far. The woman barks out something, maybe a warning, I think, because he dashes out the same way he entered.

"Stop! Police!" I call out. I jump off my bike, pushing away a gigantic stuffed panda to follow him through a hallway into a darkened storage area. The back door opens, a rectangle of light filling the room for a moment, enough for me to run after it. I reach the door before it closes completely. I wrench it open and my eyes adjust to the blinding sun outside.

Boyd and Azusa must have been close, because they're already here in a patrol car; it's parked in the middle of the narrow street. They stand in the street, their hands on their guns. The suspect clearly knows the drill. He immediately raises his arms and falls down on his knees.

As Azusa cuffs him, Boyd checks with me.

"Yeah, that was the guy," I confirm. Torn T-shirt is actually much older close up. He gives me a side eye of hate.

"So where's the bike?"

"I think he placed it here." I go back through the metal door in the storefront storage area and turn on the light. It takes me a few seconds before I fully absorb what's in front of me: at least a hundred bicycles stacked on top of one another, some missing front tires, some with sawed-off frames. Newish-looking tires are piled in the middle of the room, next to large tubs of paint. There's a faint smell of chemicals in the air.

Boyd, probably wondering what was taking me so long, joins me inside. "Wow, Rush," he says, as he props up his sunglasses on top of his head. "You've hit the mother lode."

Officer Jorge Mendez, our official LAPD liaison with the bicycling community, is beside himself. He keeps walking from one side of the warehouse to the other and swearing, not in anger but in amazement. I'm working as hard as I can to tag all the bicycles with a case number, date and time, location, and the name of the officer who found the property (me!). Other officers are taking photographs, and evidence clerks have come in vans to take the tagged items to police storage.

"Ruuuuuush," Jorge says my name like a sports cheer. And then goes back to more swearing.

I've tagged at least fifty bicycles. At least fifty more to go.

"Biggest bike theft ring in maybe the history of downtown LA—put down by the Central's Bicycle Coordination

Unit," Jorge says to no one in particular. "Take a break," he says to me. "Stand up."

"Why?" I murmur. I want to finish before my shift ends.

"I want to take your photo for my Twitter feed." He aims his iPhone toward me and I scowl in response.

"Your Twitter feed? I thought that we stopped all that."

"Not the bicycle units. All the bike groups are active on social media. They'll Retweet this for sure."

Before I can grab his phone, Captain Randle enters the warehouse. "Mother of God," he mutters as he stares at the stacks of bikes.

"Media Relations is already working on this," Jorge says to Captain Randle. "There will be a press conference on Monday. Haines will be calling you."

Captain Randle nods.

"And you!" Jorge turns to me. "I *have* to take you out for at least one beer."

The captain smiles his approval. "You deserve it, Rush. If I didn't have this dinner to go to with my wife, I'd even join you."

"How about it, Rush?" Jorge extends his arms. If it's good enough for Captain Randle, I guess it should be good enough for me.

"I have to finish tagging," I tell him. It would be nice if someone else were helping me.

"Of course," says Jorge. "And you have your police report, too. In the meantime, I have a ton of Tweets that I have to catch up on."

It takes me forty-five minutes to complete tagging, and another half hour to write some detailed notes, which will be helpful when I complete my report. I want to start on it now, but my shift is over. It'll have to wait until first thing tomorrow morning.

Jorge and I go to the Far Bar, which is on the same block as Osaka's. The bar is an extension of Far East café, which used to be one of Grandma Toma's favorite restaurants. The restaurant now is more like a sports bar, but apparently at one time it was the place to go for "chop suey." I've never quite understood why Japanese Americans of my grandparents' era liked to eat "fake" Chinese food, as Noah calls it. (Noah considers himself the Anthony Bourdain of all Chinese food just because his best friend, Simon, has roots in Taiwan.)

The Far Bar is not a claustrophobic hangout. It's mostly outdoors, in between two brick buildings, so you feel like you're at a friend's house in New York City or something. It's casual, and best of all, it's open, so I feel that I can make a quick getaway if need be. Although it's not like Jorge and I are here on a date or anything, right?

We sit on the side, away from a large group making a lot of noise. The waiter delivers our drinks. I ordered a martini for the heck of it, since Jorge did say that he was buying.

"So," he says after taking a sip of his scotch and soda. "Tell me about yourself, Rush."

Surprised, I look up from my martini. Jorge's a nice enough guy and good-looking in a fresh-faced way, but he's always been a bit self-absorbed. I know that he grew up in East LA, close to where Eduardo Fuentes's funeral was, and that he went to Don Benito High School. That his mother is a school clerk and that his father works in Parks and Rec. I know these things because he's told me his background without ever asking for mine. Until now.

"What do you want to know?"

"Well, I know that you're part Japanese. You're the assistant chief's niece, right?"

So news has spread to Jorge's ears, too. There's no use denying it.

"Yup." I bite into the olive. Its saltiness makes me cringe for a second.

"What's the other half?"

I hate that question. It's like I'm split down the middle, some kind of human mutant. "White and other stuff." I don't want to get into the "other stuff" right now, because that would mean thinking about Fernandes.

"Well, we're all mixed in America. Mutts. It doesn't matter if you're white, red or green. People are people."

"But we wouldn't be people if we were green," I say. "We'd be aliens."

Jorge lets out a weird hacking laugh. "I didn't know that you were funny, Rush."

I finish off my drink and chew on the plastic stick from the olives.

"Seriously, that was good work today. The bike coalition groups are stoked. Turns out, one of the bikes in there is their former president's. That baby is worth two grand."

My eyes grow big. "You're kidding me."

"Yup, that's grand theft, right there." The party next to us break out in laughter—some inside joke.

"Robbery detectives are questioning the suspect. There might even be another branch of their operation on the other side of downtown." Jorge flags a waitress. "You pulled a real coup today. By just paying attention. Detective material, Rush."

* * *

Jorge wants to buy me another drink, but I turn him down. I drove today and the last thing I need is a DUI to ruin my best day of work so far. I wish that I could be celebrating with Nay. Rickie is busy with some sort of school project and Benjamin is still spending most of his free time in the hospital. All I have is this one martini with a cop with a shiny forehead. I shouldn't be complaining, but I am. I leave Jorge at the Far Bar, giving an excuse that there's somewhere else I need to be.

I decide to stop by my parents' house and celebrate my victory with my family. But when I turn on their street, I notice that my dad's hybrid is not parked in their driveway.

I ring the doorbell a couple of times, but there's no answer. I have my own set of keys and dig in my backpack to get them, when I hear the double lock turning. "Hold your horses." The muffled voice of my grandmother before she opens the door to me.

"Where is everybody?" I say, immediately embarrassed to imply that Grandma Toma is a nobody.

Of course, she's oblivious to the slight. "Goofing around," she says and walks back into the hallway. She then turns back to me. "You've been drinking?"

I follow her inside. "Why do you say that?"

"Your earlobes are all red. Your grandfather's earlobes always got red when he drank."

I don't know how to take this new piece of information. "It was just one drink. And it was to celebrate."

Grandma Toma stops in mid-shuffle. "You got a raise?"

"No, not until I get a higher rank."

"When will that be?"

"Grandma, can I just tell you my piece of good news?"

Grandma Toma dutifully nods and situates herself on the couch. "What is it?"

"I busted a bicycle theft ring."

"Well, that's very nice."

"This is a big deal. Some of these bicycles are worth two thousand dollars."

"Why on earth would someone be riding around on a bicycle worth that much money? Don't they know that you can get a perfectly good one from Costco for a hundred dollars?"

Only Grandma Toma could pour such cold water on my accomplishment so fast. Wait a minute; I take that back. Mom could probably do it in even less time. *What am I doing here?*

"Have you heard from Lita?" I ask.

"She was here for dinner. All of them are at Fosselman's getting ice cream for dessert."

"You didn't tell me that." Fosselman's is the best place in Los Angeles County for ice cream, which they actually make there on the premises. "Why didn't you go?"

"Ice cream gives me the runs."

"There are pills to prevent that, Grandma."

"I take too many pills as it is. Don't need to take another one just so I can eat a scoop of lychee ice cream." Grandma Toma is crankier than usual tonight. "She's been here every night for dinner."

"Who?"

"Your other grandmother."

"She has?"

"She says that she's sworn off men. She's been a lousy mother, she says. So now we get to see her every night." Grandma Toma looks weary. "I don't know how long I can take this."

"Maybe you could introduce her to somebody."

"What do you mean?"

"You were part of that widowed group or something. Any available widowers?"

"Are you crazy? There are ten women to every man. It gets scary sometimes. That's why I stopped going."

"Well, I bet there's no one like Lita in that group."

Grandma Toma contemplates this, jutting her chin forward. She rises. "I'm going to make some calls."

With Grandma Toma on the phone, now there's really no one to talk to at my family's house, so I go home. I give Shippo some extra treats in celebration of the arrests today, but my heart isn't fully in it. I'm not in the mood to take him for a walk. I just want to curl up in my bed and watch more episodes of *Dawson's Creek*. There's absolutely nothing good to eat in my house, so I take some hard nuggets of brown sugar and pop them in my mouth like candy. I don't text Nay, because I've already left too many texts as it is. What they say is definitely true. I know that I sound like a lame country singer, but if there's no one to share your successes with, what does it really matter?

THIRTEEN

The next morning, I wake up feeling much better. I figure that martini, being a depressant, probably didn't help my dark mood. Besides, with the sun streaming in through my mini-venetian blinds, how can I not feel hopeful?

I work an antiquarian book festival at USC on Saturday—not many criminals spotted there, but there were some really cool old books and even old-school mechanical typewriters. I'm partnered with Johnny, who is bored out of his mind, probably imagining the Bunker Hill divorcée in various revealing yoga positions. Day off on Sunday—I actually go off the grid and take a long bike ride on the beach, leaving my phone in the trunk of my car. Lately, between everything going on with Puddy and Xu and Nay, I've been feeling unsettled, distracted. Uncovering this bicycle theft ring reminds me what I'm supposed to be doing in my job. *Focus, Ellie, focus.*

My sunny delight follows me to work on Monday. Today

is the press conference, Jorge said. A part of me is surprised that I wasn't called in early or told to come into work wearing my full uniform. I mean, I don't expect that I'm going to be on television or anything; but then again, maybe I do.

That feeling intensifies during the roll call, which is all about me. Well, actually, just the beginning is, but the glow stays with me throughout even the boring parts of the meeting. Mac, I notice, sits in the back, his arms crossed over his chest as if he doesn't want any Ellie Rush love to touch him.

After the roll call, a few officers come up and congratulate me. We're a bureau that gets knocked for targeting the homeless and jaywalkers, and it's nice to get some positive attention for once.

I'm working on my report when I hear someone turn up our television set. "Captain Randle's on," someone shouts, and I, like everyone else, crowd around the monitor.

Captain Randle is indeed there, looking as distinguished as ever in his uniform, explaining the details of the bike ring found in the former warehouse. "This is the largest discovery of stolen bicycles in the history of our division," he says. "This case was cracked due to the hard work and perceptive actions of our officers." My heart burns with pride as I wait to hear him say my name—Officer Eleanor Rush.

But the broadcast then cuts to Jorge, looking even shinier and more scrubbed than usual. "Since its inception, the Bicycle Coordination Unit has been working to support the enjoyment of bicycling in our city. These arrests and the recovery of stolen goods are proof of our commitment and hard work."

Everyone is hooting and hollering, but I sit there, feeling numb. *Our?* What happened to a certain officer named Ellie

Rush who used her wits and observational skills to catch these thieving suckers? I know I'm being self-absorbed, but I can't help it. I try to snap out of my personal pity party, then catch Mac's gaze. He's been watching me this whole time, and based on the sly smile on his face, he knows that I'm feeling dissed.

To further relish my discomfort, he saunters over toward me. "Nice press conference, huh, Rush?"

"Yup, Captain Randle was great."

"I noticed that you were not at all mentioned, although apparently you were the one who found the bikes."

"Well, you know, we are a team." *Team LAPD, rah-rah.*

"I didn't know that you were such a team player."

"Hey, Rush, you have a phone call. It's Deputy Chief Toma," one of our clerks calls out.

Perfect timing, I think. As I get up, Mac sneers. I can read his thoughts: *little Ellie, running to her aunt Cheryl.*

"Hello, this is Officer Ellie Rush." Might as well make it as professional as possible.

"Ellie, I am so, so proud of you. Well done."

"Thank you, Chief." Using the title *Chief* adds more professional distance between us.

"Come by my office today, okay? Maybe around two o'clock? I've already made the request to your CO."

I agree—I mean, am I going to refuse? I do wonder what our meeting is all about. A special citation? A photo op? Or . . . hell, could it be about Fernandes? I haven't found out anything new. Nothing good, at least.

I return to the computer station, trying to concentrate on completing my report. I read the same paragraph about twelve times. I'm still sore over not getting public kudos for the arrests on Friday. The little screaming meemies inside of me cry: *Doesn't matter how hard you work; other people—especially older guys—are always going to get the recognition. Remember in your poli sci course when that do-nothing big mouth got all the credit for your "A" project?*

"Oh, hi, Brad Pitt." Some officers let out some fake screams. Jorge has returned to the Central Division.

Brad Pitt? Give me a break. More like a poor man's Jimmy Fallon. A very poor man's version. A few guys stop Jorge and chat with him for a few minutes. I keep my eyes on my computer screen.

Finally the fifteen-second TV star makes his way to me. "I feel like you're avoiding me."

"Nope," I lie, pretending that I'm mesmerized by what I'm proofreading. "You did great at the press conference. Very articulate."

"You know, a lot of the TV stations cut off my full state-ment."

"Oh yeah?" I say. *Which part? The part where you say you're God's gift to the women of LA?*

He stands there awkwardly for a moment, then leaves my desk. I check whether he's really out of the area, and then click to the World Wide Web.

Bicycle News has the complete transcript of the press conference. I read Jorge's part:

Officer Eleanor Rush of Central's BCU was the one who noticed that the same bicycle that was locked in front of a hospital on Hill Street was being moved, its front tire missing, to the warehouse location on Alameda. It's the diligence and professionalism of new officers like Officer Rush that has greatly enhanced our apprehension of bicycle thieves in the past couple of months.

I feel like such a dork. Jorge gave me plenty of props and then some. It was just like he said: his quote had been cut down to fit the broadcast news segment.

I get up and look for Jorge. "Anyone knows where Mendez went?" I just put out the question to anyone who hears it.

"Think that he went to meet some bicycling groups."

I find his digits on my phone. After one ring, he picks up. "Hey, it's Ellie."

"You still mad at me?"

"I read the complete transcript on one of those bicycling websites." I take a deep breath of apology. "Thanks for the shout-out."

"Everyone in the department knows it was you, Ellie."

"No, it really was the team. If Boyd and Azusa hadn't come when they did, the perps would have been long gone." And even Johnny—silly, divorcée-chasing Johnny—if he hadn't had his reality TV meeting at Philippe's, I probably wouldn't have gone that far north on Alameda. "But thanks, Jorge. I really appreciate it."

"Let's hang out again sometime. The Far Bar was fun."

It was okay, I think, *but it would have been more fun with Nay, Rickie and Benjamin.* Jorge, however, doesn't need to know that. "Sure," I say. "You know where to find me."

I ride along Main Street toward First, where the LAPD headquarters now stand. My dad claims that at one time he wouldn't walk down Main Street, neither alone nor with ten people. The alleys in the area were littered with hypodermic needles, and vehicles were constantly broken into, hustlers literally carrying lifted car batteries in the street. Pimps and prostitutes were common, and a porno movie house stood where a Japanese theater once was.

All I can say is that Main Street cleans up good. Nowadays you can fortify yourself with a bacon maple donut at the Nickel Diner, which still has a faint rough-and-tumble air about it. The building on the corner still has Victorian architectural features like turrets, bay windows, and dormers. The Grecian columns of the Farmers and Merchants Bank building proudly announce that there was once money there. The San Fernando Building on Fourth and Main has all this beautiful filigree, like a classic, fancy cake in a British bakery.

I arrive early at the modern, glass police headquarters. The auditorium, where an Asian American police association recently honored my aunt, stands alone on the northeast corner of the block. Behind it are grass steps, amphitheater style, which lead to a new memorial of fallen officers. It's all brass plaques, each inscribed with an officer's name, rank and date of death. The thin rectangles are a limestone wall, a wall that represents us, the LAPD. The memorial looks the most dramatic during the evening, when it's lit up from the bottom. Even now, as the afternoon sun bears down and I can see the cupola of the old St. Vibiana Church in the background, I get a little choked up.

I take a seat on a concrete bench and make some phone calls, starting with Sally Choi, Benjamin's sister and one of the best-known criminal attorneys in the city.

"Sally, it's Ellie."

"Ellie, it was so good to see you the other day."

"How's your mom?"

"Better. She's been moved from ICU to her own room."

"Yeah, I heard." In all the craziness of everything, I haven't been able to get to the hospital again. "I plan on coming by soon."

"Good. She's been asking about you."

I like Mrs. Choi. She's direct and touchy-feely in a good way.

"I had a question for you. A kind of legal question. I need to see a criminal file from an old case. Way back from nineteen sixty-four."

"Nineteen sixty-four? Hmmm. I've had to dig up some old files from time to time. It's a pain in the butt. Do you have the case number?"

"I can probably get it."

"That'll save you a lot of time. You'll have to go to Foltz on Temple Street," she says, referring to our criminal courts building. "You also may be able to find something in the newspapers. A lot of them are digitized now."

I thank Sally, telling her to give my best to her mother.

About fifteen minutes before my appointment, I make my way through the building and up the elevators.

"I have a two o'clock appointment with Deputy Chief Toma," I announce to Aunt Cheryl's assistant, who is wearing a telephone headset.

"Oh, hi, Ellie." The assistant acts much less formal to me than usual. "Go ahead and wait inside. Chief Toma is running late."

My aunt's office is immaculate. Even where she has piles

of manila folders, they are stacked completely straight, the edges all crisp and lined up. She uses only one pen, a Montblanc that Grandma Toma gave her when she made detective. She keeps it in its original case.

I hear the fast-paced clicking noise of high heels in the hallway. Aunt Cheryl has arrived. She's wearing some kickass shoes, white pumps with a red and black trim.

"Hi, Chief," I say as my aunt appears in her office.

Hearing my greeting, Aunt Cheryl gets a funny look on her face. I rarely call her by her title when we're alone.

We spend some time talking about Friday's arrest. About how I noticed the hospital worker with his pink bicycle and basket, and later spotted the same bicycle being stowed away in the warehouse.

"Why were you that far north on Alameda, anyway? Were you following the suspect?"

"No, just happened to stumble on him," I say. I don't mention the part about seeing Cortez with another woman.

Aunt Cheryl rises from her throne and closes her door completely, which has been a little ajar. "Listen," she says, standing in front of me, "we've started meeting with the FBI on the Old Lady Bandit case."

"Oh, that makes sense."

"I told the agents that the Pascoal Fernandes tip came in anonymously, directly to me. You didn't tell anyone outside our family about Pascoal, did you?"

I don't respond right away. Aunt Cheryl gives me her dagger-eyed stare that would make an inmate on death row blubber and cry.

I clear my throat. "No, of course not," I lie. I pray to God that Cortez has kept his lips sealed.

"Good. Nobody can know that you are related."

My head is down.

"Ellie, do you hear me?"

"Yes." I raise my head. "Yes, Chief."

I slink out of Aunt Cheryl's office as if I've been released by the vice principal at high school. Her assistant has left her station, so at least no one has to see me leave.

I get in the elevator. I'm alone, so I let out a long breath.

The elevator stops at practically every floor. Plainclothes detectives, some of whom I recognize, come in and out—including the man I need to talk to, Detective Cortez Williams.

He almost doesn't get in when he sees me. He's wearing a peach-colored dress shirt, a teal green and brown striped tie, and brown pants. Yes, I notice these things.

"I hear congratulations are in order," he finally says as he stands next to me. I can feel the temperature rise in the elevator.

"Oh, yeah."

"That's great, Ellie. Really. I would have called to congratulate you sooner, but things are moving with some cases."

One of the cases involves the Old Lady Bandit. A crowded elevator in police headquarters is an inappropriate place for me to bring up Puddy Fernandes, but I need to talk to Cortez about him—soon. "There's something I need to discuss with you," I tell him in a low voice. I don't want to whisper, because that will draw even more attention.

"Sure, give me a call."

"Ah, it's kind of important."

We lock eyes for a moment. He knows I'm serious.

"Okay, just let me know." He gets off on the second floor, gives me a quick glance good-bye and the door closes.

As soon as I'm outside of headquarters, I leave him a voice message. I try to be as formal as possible. "Officer Ellie Rush here," I say. "I just wanted to go over some details of a recent case. It's probably good if we go over it in person."

The rest of the day is boring and I'm so thankful for it. Back at the station, I again help Captain Randle proofread police reports. When I ask the captain where old paperwork is filed, he just groans. He says that he was recently able to get almost a hundred boxes of investigator's case envelopes and property disposition requests that were stored in our station onto the destroy list. Like Sally warned me, getting access to Puddy's old records will be a challenge. I think about what she suggested, checking out newspaper records.

Since I've lost my Los Angeles Public Library card, I decide to visit the mother ship. Central Library. I change into my street clothes in the locker room and just walk the eight blocks. It's still light out and I remember something about parking—even validated parking—costing a fortune at certain hours.

Fifth Street is bustling around rush hour. There're a ton of restaurants and small shops. Everyone wants to make a buck, or at least ten or twenty, to cover the high rents. I pull down my fanny pack so it's not obvious that I'm carrying a gun. Then I remember the metal detectors, and it occurs to me that I'll have to identify myself as an LAPD officer when I go in the library.

The library security department is pretty extensive for the

downtown branch. If you think about it, a library is a haven for all—the downtrodden, homeless and so on. It attracts all kinds of people, from the richest of the rich who sit on its board, to literally the poorest of the poor. Those with fat wallets, and those who want to take those fat wallets, are all sitting under the same roof, so there's bound to be some trouble.

I walk through the shady garden that greets library patrons first—the Japanese peace bell, the long rectangular pools of water, lines from nineteen different languages embossed in the stairs. There are a bunch of people here: lovers making out, both secretly and publicly; men with stuffed grocery store carts taking a breather; latchkey kids.

With its magnificent Egyptian-like pyramid tower outside, Central Library is even more amazing inside. It's airy, with colorful modern chandeliers hanging from its celestial ceilings. The library is really old and timeless at the same time. It's my kind of place.

Taking off my fanny pack, I show my ID, badge and gun to the security guard. He takes a long time with my ID. It's like he can't really believe that I, who look as young as a high school senior, could really be a police officer. He radios someone and I drum my fingers on his little table at the front entrance. Really?

An older security guard emerges from the main lobby. He takes his time walking toward us and greets me with a big smile. We've met before, over a rash of pickpocketing in the library. "She's okay," is his endorsement for me.

I put away all the items that identify me as law enforcement and make my way to the checkout desk. In minutes I have a new library card and I'm already at a computer terminal on one of the lower levels, plugging in my patron ID number.

It's only been a year and a half since I was a student, but even in that short amount of time, technology has advanced. I'm able to quickly access the *LA Times* archives and from there, even search by keyword. It goes back, way back, even to the 1800s. I, however, just need the decade of the sixties. I type in "Pascoal Fernandes" and get all sorts of links to strange articles ranging from home improvement to cartoons. I add "bank robbery," and the list is dramatically shortened to a single entry in September of 1964.

The original article is scanned, and it's super brief, only about two inches long. The gist of it: *Pascoal Fernandes, 21, is accused of planning and driving the getaway car in a North Hollywood bank robbery.*

There's no mention of Ronald Sullivan, confirming the information Aunt Cheryl got from the retired detective. But the getaway car—that's new information.

I do searches with different combinations. Nothing. I dangle my legs and people-watch for a while. A woman keeps walking by, muttering to herself. A man in a suit spends a lot of time poring over a corporate directory. The reference librarian sits on a high chair like I do, listening to whispered requests, typing on his keyboard, and filling out forms.

My mind wanders. Then, why not? I type in "Old Lady Bandit," complete with the quotation marks. A few hits, including one in 1952. A suspect was arrested in three bank robberies, but it seems to have nothing to do with either Ronald Sullivan or my grandfather. And then there's one in 1969.

Neither the bank's name nor its exact location is identified, but the dateline is Los Angeles. I don't know whether that was a curious journalistic practice of the time—to hide the exact address of the crime (perhaps not to impede the investigation?). The story mentions that $20,000 was stolen. Judging from the size of the headline, this was a small fortune. The suspects apparently got away. The Old Lady Bandit escaped on foot, but a car presumed to have been intended as the getaway vehicle quickly followed. The vehicle is identified in the story as a yellow Buick Skylark, thought to be brand-spanking-new.

Oh no, I think. I cannot believe this. My beloved Green Mile could have been the getaway car in a heist, a heist involving my grandfather. And Lita may have known this the whole time.

Math is not my strong suit. It never was, despite the stereotype that all Asians are supposed to be good in math. Mom is good at calculating grade point averages and totals on grocery store receipts, but not much beyond that. Dad, with his Scottish (and now Portuguese) blood, is the mathematician of the family. That's probably why the obvious never occurred to me. Like if the Green Mile was around before Dad was born, how come its model year is five years after Dad's birth year?

"Lita, you lied to me!" I say to her through her screen door before she has time to open it.

"*Querida*, you going to scream at me in front of the neighbors?" she says, waiting for me to cool down on her doorstep.

I do and I quietly enter her living room.

I try to keep my voice steady and monotone. "You told

me that Puddy Fernandes had the Green Mile when you first met him. Well, that's impossible. Because the car is a 1969 model. Dad was born in 1964."

"I didn't quite say that."

"But you made me believe it. What is going on?" It doesn't take me long to lose it, but I'm pissed. I'm discovering that many of the elders in my life are liars. And not onetime liars, but perpetual ones.

"Sit down, sit down." Lita gestures toward her rattan love chair. I grudgingly settle in one corner.

Lita sits in her matching rattan chair. "After serving his jail time for that first robbery, Puddy turns up one day at my mother's house. Your father may have been five years old. My mother wouldn't let him in. Told him that I had moved away. Far, far away. He didn't know about your father. He left the Skylark for me with some strict instructions."

"What were the instructions?"

"To get it painted and not to ever sell it."

"Why didn't you tell me this in the first place?"

"I didn't want you to know that the Skylark was involved in something untoward."

"Untoward? Lita, this is really serious. The Green Mile was the getaway car in a 1969 robbery."

"Isn't there a statute of limitations? Nobody was hurt."

I don't know enough about the law to answer. Armed robbery involves the feds, and then there are a lot of other technicalities that people don't know about.

"You painted the car. You conspired to hide evidence. Lita, you could be in big trouble, too."

That thought does rattle Lita. "Get rid of the car, *querida*. Send it to the junkyard. Crush it down. Make it disappear."

"We can't do that, Lita. It'll make us all the more suspicious. The safest thing to do is to hang on to the Green Mile." *Forever.* While driving to Lita's house, I also came up with a theory. Far-fetched, yes, but then, all of this is. I give voice to my theory. "Puddy is not out here to save people's lives. He's here to find Ron Sullivan to collect his share of the money from when he drove the getaway car. Most likely, with interest and then some."

FOURTEEN

I'm early again for the next day's roll call. It's amazing how experiencing some success at your job will help your punctuality.

I sit in our meeting room by myself, fiddling with my cell phone. Nay's latest article on arrests happening in China has been posted on the *Squeeze* website. The latest officer to be arrested is named Zhiyun Xu. He is accused of taking huge bribes and dispersing the monies to his wife and relatives. His whereabouts, as well as his family members' locations, are unknown. I don't know how common the surname "Xu" is—is it just a coincidence, or was this the high-ranking leader in the Communist Party mentioned in Kendra Prescott's article? Xu's uncle, the one who had presented him with the cello? Nay refers to a number of anonymous sources, and I wonder whether any of them are Washington Jeung.

For the heck of it, I try texting her again: *Congrats on your story. Just read it. Hope it wins a Pacemaker.* After I press send, I immediately regret the line about the Pacemaker Award. I worry it sounds sarcastic, but it's not. I honestly think, especially for a school newspaper, that her article rocks.

I stare at my phone's blank screen. The friend vacay continues.

"Hey." Someone enters the room.

I turn around. It's Jorge. "Oh, hi." He doesn't always show up for our meetings, so I'm a little surprised to see him.

He comes close to me, enough to make me a tad uncomfortable. "What are you doing after work?"

"Uh." Watching more episodes of *Dawson's Creek* with Shippo at my side.

"Music Center is having one of their dance nights."

"You dance?" I ask. Benjamin loves music, but he never danced unless he was pretty drunk. It's usually up to Nay and me to tear up the dance floor.

"Doesn't everyone?"

I like Jorge's attitude. One thing that I can say about him, he is Mr. Positive.

"Maybe I'll stop by. No promises."

"Well, I'll be there."

More officers fill the room and Jorge, thankfully, moves to sit in the front corner. Other than Johnny, most guys don't sit next to me unless there are no other open spots. But this morning I'm a seat magnet. The early birds surround me. The only exception is Mac, who chooses a spot in a corner as far away from me as possible.

"Officer Mendez, our bicycle liaison, is here to make an announcement," says Captain Randle.

Jorge stands up and faces the rest of us. "Well, our

discovery of the stolen bicycles has generated great media attention and good will in the biking community and the public. As a result, Councilman Beachum wants to present a special commendation to the Central's bicycle unit. And he would like the unit to be represented by Officer Rush."

"Ruuuush, Ruuuush." Guys are beating their palms on their desks. Normally, I would love this. But I really don't want any special attention from our district's councilman.

"Officer Lambert will be presented with a commendation, as well. You're aware of this, right, Lambert?"

"What's it for, Mac?" someone calls out.

Mac sits silently in the back corner, biting his fingernail and looking uncomfortable. I don't get it. He doesn't respond, so Jorge moves on and eventually lets the captain continue with the meeting.

"Wear your uniform tomorrow for the council meeting," Jorge advises me before he leaves. He doesn't mention the Grand Park dance night again, thank God. That's all I need at work, rumors that the bicycle liaison and I are an item.

Six of us, including Johnny, Armine and me, are assigned to an independent movie shoot next to the downtown architectural school. It's on the eastern side of the Arts District, next to the Los Angeles River. I never even knew that the school existed until I started working for the Central Division. It's in an old freight terminal for the Santa Fe Railroad, a long narrow building that spans four blocks.

I'm not quite sure what kind of movie they're shooting. It's called *Renegade Flats*, and I don't recognize any of the actors. Most of them are dressed in street gear, all black. Doesn't seem like the kind of thing I'll be watching, even if the filmmakers offer it free on the web.

I move my bike closer to Johnny. He seems bummed out. "What's happening with the *Divorcée*-on-the-beach episode?" I ask him.

"The chief nixed it."

No wonder Johnny is so down. "Sorry."

"Yeah, he said that he doesn't think it would put the department in a good light."

Thank God for the chief, I think.

"Hey, maybe your aunt can put in a good word for us," Johnny suggests.

"Ah, no. I can't ask her for any favors." Especially if she finds out that I've spilled the beans to Cortez about Puddy. Speaking of Cortez, no return phone call.

We watch as the lighting crew move equipment around.

"Chale must have been disappointed," I say.

"Heck, yeah. She doesn't even want to hang out anymore."

And you're surprised? My poor sometimes-partner is one deluded man.

"Too bad for Misty, too," I say.

"She doesn't care. It's more her husband."

"Her husband?"

"He's an exec with the cable network. He's best friends with Cortez Williams. That's why Williams even agreed to meet with us."

I readjust my sunglasses. So that's why Misty seemed so cozy with Cortez. He's tight with her husband. They're friends. Legitimate friends. Once again, my paranoia, jealousy, has gotten the best of me. I wish I could just turn off that side of me, like a faucet or a spigot. I need that slogan "Keep Calm and Carry On" tattooed to my brain.

"Anyway, Misty's husband has plans for us, Ellie. A kind of *Baywatch* on bikes. A reality show."

"Good luck with that, okay?"

"Oh no, if it gets off the ground, you'll have to be a part of it."

Not a chance. I ride my bike to the other side of the production and look away from the lights, actors and reflective screens. I know that the river, shallow fingers of water carrying mud and trash, is just a few blocks away. I feel more connected to the river, no matter how dirty and pitiful, than all the glitz right in front of me. The river smells real and is going to be there tomorrow, whereas this whole film crew will be gone, leaving the streets empty again.

Toward the end of the day I receive a text from Jorge: *60s nite!!! Music Center. 7.*

His exclamation marks crack me up. I don't know of any other guys who would use so many—or even one—in a text. Circles of people at the shoot have gathered, smoking cigarettes and laughing. They've invited a few of us, including Johnny and me, to drinks at the local bar. I don't feel like standing around, a beer in my hand, talking BS. But I also don't feel like playing dog lady again, spending another night with Shippo and *Dawson's Creek*, so I text Jorge that I'll meet him there.

I go home to feed Shippo and to change. I'm certainly not going to dress in tie-dye, macramé vests, or whatever they wore then. In defiance of the theme, I wear a Nike Lycra running shirt and shorts.

I drive the Green Mile, prepared to pay for parking. The

lot is already filled with young people my age trying to find their inner flower children, judging from the outfits they're wearing. There are also plenty of people in regular T-shirts and jeans like me.

"Hey, I like your outfit. Prefontaine," a skinny black guy wearing a halter top says to me.

I've heard of Prefontaine before. He was a runner who ran in Oregon, where Nike's waffle-iron sole was created. While trying to rebel against the event's theme, I guess I fell smack-dab in the middle of it.

I go up the stairs toward the Music Center plaza. There are about two hundred people already on a laminate dance floor that they've placed on the concrete. The DJs on the stage, at their turntables, are spinning the vinyl. Strings of paper lanterns above. It's completely insane.

"El-lie!" I hear a male voice shouting, but it doesn't sound like Jorge. Rickie comes running toward me, his Mohawk standing straight up with God knows how many layers of hair product.

"It's the sixties, Rickie. Way before the Village People."

"Don't be such a smart-ass. It's not how you look; it's not even about how you move. It's about just showing up and being with everyone."

I give Rickie a sideways look.

"Why are you here, anyways? Didn't think these dance jams would be your thing," he says.

"Maybe I'm branching out."

"Are you with someone?"

"Not necessarily." I regret my ambiguous remark.

Just then I hear Jorge calling my name. He's wearing a pair of tight jeans and a loose wine-colored V-neck T-shirt.

On his head is one of those hipster hats that I usually can't stand. But he actually looks pretty cute in it. Lessens the glow of his shiny forehead.

"Hey," I say when Jorge joins us. "I'm here."

"It's even more crowded than usual." Jorge notices Rickie. "Hi." He extends his hand.

"Jorge, Rickie. Jorge and I work together. Rickie and I are friends from college."

From the stage the music changes to Sly and the Family Stone's "Dance to the Music." I love the beginning of this song—the horns blasting, the tambourine shaking, and someone—maybe Sly Stone—yelling in that raspy voice, "Hey, get up and dance to the music." Rickie starts jumping up and down, and in this crowd, it's totally appropriate.

Jorge cups his mouth as he says to me, "So, is he your boyfriend?"

I make a face. "No. Are you kidding me?"

We make our way to the dance floor, and yes, we start dancing to the music. Some folks are doing some choreographed moves, but we choose to just lose ourselves in the rhythm. At one point, I literally lose Jorge in the crowd.

Rickie hops toward me. "So, is he your new boyfriend?"

I laugh. "That's funny. That's what he asked me earlier about you."

"You're not my type."

"Amen to that."

More hip and butt shaking. Hands clapping. Cymbals banging.

Rickie hops to me again. "He's kind of One Direction–ish. Looks like that half-Pakistani one, you know, Malik."

Jorge? You'd have to squint really hard to make that

connection. "Whatever. He's just a friend. Wait a minute, I want to amend that. He's just a coworker."

The song ends and a new one comes on. Jorge comes back. The rhythm of an electric guitar. The DJ introduces it as the Kinks' "You Really Got Me," and the older people on the dance floor go wild. I've heard the song before, too, and both Jorge and I start bouncing around on the laminate floor. Colors flash. Beats ring. My body lets go.

Jorge jumps, his shirt rising up. I'm surprised to see a tattoo by his belly button. It's of a skeleton with a smoking gun. *Why does he have a gang tattoo?* I wonder. He takes hold of my elbows. The two of us are now leaping together like fools. And before I know it, his mouth is on mine.

"No, no," I say, feeling the wetness of his kiss. "This is not going to happen." I pull myself from him and walk off the dance floor.

"Sorry, sorry. I didn't mean anything by it." He follows me.

"We work together."

"I'm sorry," he says again. He's removed his hat; sweat is dripping down the sides of his face. "But as for us working together, I mean, how else are people supposed to meet after you leave school, anyway? Besides the Internet."

"I know. It's just that . . ." I can make up dozens of good reasons; the best one is that I'm still recovering from a breakup. But he's not proposing marriage or even a relationship. "It's just not a good idea."

"I get it, I get it." He doesn't verbalize what he gets. The thing is, we both know now that I don't want to be kissed by him. That part is clear.

He disappears in the sea of people and I don't bother chasing after him.

The song changes to "I Heard It Through the Grapevine." A dance instructor is giving the crowd some coordinated steps.

A Mohawk nears. "Hey, what happened to Mr. No Direction?"

"He took off. I think that he's pissed."

"What did you do?"

"He kissed me."

"And . . ."

"I didn't want to be kissed by him."

"Oh. Harsh."

"I wasn't mean about it. I figured it was better not to lead him on, right?"

"Poor George."

"You know he spells it J-O-R-G-E."

"But he pronounces it George, not Jorge?" Rickie says it the Spanish way, sounded the *J* as an *H*. "That's sacrilegious, man."

"See," I say, as if that's my reason for rejecting him. "He also had a tat on him."

"Who doesn't?"

"No, I mean it's a gang tat. From East LA."

"Maybe he's just a poser. I mean, George?"

I shake my head and then check my phone. While I was dancing, I'd received a voice mail message. I say good night to Rickie and then listen to my message as I make my way back to the car.

It's my mother. "Congratulations on your arrest of the bicycle thieves. Your boss must be very happy."

Even though it's late, almost eleven, I call my mom back. Ever since she went through chemo, her sleeping patterns are all messed up. She now barely sleeps, making her both a night owl and an early-morning person.

"Hi, Mom, sorry to call so late."

"I'm up. Reading for my book club."

"Book club? Since when did you start doing that?"

"Janice got me into it. They read the most depressing books. It's almost like the more suffering, the better."

"Oh." I give it another month before Mom picks up a different activity. "Anyway, you called?"

"Yes, I read the post on *Bicycle News*."

"Since when do you read the *Bicycle News*?"

"I have you on Google Alerts."

"Why would you have me on Google Alerts?"

"Well, you don't tell me anything. How else can I find out things about you?"

Even more reason not to be on social media.

"Anyway, congratulations on solving the case." Mom makes me sound like Nancy Drew. Ellie Rush and the Missing Pink Bicycle.

"Thanks, Mom. It was actually kind of an accident—"

"No, no, don't do that. Don't sell yourself short," Mom says. "You did something of note in your field, and you need to be proud of it. I am."

When my mother says things like this, it always throws me for a loop. Lately she's been giving me more compliments and I don't know what to do with it. So I change the subject. "By the way," I say. "I have some bad news. Benjamin's mother was diagnosed with ovarian cancer."

"Ovarian cancer. Oh, that's not good. Hard to detect."

"She had a hysterectomy. The surgeon found some cancer cells in her lymph nodes, but they think they got all of it."

"She's about my age?" Mom has met Mrs. Choi only a couple of times.

"I don't know. Maybe."

"I'm so sorry, Ellie. Tell Benjamin that I'll be cheering her on. She'll get through it. And if she ever wants to talk to someone . . ."

My mother's nurturing mood gets me to further open up. "By the way, has Aunt Cheryl mentioned if she was dating anyone?"

"What?" Mom is scandalized. "Who is she dating?"

"I'm not sure, or even if she is. I was just wondering if she'd said anything to you or Grandma."

"Well," Mom says, "I have your aunt on Google Alerts, too, and so far I haven't seen anything new."

See, NSA, if you have a need for a middle-aged Japanese American woman, I have the perfect candidate for you.

FIFTEEN

I'm at Grand Central Market on Monday morning, sitting at the counter of a popular breakfast place that specializes in organic coddled eggs. It's early, a little after eight a.m., and I'm in my full uniform. After playing telephone tag with Cortez, we've finally made a time to meet up. It's for less than an hour before work, but with the LAPD's joint investigation of the Old Lady Bandit robberies, I'll have to take what I can get.

I check my phone. Cortez is a few minutes late; it's not like him, but no message, so he must be on his way.

And then, magically, he appears in the empty seat next to me.

"Sorry," he says, "accident on the 10." He does a double take. "Hey, you look nice."

Yes, I've actually pinned my long horse hair into a bun (took me two packages of bobby pins), rubbed some tinted moisturizer on my face, and even applied a couple of wands of mascara. I'm going to receive a commendation at City

Council chambers today, so I might as well look respectable, even if I'll be receiving that commendation from a man I don't have any respect for.

"Thanks," I say. "You've been busy."

"Worked all through the weekend."

We both order coffee and our expensive breakfasts.

"I know that you can't say much about the investigation, but you haven't mentioned anything, have you? About Puddy Fernandes being related to me?" *Or, more important, to Aunt Cheryl?*

Cortez frowns. "No, no. That would never—I keep my word, Ellie. Is that why you wanted to see me?"

"Ah, well, I've been thinking . . ." I say. Actually, I have been thinking nonstop for the past three days, both during work and on my day off on Sunday. I trace a finger on a glass saltshaker on the counter. "I just want to say that I'm sorry if I seemed weird that day at Philippe's. I should have been nicer to your friends."

"Not really my friends. Just Misty. She's my best friend's wife."

"Yeah, I heard," I say. I am such a doofus.

"Anyway, I don't think Misty noticed."

"But you did."

Cortez smiles. "I did."

Our expensive but beautiful breakfasts arrive. "By the way," I announce, "this is my treat."

"Oh really?"

"This is my 'I admit that I've been slightly crazy' apology."

"Well, okay. I'll take it."

For the next half hour, it's like when we first met earlier this year. We tease, laugh and share silly stories. It's light.

Comfortable. I want it to keep going. Then Cortez has to go and ruin it by saying, "So what is this we're doing, Ellie?"

"What do you mean?"

"I like you, Ellie. I want to spend more time with you. Alone. I don't want you to get upset at me when I don't even know what I've done."

It would be so easy for me to say back, *I like you, too, Cortez.* But saying those words scare me. I don't know whether it means going through a door I'm not ready for.

Cortez glances at his watch. "I need to go. You don't need to say anything to me right now. Just think about it, okay?"

As I enter the City Council chamber, the Media Relations guy, Officer Marc Haines, greets me at the door. He's all happy, practically panting like Shippo does when I open up some new treats. It's pretty pathetic.

I've been inside this room a few times before; the first time was probably when I was in grade school and Aunt Cheryl was receiving a commendation of her own. With its steepled ceilings, hanging lights and tile mosaics, it made me feel like I'd stepped back in time to some foreign place in Europe with kings and knights. Indeed, even today, the chamber feels like a slightly religious place—at least, until the proceedings start. Then you feel like you've walked into some Shakespearean play with one too many fools, most of them politicians.

Jorge looks miserable when he sees me, and so does Mac. A morning of awkwardness. Fantastic.

Each of us sits in a different pew, but Haines gathers us together like a high school sports team. I'm just waiting for him to pull out a whistle and make us huddle and cheer, "Go LAPD!"

Mac is up first. I have no idea why he's going to be commended. The council agenda gives no clue.

Mac stands next to a councilman for the San Fernando Valley. All fifteen members of the council sit at a curved wooden desk and face us in the wooden pews in the public gallery.

I'm confused. I know Mac lives in the Valley, but we in the Central Division service downtown LA. The councilman is older and has been in his seat for a number of years. I recognize his name. I think there's a middle school named after him.

The councilman tells all of us to wait one minute and then a young man in a suit—maybe one of his aides—hands him a small package. At first I think it may be a gift of some kind, but no, it's alive. It's a Yorkshire terrier about a third of Shippo's size.

The crowd coos. The terrier is adorable. But I'm still scratching my head. What does this have to do with Mac?

Then the councilman tells his story. "I was going for my morning walk with Lemon Drop here; we call her LD for short. We were in the local city park in the neighborhood." LD then licks his owner's face. The crowd *ooh*s and *ahh*s again. "And then these three dastardly, wicked—"

I'm waiting for gangsters, or maybe teenagers, but no, it's . . .

"—*squirrels* began to attack LD. A totally unprovoked attack! I had never seen anything like this before." I glance at Jorge next to me. He can't believe this, either.

"I was struggling to save LD and then this man, this fine representative of our city's LAPD bicycle unit, comes riding in with a water bottle to save the day. Scares those scoundrels with squirts of smartwater. LD needed ten stitches. The squirrels, of course, escaped."

Jorge presses his mouth closed so he doesn't bust out in laughter. I bare-knuckle the bottom of the seat in our pew. Haines frowns at us. We are being impertinent. Rude.

"This is proof that we need to ban the feeding of all wildlife in parks and nature areas. We cannot let these aggressive animals terrorize our citizens."

During the councilman's whole tirade, Mac has been wearing the biggest fake smile ever. All his top teeth, aside from his molars, are visible. The ends of his mouth are starting to tremble.

He is presented with his commendation, and bombarded with flash from camera phones and even legitimate cameras.

When it's all over, Mac passes me by, murmuring, "You tell anyone about this, you die."

No worries. I see Haines has been taking plenty of digital photos. This is going to end up on Twitter for sure.

Councilman Beachum then steps from his desk, calling Jorge and me up forward. I secure my cap on my head; I'm totally official now. I have to say, Jorge is also looking pretty darn respectable.

As we turn toward the public gallery, I note a familiar blue Windbreaker in the third pew. It can't be, but it is. My father, taking time off from his Metro job? Next to him is my mother, aiming her iPhone camera right at me. And believe it or not, next to her is Grandma Toma, her hair again freshly dyed. She always seems to break out the box of L'Oréal when one of her family members does good.

Beachum can talk, that's for sure. He goes on and on about how he's committed to biking and bike lanes. And how thefts of bikes cannot be tolerated. He gives the BCU and specifically me props and then some.

The longer he goes on, the more I feel like a fake. I can't stand Beachum, and at the moment I don't think Jorge can stand me.

"Officer Rush showed alertness in following up on a possible stolen bicycle. That alertness led to her discovery of the largest bike theft ring in the city.

"Through the work of Rush and the BCU unit, individuals can be reunited with their primary form of transportation, including Kenyon Low, an orderly at the hospital in Chinatown. He needs that bicycle to get to work each day."

The man I'd seen locking up the pink bicycle rises from the front pew. He's wearing his hospital scrubs, and for a moment, I'm seriously taken aback. He shakes Jorge's hand quickly but grips mine extra hard. "Thank you, Officer," he says to me. "I'm raising my daughter on my own. That bike is the only way I can easily get to the hospital."

I blink away some tears and all of us pose for more photos, including some for the Rush family's personal collection.

When the council moves on to the next agenda item, we begin to file out. My family follows me into the hallway.

"I didn't know you guys were coming," I tell them. "How did you find out about this?"

"Your mother saw it on her Google Alerts," Dad says. He seems perfectly fine, back to normal.

Who's worried about the NSA? It's Google Alerts that we should be afraid of, I think.

"That Councilman Beachum is a tall man," Mom says, admiring his height.

"You've seen him before," I say.

"I just never noticed how tall he was."

"He's tall," Grandma Toma agrees.

"Can we stop talking about Councilman Beachum?"

Just then Mac walks out of the chambers, followed by a couple of older women who want to pose for a photo with him and LD.

"Say cheese, Lemon Drop," they coo to the dog.

I inadvertently lock eyes with Mac, but just for a second. *Smile,* I say to him silently. *Smile for the camera.*

The rest of day is delete-able. That's actually Nay's word for any time spent on anything mundane. Delete. Cannot get back. Delete. Like old e-mails crowding your in-box, old texts eating up your phone's memory, delete-able moments just suck up our time. In my case, however, they are also providing me with a paycheck.

Although I acted annoyed when I saw my family at City Council chambers, it actually means a lot to me. It may have been the first time—other than my graduation from the Police Academy—when my mom seemed proud of me for being myself. Not the way she wants to see me, but the way I see myself and hope to be in the future.

When I drive home later, the grayness of the day seems to have really taken hold. LA is strange around this time, late May and June. There is a gloom to it, almost an indecision on whether the world should be warm with possibilities or damp with dread.

The light in the house next to the corner church is on. I park the Green Mile and press the intercom. After a couple of minutes, the door opens.

"Sorry to interrupt you, Father Kwame," I say. A few aphids circle the lightbulb at the top of the alcove.

"Ellie, you look so official."

I smile. From anyone else, I'd take that comment as a dis.

From Father Kwame, however, it's what it is. An honest observation.

We go inside and Father Kwame takes his regular seat in the corner. There's a Bible on the table. It's doesn't look like it's in English. "Was just doing some reading," he says. "Related to Mr. Fuentes's church. The gardener," he adds, as if I wouldn't remember. "I've actually been in touch with the minister. He was telling me that he's doing a series of sermons on the crucifixion of Jesus."

"But Easter was, like, over a month ago."

"I know. But I guess his congregation was mesmerized about the story of Barabbas, so he wants to devote some special sermons to it."

"Wait, what did you say?"

"The crucifixion?"

"No, the guy's name."

"Barabbas."

"What's his story? This Barabbas guy?"

"Barabbas was in line to be executed. He and Jesus were imprisoned together. But the crowds started to call out for Barabbas, the guilty one, to be freed. So Barabbas was, and Jesus assumed his position."

I hadn't heard this story before. Or if I had, I hadn't been paying attention. My face feels hot. That's what Eduardo Fuentes had said to me. Not Barbara, but Barabbas.

"The pastor was saying that there are times when we need to step forward in place of a Barabbas. A very interesting interpretation. Has given me much—"

"Thank you, Father," I interrupt him. I rise from my seat. "You've really helped me."

"I'm glad, Ellie, but how?"

SIXTEEN

I'm off the next day, but it doesn't mean that I'm not working, at least in trying to connect some dots. I have RJ's work number from the day I first met him. I call, and when I tell the woman who answers that I need to talk to RJ in person about something important, she dutifully gives me the address in Alhambra where he's working. It's amazing what people will tell a complete stranger over the phone. No wonder those telecom shysters are able to wrestle away the life fortunes of vulnerable seniors with cold calls.

Alhambra is not far from Highland Park. Only thing, there's no direct way to get there via freeway, so I take the back streets, mostly treelined and idyllic. I drive east through San Marino, which is even more moneyed than South Pas. There seem to be no apartments in that town, only expensive houses, and few people walking the streets. San Marino's shopping area is divided along two parallel boulevards, with few opportunities for people to run into their neighbors and friends.

Alhambra, on the other hand, has plenty of apartments and condominiums, and its Main Street is an actual main street with movie theaters, Chinese and American eateries, a beautiful library and City Hall. Where I'm going is only a few blocks north of that artery.

It's not difficult to find RJ, between the sound of the lawn mower and the white truck with LANDSCAPING AND GARDEN-ING painted on the driver's-side door.

The house itself is ranch-style and neat. Nothing awe-inspiring, but still probably worth a million dollars.

RJ, wearing a straw hat, notices me get out of the Skylark. He looks disturbed, as if I've crossed over a line of privacy. Sweat is dripping down onto his long-sleeved cotton shirt. I don't know how gardeners in LA can work with so much clothing on, but I guess it protects them from the UV rays. He has two other helpers—one is cutting the hedges and another is pulling weeds out of a flower bed. He stops the lawn mower. "What are you doing here?"

"I heard I could find you here."

He doesn't look that hospitable, so I get right to the point. "What were you going to do after you stole it?"

"Don't know what you saying," RJ stonewalls.

"The cello. It's not like you could take it to a pawnshop. You must have had a connection."

"You need to leave. This private property."

I'm careful to stand on the sidewalk. "Not where I am. What, you gonna call the police and report a public distur-bance?" I hate to play the cop card, but I need RJ to open up. "Your uncle knew about your plans. He was trying to stop you by stealing it himself." The words have truth in them. I know because tears come to RJ's eyes.

"Uncle Eduardo didn't understand. I wasn't going to steal and sell. How could I be stealing for the owner?"

I am stunned for a few moments; then I slowly recover. "Are you saying Xu asked you to take the cello?"

"The old man. The father. I was supposed to take it after the concert. The translator was with him. They told me that no one would get hurt."

"Why didn't you tell the police after your uncle got hurt?"

"I was going to. Believe me, I was. But those men—that translator told me if I spoke up, I'd get into trouble. That Mr. Xu's son was famous, a star, so who would believe me? And everything was on the TV, and my *prima*, Marta, was so upset. How could I tell her that I was behind what had happened to her father?"

"Wait a minute. I still don't understand. The man who pushed your uncle down the stairs asked you to steal the cello? After Xu had performed?"

RJ nods. His chin drops to his chest and he presses down on his hat so I can't see his face. He rubs the edge of his shirtsleeve over his eyes and finally looks up.

"And then what? Where would you keep it?"

"I was supposed to take it home and then burn it."

What? This was absurd. Crazy. I say pretty much that in Spanish. RJ stays silent. He bites his lip and looks away.

"They offered you money." Because what else could there be?

RJ nods his head. He is ashamed that he would pimp himself out in this way. I'm ashamed for him, too. "Tío Eduardo told me to have nothing to do with it. To go to the police.

But I need to grow my business. My wife and me, we are having a baby. I don't want my kid to do what I have to do every day."

The cello was a fake; I was pretty sure of that. Mr. Xu wanted its origin to be hidden. But why take such severe measures?

"What you going to do?" RJ asks me. Now that his secret has been uncovered, he seems almost relieved.

"It's not what I'm going to do," I tell him, "but what you are."

I wait downstairs in the parking lot at Disney Hall. Leaning against the Green Mile, I check the reception on my phone. Not good. I don't know where Mr. Xu is anymore. Or Xu. But I do know where one person who has been linked to them is.

Cece comes out, carrying a viola case. I wonder how much *her* instrument is worth.

Probably not five million dollars.

I take a few steps toward her, causing her to slow her gait. "Hello, I'm Officer Ellie Rush."

"I know about you," she says and starts walking faster. "I'm not talking to you. I know my rights."

I follow her to her BMW. "I spoke to RJ Santiago. He told me about the deal, how Fang Xu was going to pay him to steal Xu's cello after the performance."

Cece's chin hardens and she attempts to get to her driver's-side door. I keep the door closed with the side of my body. I may not be the biggest person in the world, but I'm strong enough to take on the Philharmonic's star violist.

Unable to wrench open her door, Cece is utterly frustrated. "I'm going to call—"

"Who? The police?"

"Well, someone who doesn't ride a bicycle, that's for sure."

"RJ is going to be talking to the detectives today. He's coming clean about the deal he made with Fang Xu."

Cece doesn't bat an eyelash. She acts like she couldn't care less.

"I can tell the detectives to call you in next. Unless you explain to me how you're involved."

She takes a deep breath. She has a beautiful face. I wonder what she would look like with her natural hair color.

"You married?" she finally asks me.

I shake my head.

"No, you're still young," she says, even though we're probably about the same age. "But you've been in love? You must have been in love at least once."

I think that I know where this is going.

Cece hugs her viola case to her chest. "Xu and I met in Philadelphia, both teenagers in the conservancy. Xu's father came with him. To make sure he rehearsed every night. Every day. Only breaks for class and meals. Fang Xu is a man obsessed. Feels like the only way he can make his mark is through his son's performance."

Classic tiger father, I think.

"Mr. Xu always positioned himself to be greater than he really was. That's why he got a British language tutor for Xu. In his mind, Europe, the home of classical composers, was the best. But Xu didn't get into the conservancies there. America was his father's second choice."

"We fell in love through our music. Even though we didn't have many opportunities to talk, to be alone, whenever we were playing in the same room, we played for each other."

I'm not a romantic, not by a long shot, but even I cannot help being a little affected by Cece's story of their courtship.

"But I'm from Taiwan. Xu, mainland China. It's not impossible for other couples, but it was impossible for Xu and me. First of all, there was Xu's father. Practice, practice, practice. No time for girls. And then there was Xu's uncle, a rising star in the Party."

She registers my blank look. "You know, the Communist Party."

Although Benjamin often derides me for my lack of knowledge when it comes to Asian international affairs, I do know enough to be aware that there's tension between the "two Chinas," because mainland China doesn't recognize Taiwan as an independent country. Relations between the two entities seem to go back and forth. Here in LA, mainland Chinese and Taiwanese sit together in the same restaurants, shop in the same grocery stores (sometimes even in Japanese ones!). The things that divide people overseas don't seem to have the same pull over here in California.

"Then his father was called back to China by his wife for a brief time. That's when Xu and I were able to spend time together, one-on-one."

I know what she's saying with that.

"When Mr. Xu returned, he told his father that we wanted to be together. We wanted to be married. Technically, we were of age. We could have run off. But Xu is a dutiful son. He didn't want to go against his father. His father exploded. He flew into a rage. He said that by marrying me, Xu would be a disgrace, not only to his family, but to his country. Xu was miserable, crushed. He didn't know what to do. He fell in a deep depression."

Cece starts to blink faster. "Then came word about the Stradivarius. The long-lost cello, brought over to China by Italian monks and protected during the Cultural Revolution. This was to be presented to Xu by his uncle. A precious gift from this country. That instrument saved him but would ruin us because how could he turn his back on such a gift? So I made it easy for him. I broke it off. I knew that he would have chosen me, sacrificed his music career, his family, his country, even his instrument for me. But I couldn't let him do that."

She moistens her lips. "So we separated, but it was eating my soul. It didn't make my feelings go away. Then the following year, the concert season for this year was announced. Xu was coming to Los Angeles to play with us."

"And he wanted to see you."

Cece nodded. "And I, more than anything, wanted to see him. During the rehearsals, we were again speaking through our music. Our love was still there. We knew that we needed to be together. But how could we speak freely, with Xu's father constantly at his side? Then the accident happened with the gardener. That changed everything. Fang Xu has been distracted, constantly on the phone with China. Through that tragedy our love could once again bloom."

Good for you, I think. *Not so good for Fuentes's family.* "I saw you. The night of Xu's concert. Here in the parking lot. Here, in fact. You were arguing with someone."

Raising one of her perfectly manicured eyebrows, Cece practically dares me to identify the person.

"You were arguing with Fang Xu. You didn't want them to leave for China."

"Xu was *not* going back to China."

"Then where is he? The police need to speak with him."

"I have no idea where he is." Cece says the words in a string of staccatos. "I've told you everything. Can I leave now?"

I nod. I stand back as she gets in her car, puts it in reverse and speeds out of the artists' parking level. A part of me wants to charge after her, *Fast and Furious* style. I believe she's telling most of the truth, but not all of it. I have no doubt that she knows exactly where Xu is, and maybe his father, too.

SEVENTEEN

I come home relatively early from work the next day. I feed Shippo and then change into shorts and a T-shirt to go jogging. As I run on the sidewalks broken by age or buckled by roots of old trees, I can't help but keep thinking about Eduardo Fuentes. I have no idea whether RJ's admission is going to clear his uncle's name in any way. Could Fang Xu be charged with something? And since the LAPD has no clue where he is, does it even matter?

I run faster, running past the Police Museum on York Boulevard, where a 1929 Model A police car is on display behind a gated driveway. I almost trip on some hard round fruit fallen from an overhanging tree beside an income tax business in a barred house. I keep going until I cross the street on the corner of Galco's Old World Grocery, seller of vintage and specialty glass-bottled sodas and candy like sarsaparillas, cucumber soda and wax lips.

As my breathing quickens, I stop thinking about Cece, Xu or the cello. I don't think about Cortez, Puddy or Aunt Cheryl. And last of all, Nay, Benjamin and Benjamin's mother all slip and dissolve away. My running shoes hit the pavement. Air pushes out from my lungs, up my throat, nose and mouth. The rhythm of running is all I feel. I'm just in the now, right this moment, nowhere else.

When I return home and unlock the door of my house, I sink in my chair, stinky and sweaty. Then I do a double take at the sight of Shippo sitting placidly at my feet, his corkscrew tail moving back and forth. Usually he greets me, jumps all over me to beg for either a treat or his next meal. *What's going on?*

Then I spy something at my feet. There are two pieces. Brown and exactly the same size. Damn, is it dog poop? I get down on my knees for a closer look. Shippo wanders toward them and I shoo him away. I get up to retrieve a poop bag and gingerly pick one of them up. It's hard and cold. *What the hell?*

It's obviously not poop, but some kind of fancy dog treat. I recognize it from the high-end natural dog food store down the street, something gourmet, duck or bison. How did it get in my house? Since they are still cold, the food was scattered recently. Like perhaps minutes ago.

I carefully search my house, the living room first. The windows are all secured closed. This house is ancient, probably from the fifties, and the landlord just adds a fresh coat of paint for each new tenant. So the windows, unfortunately, are pretty much painted shut. The one in the bathroom is the only one that actually goes up and down—it's closed, but I see a lot of paint chips on the floor by the toilet. My window is small; I could barely fit through it. An adult would have to be quite the contortionist to get their body through there.

Then in the bedroom, I notice that my dresser drawer is open, just a crack. No. No friggin' way.

But it's true. I pull open the drawer and my laptop is still there. But next to it, where my Glock should be, is an empty space. I swear, long and repeatedly. I sit on the edge of my couch and cover my face. Who else knew where I stored my gun? Who else would take my Glock but not my computer? Shippo comes over to me and jumps on my knees. He senses that I'm upset.

"It's not your fault, Shippo." I pet his head. I took him to the groomer on my day off and he still smells sweet from the oatmeal shampoo. There's something caught in his collar—a piece of black string? No, it's a long curly hair. Hair from a poodle.

I curse again. Proof that my effing long-lost grandfather has stolen my gun.

It doesn't matter if I report it missing; if someone does anything illegal while using my gun, I'll be sunk. The media will be unforgiving. If my gun, an LAPD officer's gun, gets used in the commission of a crime, the public won't care about the illegal circumstances in which it was obtained. They will just stamp the department as BAD and the officer who owned the gun as the WORST.

I can't even tell Aunt Cheryl that my gun has been stolen. If she tries to cover it up in some way, she'll get in trouble. Then again, if she doesn't know about it, she'll be in trouble, too.

I rub my eyelids with my fingers. I'm all sweaty and filthy. Definitely apropos. *Get a grip, Ellie. Think.* I'm so scattered and freaked-out, I can't even find my cell phone for a moment, and then I realize that it's in the pocket of my shorts.

"Lita, it's me, Ellie."

"*Querida*, so nice—"

"I don't have time for all that." I'm being super rude, but I can't help it. "I need to figure out where Fernandes might be. Or maybe that other guy, Ron Sullivan."

"But why?"

"Lita, please."

"I have no idea. You were the one who told me that Puddy lived in San Bernardino."

"What if he needed to hang out somewhere close by? Aunt Cheryl says the taxi dropped him off in North Hollywood on Mother's Day."

"Well, he used to hang out in this bar in North Hollywood. That's where we met. But that was sixty years ago, *querida*. Many lifetimes ago. Although . . ."

"Yes, Lita?"

"Although I heard that it was going to reopen. Some younger relatives of the original owner."

It's a long shot. An extreme long shot. But I'm desperate. I tell her, "I'm in trouble, Lita. I think that Fernandes might have stolen my gun."

"I'll be there in fifteen minutes," she says.

"Wait, what?"

"You stay put. We'll handle this together."

Lita actually makes it in thirteen minutes and quickly agrees with my initial attribution of the theft to Fernandes's handiwork. "Who else could it be? He probably snooped around and saw it there the other day when he went through your room to the bathroom. He knew exactly where to find it."

We drive in Lita's yellow Cadillac. I'm thankful that she is literally taking over the wheel. My hands are wet with nervous sweat and starting to shake. How could this guy—the man who claims to be my flesh and blood, my grandfather—do this to me? I wish I'd never met him. I wish that he'd never come back into Lita's life. We were all better off without him.

The other reason I'm glad Lita is driving is that she knows exactly where we're going. She doesn't need a GPS or Google Maps to tell her where to go. She has an internal compass that pulls both of us through the freeways and streets of Los Angeles and now North Hollywood.

We finally park on Lankershim, one of the main boulevards in the city, in front of a construction site. The facade of an older building in the back is still visible; it's a dome, shaped like a German beer stein. Dirt is everywhere. A blue Porta-Potty is off to one side.

A man about my father's age with a graying beard seems to be the person in charge.

"Hel-lo!" Lita says to him. It's amazing to see my seventysomething grandmother turn on the charm with someone who could be her son.

"Hi." He brushes his hands on his dirty jeans and walks over to us.

"I'm an old-time customer here. So excited to see it reopen."

"Me, too. We've been working seven days a week to make it happen. It was my father's place. I actually grew up here. I want to make it what it was back then. Like *Cheers*, right?"

"You're Saunders's son?"

The bearded man nods. "He died a couple of years ago. I came back home to help my mother take care of her affairs. That actually gave me the idea to do something with this property again. Would you like to take a look?"

We walk past an outdoor deck where most of the renovations are taking place. When we go inside the building, Lita immediately comments on the sunroof. "I like all the light. It used to be so dark in here," she says.

The bar owner nods. "We are definitely going to be mixing the new with the old." An old door, a makeshift table on two sawhorses, is in the middle of the room. On top of it are all sorts of old furnishings that do look fifty years old: doorknobs, switch and light socket plates, and grills.

I'm getting a bit impatient about their leisurely pace of conversation. This is not a nostalgia tour. "We're actually in search of an old customer," I interrupt.

"A lot of them have actually been coming around. Excited about the eventual opening, I guess."

"Pascoal Fernandes. He could also be going by Puddy."

"Puddy Fernandes? No, I'm afraid that that name doesn't ring a bell. And I'd remember that one."

Lita and I exchange looks. Is this just a complete dead end? I take a second look at the beat-up doorknobs and remember the rusty screws littering the backseat of the Green Mile. I quickly scroll through some photos on my phone while Lita and the bar owner engage in more small talk. I hate to do this to Dad, but I don't have that many options. "How about someone who kind of looks like this? He'd be twenty years older with a mustache."

The bar owner takes hold of my phone and stares at a photo of Dad that I took on New Year's Day. He's looking goofy and holding a big bowl of *ozoni*, a Japanese clear broth with fish and nuked mochi floating in it.

"Oh, that looks like Noah. A younger version."

"Noah?"

"Yeah, Noah Rush."

Fernandes stole my brother's name? That's low.

"Noah's been helping me go to junkyards and picking up old furnishings for me. Or picking up purchases from craigslist. But then he lost his wheels. Said his old lady took away his car."

"Oh, he did, did he?" I can see the steam rise from Lita's head. I hold her elbow. We are too close to finding him to blow it.

"Do you know where he is? It's very important. We have something valuable to give him."

"Oh, yeah? He's been talking about how he was waiting for something that was owed to him."

I bet.

"He's in that hotel down the street. You know, the Bavarian Inn?"

"The Bavarian Inn is still there?" Lita's voice is thin.

"Yeah, new owners, of course. But still hanging around."

We thank the bar owner and Lita promises to come to the grand opening in September. As we walk back to her car, she seems a bit distracted.

"Are you okay, Lita?" Perhaps all these old memories are too overwhelming.

"The Bavarian Inn," she says weakly.

"You know it?"

"That's . . . umm . . . That's where your father was conceived."

Definitely TMI for this granddaughter, though it certainly explains why Lita now resembles a limp rag.

"Lita, give me the keys." I wait until she gets in the passenger side and then buckle myself into the driver's seat. I speed up the street. The sun is just starting to go down. The

Bavarian Inn sign is in some kind of Germanic-style font. The office has a high-pitched roof with a rooster weather vane bent at a forty-five-degree angle. The rooms themselves are in a two-story building that has definitely seen better days.

"It didn't used to look like this," Lita says apologetically, as I park the car in the cracked parking lot. The paint for the parking lines has faded so that I'm not even sure if we're in a legitimate spot. Since there are only five other cars here, I think we're good.

We get out of the car, bringing with us the security club that Lita uses on her steering wheel. You never know when a club may come in handy.

Above the traffic noises, I hear something: the high-pitched sound of a dog barking, coming from the second floor. I quickly follow the barking, while Lita more slowly makes her way up the stairs behind me.

"Fernandes." I rap on the door with the end of the steering wheel club. "Let me in! It's me, Ellie."

The barking gets louder, but it sounds like it's coming from a back room. Bacall must be locked in the bathroom.

"Fernandes! I need my gun back."

Lita has finally caught up with me, her chest heaving from the physical activity.

"I don't care what you do with your life, Puddy," she says once she's caught her breath. "But you can't do this to Ellie. Give my granddaughter her gun back."

The door is unlocked and then opened a crack. I tell Lita to stay in the hallway as I slowly walk in, clutching the club in my right hand.

Bacall's barking gets more furious, but I can't see her. It's dark in the room, other than light seeping through the open door and sides of the window not covered by a dirty curtain. There are two men on the floor, their feet and hands secured by what looks like multiple rounds of Duct tape. Duct tape also covers their mouths. The two men are both alive and wriggle like worms. It's amazing that Fernandes could do this on his own, without the assistance of a partner.

As my eyes adjust to the darkness, I spot Fernandes in the far corner. He holds my Glock, first aiming it toward his hostages on the floor and then at me. I hear Bacall's paws scratch at the closed bathroom door.

"What have you done, Puddy?" I hear Lita behind me.

"Close the door," he says, and Lita enters the room with me and shuts the door behind her.

Lita visibly reacts to the older Duct-taped man. It must be Ron Sullivan.

"Is this the best you can do? Claim something you lost fifty years ago?" Lita says.

"I did time for the first heist. Didn't get my share for the second one. I deserve something for all that."

"And you want to benefit from the evil they have done? They killed a man, Puddy. You're a lot of things, but you're not a killer."

"I haven't killed anyone. Yet."

"And you're not going to kill anyone else, either. At least not with my granddaughter's gun." Lita takes a few steps forward so that she's standing next to me. She stretches out her hand. "Give it to me."

Fernandes continues to hold my gun toward us. "It's not fair. My mother died while I was in the joint. She deserved better. I deserved better."

I grip Lita's club. "One thing that my parents always

taught me was never to assume that I deserved anything. To think about other people instead. How I can help them."

Fernandes stares at me. In the dim light his eyes look like black holes. It's obvious that he hasn't slept.

"See, Puddy, you've actually received more than you have ever deserved. Than I have deserved," Lita adds. I know that she's talking about Dad and Noah and me.

First Fernandes's shoulders begin to shake. Then his arms. And then his hands and, as a result, the Glock. He's making a weird choking noise. Is he crying? I fear that he will inadvertently shoot off the gun.

"Mr. Fernandes, I need you to give me the gun." My voice sounds calm and collected, like it's not coming out of my mouth.

Fernandes steadies himself. He wipes tears from his face with a brush of his forearm. He turns the gun in his hands— for a second I fear that he's going to shoot himself—and then presents it to me, grip out.

Dropping the club, I claim my gun. I hold it in my right hand and aim it safely toward the floor.

"What's going to happen now?" Lita asks after picking up the club.

"I'm going to have to call this in," I tell her. "Assuming they're the bank robbers, then these two here killed a man."

"I know, *querida*. You're the one person in the family who does everything by the book."

I don't know how I'm going to explain everything.

The reception in the room is awful, so I step outside onto the balcony to make my call.

He finally answers.

"Cortez—" I begin.

"Listen, Ellie, I have to call you back later. We got a lead in the Old Lady Bandit case."

I hear sirens in the distance closing in on the Bavarian Inn.

"What's happening?" Lita is at my side as I quickly end my conversation with Cortez.

"Let's get out of here," I tell her.

I know I should stay, give a full report about what happened—Fernandes stealing my gun, following a hunch to the bar and then the Bavarian Inn, discovering the two men taped up, my own biological grandfather aiming a gun—my gun—at me. But it's easier to do what we are doing, sitting in Lita's Cadillac from across the street and watching the black-and-whites as well as Cortez's car drive into the parking lot.

"He must have called it in himself," I say, referring to Puddy Fernandes. He and Bacall are long gone.

"But when?"

"Probably even before we arrived."

"You mean he really was trying to help the police catch the Old Lady Bandit?"

"I don't know," I say. The car is silent for a few moments. I listen for the yapping of a dog somewhere outside, but there's only the hum of cars driving past a dilapidated motel, a motel with literally cockeyed direction, the place where my family began.

EIGHTEEN

On Sunday night, I'm looking on my laptop at stories regarding the apprehension of suspects in the Old Lady Bandit robberies. Ronald Sullivan and his nephew, Andrew Sullivan. Due to a lead by an anonymous caller, the LAPD found both of them in a hotel room, their hands and feet taped together. Their vehicle was discovered in the parking lot, and contained residue from a bank dye pack, further linking them to at least one of the robberies.

I'm getting a phone call. Midnight. It's from an unknown caller. I hesitate before I answer. Between everything that has happened these past few weeks, I've had my fill from the unknown, that's for sure.

"Hel-lo," I say with some trepidation.

"Ellie, it's Supachai. Don't be so worried, girl."

I stare at my phone. Has Supachai somehow wired it with a camera? "Can you see me?"

Supachai starts laughing. His laugh sounds like a chimpanzee on crack. "Can't pull a fast one on you. I'm trying out my new software. It analyzes the mood of humans through audio. Kind of like a mood ring for the voice."

"That's creepy. I thought that you weren't going to do all that invasive stuff anymore."

"Well, this will be used for good, not evil."

"Right." A polygraph without wires. Actually, I'm sure the LAPD would love to have access to Supachai's software.

"How have you been?"

"You tell me."

"I turned it off, okay?"

I'm afraid to say anything, so I don't.

"Anyway, the reason I'm calling—you remember back when I asked you and Nay to be on the beta test team for an app I was developing. Sinker?"

"Oh, yeah. That was for hookups, right? I deactivated it, Supachai. Sorry. Wasn't my thing."

"No, no, it was a silly school project. Never really did anything with it. But I noticed earlier today that Nay didn't deactivate it. She's still on it."

"You've got to be kidding me." Nay has probably forty thousand apps on her phone.

"Anyway, you seemed all concerned about Nay when you came by my offices the other day. I normally don't do these things, but if you want to know where her phone is right now, I can help you out."

He gives me an address, and I get to Google Maps and start typing. It's in Van Nuys. A hotel, two blocks away from the airport.

"She's been there all day," Supachai reports. He agrees

to keep me updated if I add a tres leches cake to the sangria I owe him.

"I'll hold you to it," he says, and we say our good-byes.

I have work in eight hours and I'm not going to run over to Van Nuys in the middle of the night. I'm just relieved to see that Nay's phone is charged and working. And that she's still in the continental U.S.

There is more report writing awaiting me at the station. I actually don't mind; there's been too much going on, both at work and outside of it. I wish I had my own desk, but there's no room for that. Today I find the guys crowding around one of our larger computer monitors, yelping in laughter. It can't be porn; Captain Randle has a no-tolerance policy on that. Most likely it's some stupid Jack Ass–type site.

Mac finally attempts to join the fun. "What's going on?"

It's like the parting of the Red Sea, and I get a clear shot of the monitor—it's a full-screen photo of Mac, Lemon Drop the dog, and the two women from the City Council meeting. It's from one of the women's blog (does everyone have a blog now, BTW?).

"Lemon Drop, Lemon Drop, Lemon Drop." They are hooting and hollering.

Mac's face is beet red. He's used to bullying, not being bullied. I know that I should be enjoying this—I mean, a part of me is—but a larger part of me is not.

I know that I could come to his rescue on a white horse ("stop it, guys"), but that would make it way worse. Instead, I pick up my files and plant myself at another station, somewhere I can't see the TV monitor or can't hear laughter at the expense of a fool.

"Rush, you want something from El Tepeyac?" Cherniss asks me. A clerk is going to make a run into Boyle Heights; El Tepeyac is famous for its Hollenbeck special, a humongous burrito filled with delicious stewed pork chunks that can literally—I mean literally—feed a small family.

I've just touched base with Supachai and he's confirmed that Nay is still at the hotel. Here's my opportunity to come clean with my CO.

I spend the next fifteen minutes explaining that I may know why the Xus have gone MIA for the past several days.

The bicycle ring bust has bought me a lot of goodwill. Cherniss says that he will inform the district attorney, and later clears me to go find Nay and see what she might know.

Even though it's midday, the traffic to Van Nuys, again, is terrible. It's stop-and-go, and I pass one car on the freeway that has already overheated. I was offered use of a patrol car, but opted to use the Green Mile. I pat the dashboard. *GM, you have what it takes to get me to where I need to go. You're like a cat. Nine lives.*

The hotel in Van Nuys is dated, and reminds me of a large library building circa 1970s. Luckily, there's plenty of free parking.

I pick up one of the hotel courtesy phones and ask the operator for Nay Pram's room.

"I'm sorry; there's no guest by that name."

"Xu, spelled *X* and *U*."

"No."

"Cece Lin."

"No."

I'm out of luck, so I go to the front desk. This time I do play the cop card and show my badge. "I'm looking for a guest. She's twenty-three. Asian American. On the chubby side."

Nay would kill me for describing her this way, but it apparently works, because another person at the front desk nods. "Oh, the journalist? I think they're sitting by the pool."

I walk through the hotel to a small pool with a number of round tables arranged around it. Each table has an umbrella as well as some plastic patio chairs.

Around one of the tables are three people. Nay, doing her best Barbara Walters imitation, is holding court with Xu and Cece. They don't seem the slightest bit surprised to see me.

"Hey," Nay says. "We were wondering how long it was going to take for you to find us."

Xu and Cece are seated as close as two people in separate patio chairs can be. Their hands are entwined and I notice that Cece has removed one of her sandals. Her bare foot slides against Xu's bare ankle. That's a real sign of love, I think. Not the gross public displays of affection, but the little tiny things that no one else really notices.

I feel like shaking Nay. *You've been MIA with these two?* I think.

"I told them they can trust you," she says to me. And then to the power couple, "Go ahead."

"We'll tell you everything," Xu says. "But only if you give us something in return."

The celebrity cellist wants a deal from me? "I can't promise you anything. You'll have to speak to the district attorney for that."

"Then call the DA."

"He won't do me any favors. Whatever you tell him has got to be good," I say.

A familiar figure approaches from the other side of the swimming pool. Fang Xu has obviously taken a shower and gotten some rest. He's wearing a T-shirt that reads I HEART LA, most likely a purchase from the hotel gift shop. He says the first English words I've heard him express: "I confess."

The district attorney, Mitch Tocher, doesn't think much of me. He must not be in Aunt Cheryl's camp, either, because even though he knows I'm her niece, that doesn't soften the douche-bag way that he treats me. He shows up in about an hour, but he's not alone. He's accompanied by Cortez's partner, Garibaldi.

He opens the metal gate and both of them make their way over to us. Nay has already returned to her hotel room, claiming that she had some calls she had to make.

"You can go now, Rush," says Garibaldi.

What an ass. I get up to leave, but then Xu says firmly, "She stays. Or we won't cooperate."

The detective curses and shakes his head. Even though the DA is probably thinking the same thing, he has enough sophistication to just grit his teeth and move on.

They begin to deal. The Xus and Cece should have legal representation, I think, but I'm in no position to advocate for that.

Just in the knick of time, a familiar slim Asian woman walks in.

"Hello, gentlemen," she says and then acknowledges me. "Officer Rush." I nod. "I'm Sally Choi, and I've been retained as legal counsel to the Xus and Cece Lin. I hope you don't mind if I confer with my clients."

She takes them to the other side of the pool, leaving me stuck with the district attorney and Garibaldi. "Funny that you should be involved with this," Garibaldi says to me. "Seems like you and your aunt have your fingers in practically everything." The DA grins. I don't like it. I wonder whether he's interested in being mayor.

With her clients trailing after her, Sally finally returns to the table. She pulls up a patio chair, and Xu, after getting a nod of approval from his legal counsel, begins to speak: "My uncle, a high-ranking officer in the Communist Party, has been arrested for misuse of funds in my country. They are now looking at my father and, yes, even me. My father, I have just learned, has been involved in the manufacture of violins and cellos in China and falsely labeling them as being produced in Europe." Fang Xu hangs his head down. "So my father made a deal with Eduardo Fuentes's nephew. My cello would be stolen, after my concert, and therefore there would be no evidence when we returned to Shanghai the next day."

Cece grabs hold of Xu's hand in a show of support, and he continues. "But then Eduardo Fuentes stepped in—I don't know exactly why—and the counterfeit instrument is now in the hands of the Chinese government. And now my father is a wanted man. We want political asylum here. There is no way my father will get a fair trial in China at this time."

Sally, who has been madly scribbling on yellow lined paper, peers in the faces of the DA and Garibaldi. "Satisfied?"

The DA jots down notes on his notebook. "For now."

"The county clerk's office, then?" Sally asks about our next destination.

"The wedding chapel. As agreed," the DA says.

Nay, freshly coiffed and wearing a new outfit, has rejoined us. She's carrying a plastic bag weighed down with something. She's also wearing her press pass, and I suppress the urge to roll my eyes. I guess I have to get used to my BFF's role as PPW's star reporter. Based on her report about the crackdown on graft in China, she definitely has the goods.

Garibaldi takes a long look at her. The idiot is such a perv. "Rush, since you're here anyway, you might as well be useful and come with us," he says. I'm not that eager to play his wingman, but he does outrank me.

"You don't need to cuff them, do you?" Sally says. "You haven't charged them with anything."

"Officer Rush will just keep them company."

I give the Green Mile's car keys to Nay, and stand between Xu and Cece. As I gently grasp the crook of their arms, I feel that we are marching down the wedding aisle together, which, essentially, is what we all will be doing in a few minutes.

The three of us get into the backseat of Garibaldi's unmarked car. Mr. Xu rides with Sally. The DA rides alone.

It's a short drive to the county clerk branch in Van Nuys, but as I sit in between the two lovers, I feel the electricity of their passion for each other. It's a little awkward, but it also makes me realize that I want to feel that kind of passion myself.

The marriage ceremony itself is short and uneventful. The DA goes into the county clerk's office first, and through his influence, we're able to get preferential treatment. I can tell that this irritates those waiting in line, including a few men in yarmulkes, and since this is LA, one of them is speaking Spanish.

Nay buys a bouquet of flowers from a vendor outside. It's a colorful assortment, mostly dyed daisies in an arrangement of foxtail greens.

The officiant is a short, bald man who seems happy with his job. We assemble in the wedding chapel, which turns out to be a small room with the round county seal on the wall. Fang Xu conspicuously stands in the back. A ruined man, now he must witness the union that he had fought so hard in the past. This may be more punishment than he will experience in the future—whether it be in the U.S. or China.

While the officiant recites his wedding script, I stand next to Nay in the back on the other side of the room from the father of the groom. There's no time to get rings, so Sally has located one of her daughter Camila's, a plastic ring with a butterfly, from her purse. For Xu, we use a plain aluminum ring off of my key chain.

Cece, clutching the $5.99 bouquet, looks beautiful. Her porcelain skin glistens and her eyes shine as she looks up at Xu. "I do," she says.

"Spoke to Washington," I whisper to Nay.

"Royal asshole," she hisses.

"He thinks you used him."

Nay snorts. "He's calling *me* a user? He was the one keeping tabs on me so that I didn't write anything damaging about his 'client.' I'm sure the police will be going after him next."

Why do I think that another article will be published under the Nay Pram byline soon?

"Sorry that I had to be so secret agent," Nay murmurs. "You missed me, huh?"

"Isn't it obvious?"

"I just didn't want to get you into trouble. I just kept making excuses so that I couldn't talk to you. You know I can't keep my mouth shut when I'm with you. I'm not going to stand in the way of you becoming the youngest woman to make homicide detective."

"Nay, the way things are going, I'll be lucky to be on the force for another year."

The officiant frowns at us and we both hush up. "And now, with the power vested in me by the State of California, you may kiss the bride," he says.

Xu places his elegant hands on Cece's face and plants a big one on her lips. Although I don't consider myself a romantic, I have to admit that it's pretty darn hot.

Nay takes a series of photos—a lot of them. If you flip through them fast enough, it looks like a movie.

Before we are released from the county clerk's wedding chapel, Cece presents me with her bouquet.

"Why me?" I would think Nay would be the go-to recipient of the bouquet, especially since she bought it.

"Because you made this possible," she says.

At this point, Garibaldi insists that he cuff Fang Xu for his ride to the station. Sally is upset, but Xu stops her. "He honored his side of the deal. We will honor ours. He can cuff all of us." He places his wrists together at his back.

"Rush," Garibaldi says, holding out his handcuffs.

Great, I get to do the honors.

I secure the cuffs on Xu carefully. I don't want to do anything to harm those hands. I do the same to Cece and Fang Xu. All of this feels surreal. I gently push down each one of their heads as I guide them into the backseat of Garibaldi's vehicle.

"Main headquarters?" Sally asks, and Garibaldi confirms it. From the look on his face, the DA can't believe that he has to spend the next few hours dealing with the lovebirds.

"Rush," Garibaldi says, "I can take it from here, but if Ms. Pram wants to ride with us . . ."

Yeah, you probably want her on your lap. "No, she's fine," I say. "I got her."

Nay prattles on and on while I navigate the Green Mile down Sherman Way and eventually to the 170. Her monologue is comforting, familiar. I've missed it, for sure.

"I'm actually working on a feature story right now," she announces. "Star-crossed lovers. Cece and Xu were separated by their birth countries' politics, unsupportive family members, but now they are together again. For however long it lasts."

As I transition from the 170 to the 101, I glance at Nay's open plastic bag, which she has placed on top of the emergency brake. At the top is a book with a worn cover. A translation of *Don Quixote*.

Nay follows my gaze. "Yeah, I found it at a used bookstore in Van Nuys. I've been reading stuff about Cervantes, too. Did you know that he was held by pirates for five years?"

"You're kidding me."

"These nuns had to negotiate his release. He died there, in the convent. Flat broke without a coin to his name. He was all hunchback and had only six teeth." Nay shudders when she imagines the toothless master writer.

"In the book, Don Quixote dies, you know. He renounces all the things that he was chasing before. All the knightly stuff. Do you think that he was right, Ellie? Because all of that seems pretty damn cool."

We finally arrive at PPW, where Nay's planning to stay

up all night to write her magnum opus. "I need to get it down while it's fresh in my mind," she says as she slides out. She gestures toward the flowers in the back. "Oh, you'd better put that in water right away."

"I have someplace in mind for it."

After dropping Nay off, I remain in the loading zone to send a text to Cortez. All this stuff has gotten me in a mood for romance. I don't know whether I'll get a reply.

I go up Figueroa all the way to First and make a right. And then another right on Grand Avenue at the concert hall.

I place the bouquet at the bottom of the stairs. I have no idea where Mr. Fuentes is buried, but this is where it all happened. Is Eduardo floating above, with God? Or is he here, watching over his daughter, his grandchildren, and his nephew, RJ?

I know that the flowers won't stay here long. In probably a half hour, or maybe just a matter of minutes, some security guard or flak like Kendra Prescott will come along and remove Xu and Cece's wedding bouquet and toss it in the trash. But that won't matter. Because for a moment, this moment, Eduardo Fuentes was thought of. Remembered. And absolutely no one can take that moment away.

It's dark now and the streetlights, timed to go on at the absolute latest moment, have finally brightened. It's rush hour and traffic is heavy, as usual. Jurors, released from their day's duties, cross the street from the courthouses. Attorneys pull boxes of files on rollers. A homicide detective, wearing a powder blue dress shirt and red tie, is among the crowd, his eyes on me.

I take hold of Cortez's hand and pull him up the stairs, out of public view.

"I want to hang out with you. And not as just a friend," I tell him.

"No games?"

"No games."

Cortez kisses me. And I kiss him back.

NINETEEN

"Really, do we have to do this?" Noah asks me as I park the Green Mile underneath an oak tree. It's about four o'clock on my day off. I picked up Noah after school so that we could meet Dad here in Griffith Park.

"You know he loves this place."

We get out of the car and there it is, the familiar whiff of horse dung from the neighboring pony rides. We walk away from there, toward the white building with a steeped roof and green trim. There's a window for tickets and a sign, LOS FELIZ PASSENGER STATION. Three kids stare through the bars of a gate at a small locomotive and train cars.

"You better look like you're having fun. We owe him this much," I say as we find a shady spot across from the mini–train station.

Noah lets out an audible sigh. He knows that if he hadn't spilled the beans to Puddy Fernandes, none of this craziness would have been unleashed. It ended okay, in the sense that it eventually led to the arrest of the two Old Lady Bandits (neither of whom turned out to be ladies, and only one of whom really qualified as being old). Cortez got most of the glory for those arrests, but I didn't mind. I wondered whether Ron Sullivan and his nephew had implicated Fernandes—or me and Lita—in any way. Cortez didn't mention it, and I'm certainly not going to ask him about it.

Noah wrinkles his nose when he notices the ride called the Simulator, a "roller coaster" designed for really little kids, three years and younger. It's supposed to look like a space rover, but actually more resembles a giant computer printer from maybe the eighties or something. The side door is open, revealing a row of seats with seat belts.

"That thing gave me nightmares," Noah says.

"I remember. What was up with that?"

"Well, they close the door on you in that thing and it jerks around. If that isn't child abuse, I don't know what is."

A hybrid parks next to the Green Mile.

"Hi, Dad," I call out.

He walks toward us, tugging at his pants pocket. "Do you need money for some tickets?"

"Ah, can't we just watch?" Noah is desperate to get out of this.

"Watch? Watch? No Rushes just sit back and watch."

The three kids and their mother sit in one of the train's open-air cars. The locomotive engineer is in the front seat, and the train has started to move forward.

"Too bad," Noah says. "I guess we missed the train."

"There'll be another one coming."

"Oh, joy."

"In the meantime, get us some Push-Ups." Dad gives Noah a ten-dollar bill from his wallet.

That temporarily appeases Noah, who makes his way to the snack bar in between the train station and the pony rides.

Dad joins me on the low brick planter underneath the tree. The train, with its four passengers, winds through the tracks through a man-made idyllic landscape that looks nothing like LA.

"I've always wondered about him, you know," Dad says.

"Who, Noah?"

"No, I'm talking about my father."

"Oh."

"I've never mentioned anything to Lita or your mother."

The air gets very still.

"When I found out that I had high cholesterol in my forties and could do nothing to lower it, I started thinking about him again. Did I inherit this from him, his side of the family? What is he like? Is he an ENFJ like I am?" Dad asks, referring to this Myers-Briggs personality test that he's really into. I've forgotten what the letters stand for. "I look like him," Dad declares.

"Yeah, you do," I agree. "But you're going to be way better-looking when you're his age. He obviously doesn't take care of himself."

"Now that I've seen him, I feel okay. Even better than okay."

"Really?"

"I've always wondered if he ever thought of me. Or if I was forgotten. Even worse, reviled."

"Dad!"

"My mother always referred to it as an *indiscretion*. I'm happy to know it was deeper than that. They were in love."

"They were."

"So, in that sense, I wasn't a mistake."

"Dad, don't even say that." My father will never, ever be a mistake, especially not to me.

Noah comes back with the Push-Ups. He notices the somber expressions on our faces. "What happened?"

"We're just hot," Dad says, accepting his Push-Up. "After the ice cream, it's Simulator time!"

Later, Dad has to go back to work to finish a few things, so I drive Noah back home.

"Do you think he'll be back?" Noah asks.

"Who?" I reply, knowing full well who he is talking about.

"Grandpa."

"Don't call him that."

"But I've never had a grandfather. At least not one I really remember."

"Find a surrogate, then."

"What, a fake one?"

"No, someone who will take the place of one."

"And who could that be?"

I think about all of our older relatives, our neighbors, our family friends. No good candidates come to mind. And then I think of someone in my own life. "One of these days, I'll introduce you to someone. His name is Father Kwame and he's supercool."

When Noah hears *Father*, he's immediately turned off. His run-ins with priests at his Catholic high school have left him highly suspicious of clergy.

"You'll see," I say.

"Yeah, I'll see."

As we turn onto my parents' street, I notice a Lexus driving in the opposite direction, and spot a familiar-looking woman in the passenger seat. "Was that Lita?"

"Looked like her," Noah says, without curiosity. As soon as the front door is open, he immediately goes upstairs to his room.

Mom, meanwhile, is sitting on the couch, her legs splayed apart as if she's been shocked by some news. "Lita has a new boyfriend," she tells me.

"Oh, yeah?" From the corner of my eye, I notice Grandma Toma sitting quietly on the piano bench.

"He's Nisei," she says. I know what Nisei means. Second-generation Japanese American, like Grandma Toma.

"That's nice," I say.

"He's a retired accountant. A widower."

"Well, you should be happy for her. I guess you won't be seeing her as much now."

"He has a second house in La Quinta."

"Fancy. Maybe if you're nice to Lita, she'll invite you over there sometime."

Mom stays frozen on the couch, still trying to process how her wild mother-in-law has snagged a very respectable widower.

I quickly say my good-byes. Before I leave, I raise my hand to high-five my grandma. She doesn't quite get how to do it, and instead shakes my hand awkwardly as if she is meeting me for the first time.

I decide to stop by Osaka's.

"Hey, the gang's all here," I say, when I see both Nay and Rickie at our table.

"We're not all here. Still don't know what's going on with Benjamin," Nay says. She's wearing her glasses, which means she probably did pull an all-nighter last night.

"You know something," Rickie comments, his hands full of edamame.

"She does." Nay sniffs. "Or else she's getting some. Maybe both."

Nay's wrong. I'm not getting any. At least not now. After an hour's hot and heavy make-out session last night with Cortez, I'd pulled myself away for some air. My chin was chaffed from his afternoon shadow. We actually talked about taking things slow. And then proceeded to make out again for another hour.

As for knowing something about Benjamin—technically, he should be the one telling them. I've leafed through enough of Lita's old self-help books to learn all about co-dependency. I shouldn't be speaking for Benjamin; I should let him do his own talking. But who cares, anyway.

I tell Nay and Rickie about what's been going on with Benjamin's mom, and they react pretty much the way I thought they would: they're pissed as hell.

"Why didn't he tell us? What, he didn't think that we could handle it or something?" Rickie says.

"And why did he only tell you? Have you guys gotten back together?" Nay narrows her eyes at me.

"Remember, my mom had breast cancer." *You don't really get it until you go through it,* I think. But I don't say it in exactly that way to Rickie and Nay. "He probably thought that I could relate."

"Oh, yeah," Nay says.

Rickie nods, looking uncharacteristically reflective.

"What hospital is she in?" Nay asks.

"St. Vincent's."

"Well, let's go. Before visiting hours are over."

I'm not sure how Benjamin's going to react to the three of us arriving bearing gifts from the Korean organic market in Little Tokyo, but a part of me thinks that he'll be cool with it. Maybe he always expected me to be his messenger. Codependence sometimes has its role.

We get off of the hospital elevator on Mrs. Choi's floor. Passing a full waiting room on our way to her room, we spot the Choi clan inside.

Rickie's the first to get to Benjamin. "Hey, man, sorry to hear."

Benjamin accepts Rickie's hug. And Nay's, too. She can't help a dig. "You shoulda told us."

"I heard that you were kind of distracted yourself," he says and smiles.

Sally's in the room with her husband and Camila. In the cushiest seat again is Benjamin's grandmother, who motions me to come over.

"What does she want?" I ask Benjamin.

"She wants to give you something. She made me go into Little Tokyo to buy it."

I crinkle my nose, wondering what it can be. I approach, bobbing my head.

She presents me with a long box, like a shoe box cut in half lengthwise.

"Ca-su-te-ra," his grandmother says.

Okay, doesn't help me much, but I just repeat it and bow with a smile, mouthing my thanks. After accepting the box, we move to the other side of the room.

"What is it?" I ask Benjamin. I look to Benjamin for my translation.

"It's like pound cake. The Portuguese brought it over to Japan."

"The Portuguese?" I say. "Like from Portugal?"

"Ah, yeah, that's usually where Portuguese are from." Although Benjamin is in worryland, he still can be snarky. Which is a good sign.

I start to laugh. Softly at first, like when something's caught in your throat. And then deeper, from my belly.

Benjamin both frowns and smiles at the same time. "What's so funny?"

"I'll tell you later," I say, because it really does seem like we will have all the time in the world.

Searching for the perfect mystery?

Looking for a place to get the latest clues and connect with fellow fans?

"Like" The Crime Scene on Facebook!

- Participate in author chats
- Enter book giveaways
- Learn about the latest releases
- Get book recommendations and more!

facebook.com/TheCrimeSceneBooks

Obsidian

M884G1011